Srishti Chaudhary studied creative writing from the University of Edinburgh and English literature at Lady Shri Ram College for Women. Previously, she had a series of short stories published by Juggernaut Books. Her articles have been published by BBC, Vice, Nat Geo India and the *Hindu Businessline*, amongst others. She wishes she had a cool signature, the apparent prerequisite to being a writer. She can be reached at www.srishtichaudhary.com.

EBURY PRESS

ONCE UPON A CURFEW

To the Edinburgh library salon

Srishti Chaudhary

Once upon a Curfew

Srishti Chaudhary

EBURY
PRESS

An imprint of Penguin Random House

EBURY PRESS

USA | Canada | UK | Ireland | Australia
New Zealand | India | South Africa | China

Ebury Press is part of the Penguin Random House group of companies
whose addresses can be found at global.penguinrandomhouse.com

Published by Penguin Random House India Pvt. Ltd
7th Floor, Infinity Tower C, DLF Cyber City,
Gurgaon 122 002, Haryana, India

Penguin
Random House
India

First published in Ebury Press by Penguin Random House India 2019

ISBN 9780143445968

Typeset in Adobe Garamond Pro by Manipal Digital Systems, Manipal
Printed at Replika Press Pvt. Ltd, India

www.penguin.co.in

*To Edinburgh, the city which reminded me
that—above all—I am a writer*

1

'Some *thanda*, madame? Campa? *Shikanji?*'

Indu looked at the masterji, a short, hunched man with little bristles of white beard on his dark face, thick glasses covering eyes that never stopped squinting, and a slab of sky-blue chalk held safely above his right ear, ready to mark boundaries.

She said *shukriya* and shook her head clearly. 'It would help, though, if you would not delay this any longer,' she added.

'*Bass* done, madame, it's done! Think of it as already done.'

'Don't joke, masterji. With the state of the border on the kameez, it could well be another year. And didn't I tell you I wanted brocade?'

Masterji gave a sheepish nod. The rolls of fabric at the back of the shop were propped up against each other in slants, waiting to be cut and stitched into clothes. Beneath the glass table, boxes of sample borders, sequins, laces, buttons and frills were on display. On the wall behind, there was a large calendar featuring Ganeshji, and the scent of fresh incense was in the air.

'*Arre*, why do you worry, madameji?' he asked. 'If I say it will be done before the wedding, it will be! Do you think I will let you go to the wedding in old clothes?'

'How many times have I told you to be more efficient with your work than your words, eh, masterji?'

'Uff, madame likes her little jokes . . . so what about the arm, madame? You want brocade, hun?'

'The neck, masterji, and don't make me repeat it again. I'm going to send Natty on Saturday, and it better be done by then.'

'Yes madame,' he said. 'Whose wedding is it?'

'Someone in the family,' she said before walking out of the shop; she didn't want to bother too much with explanations. While Shashi uncle was not exactly family, the marriage of his son demanded the same amount of enthusiasm.

Indu eyed the dirty water and mud on the road warily, placing her *dupatta* on her right shoulder, making sure it was perfectly balanced in the front and the back. As she attempted to cross the dirty, congested road, a couple of children began trailing her, begging for an anna. It had rained all night, so the city was obviously paralyzed. But that's not what made Indu stop in her tracks. She stared at the huge poster of Rajesh Khanna and Sharmila Tagore across the road. His head rested against Sharmila Tagore's as if in peace. The way his eyes closed in bliss, his lips on the verge of a smile . . . Indu couldn't imagine a more handsome man in the whole country.

Indu tore her gaze away from the poster and looked for Natty. There he was, at the wheel of the white Ambassador, waiting for her as he always did. She saw him see her and started the car. Holding her dupatta from both ends, careful not to let it dip in the muddy water, she got in the car and sat at the back with a sigh, pulling the door shut, blocking out the cacophony of the street.

'Is your suit stitched, madame?' Natty asked her, slowly reversing while looking into the rear-view mirror.

'Of course not, Natty,' Indu replied. It was an old, affectionate name for Natwarlal, who had spent half his life driving the family around. 'You think masterji ever finishes anything on time?'

'People change sometimes, madame,' Natty said, straight-faced.

'We'll see about that, Natty. Let's please go before the rain gets worse.'

Natty gave his usual small nod and began driving as little droplets of rain began hitting the windows. She watched the street pass by. Hawkers covered their stalls with plastic sheets to save their fruits from the rain, vegetable vendors pulled their carts under awnings to prevent them from getting spoiled, and bicycle and scooter riders shielded themselves under the flyover. The Ambassador cut through the traffic easily amid the sea of carts and bicycles.

Indu stared at the bald patch on the back of Natty's head and asked him, 'Say, Natty, what was that song that you were humming in the morning?'

She saw his face light up in the rear-view mirror. 'Oh, the latest of Kishore Kumar! '*Waada karo nahi chhodoge tum mera saath*', do you know?'

'Of course I know,' Indu replied smugly.

'Then how come you asked me, madame?'

'Because what you were actually humming sounded like a completely different song, Natty!'

'Madame likes her little jokes. I know how bored she'd be without me and my summer hits.'

Indu shook her head, stifling her laugh, and stared outside the window. While brown and yellow leaves lay muddied on the side of the road as a result of the rain, the trees looked greener than ever. The heat had dissipated a bit because of the cool winds that accompanied the rain. The streets looked especially grey against the lushness of Lutyens' Delhi. It was a city that was at its best and its worst in this season. The September rain might have brought relief from the aching heat, but had also invited disease, stagnant water and mosquitoes. Indu would rather stand the blazing heat than spend nights swatting mosquitoes.

As the car took a turn, Indu came face to face with a hoarding of Sunil Gavaskar advertising a shaving cream. The Ambassador glided through the tree-lined avenues as the roads became a little wider. There was the usual racket of horns and bicycles on the road as they went around the roundabout towards Civil Lines.

Indu's father had always maintained that a good life was a Series of Smart Decisions that for him had begun with meeting his wife, Lata. From what Indu had heard, her mother had been a beautiful, docile and cheerful young woman from a well-to-do family and had a penchant for making *karhak* ginger *chai*. It was true, Lata's *chai* was always great, but it was not what had sealed the deal. 'It was always your sisters,' her father had told her mother later. Her sisters had gushed and giggled over Ajit, the young Delhi boy. And so the decision was made even before the couple saw each other. It was the first in the Series of Smart Decisions.

Lata was a sweet, compliant bride but also a woman who fought her battles fiercely. Unshakeably religious, she was aghast to find herself with a husband who had driven all traces of God out of his home and preferred to avoid any matter of faith. Slowly and steadily, though, she was able to turn the dial in her favour. By the time Amita, their first daughter, was born, the new, happy father never missed the morning prayer. Amita was a clingy child, introverted and prone to bouts of anxiety, and so she too did whatever was asked of her, including prayers.

Perhaps it helped that their increased belief in God coincided with their prosperity. While Ajit had always been well-to-do, his career took off after he got married. Indu's grandfather had been employed by the British and had been in a high, administrative position, which had brought him into contact with Congress officials. He ended up being one of the few people who benefitted by the British both staying as well as leaving, for the house allotted to them in Civil Lines was not withdrawn by the Congress. A generous dowry from the wedding helped set up further savings, and pretty soon, her father was employed in several commissions of the government, working among members in the upper tiers of the Congress. Although never an official member of the party, he made lavish donations to it.

A year after Amita was born, and on the same day that all of Congress celebrated the birthday of the Prime Minister's daughter Indira Gandhi, Ajit and Lata's second daughter was born. There was no choice, then; the little baby girl had to be called Indira. The newly christened Indira was taken to meet her namesake as well, wrapped up in blankets in her mother's arms, her mother's own head covered by the drape of her silk sari. Indu had then received a fond kiss from the woman whose swearing in she would witness years later.

Natty stopped the car outside their house in Civil Lines, and Indu walked in to discover her parents sitting in the drawing room with some other people.

'There she is!' her mother said, her short hair expertly curled at the edges, which Indu thought was hypocritical of her since she continually dissuaded Indu from cutting her hair. Her parents were with a couple seated on the sofa opposite them.

'Namaste,' she said to Supriya aunty and Balwant uncle, who got up to hug her. She then went and sat on the settee in the middle, and found all eyes trained on her.

'Should I ask Sunita to prepare tea for you?' her mother broke in.

'No, I am alright,' she said, adjusting her *dupatta* and looking around, smiling.

'We were just talking about how difficult commuting has become these days,' Supriya aunty said. 'Just this distance of five kilometres took us an hour to cross!'

'I have to say I agree,' Indu's father replied, a few grey hairs standing out on a head of black ones, balding at the top. '*Gheras* on every corner, clogged roads, workers on strike every other day—God knows how the country is supposed to function.'

'*Arre ji*, people have too much liberty these days,' Balwant uncle said, 'and still they complain! The press is happy to publish any masala they think is news, always trying to cook up trouble. The people are also happy to lap it up, bored in their lives and ready to blame the government for anything—everyone has forgotten the times of the Raj, when nobody dared raise a voice unless they had the Mahatma standing behind them! These days, it's all hue and cry over nothing.'

'I'm telling you, Lata,' Supriya aunty added, 'these jokers are now overdoing it. Protesting is one thing, but they are hindering smooth functioning, and then the blame is placed on the government. I just don't read the newspaper these days, it's so depressing.'

'They should focus on Dilip Kumar, hun?' her mother said with a twinkle in her eye as Indu giggled.

'*Batao!* Of course! Shirtless pictures occasionally, his phone number! *Hain na Indu?* Or who is your hero again, Shammi Kapoor?'

'Rajesh Khanna, aunty,' Indu said, 'the *real* superstar.'

'Everyone thinks their hero is the real superstar only,' she said, looking at her husband. 'And what about our hero, hun?'

Balwant uncle laughed and looked at Indu. 'Indu *beti*, Rajat is leaving for London in two days. I have given his address to your mother, and he, of course, will be writing to you first. It would be great if you two could keep up a correspondence—it will be some time before he returns.'

Indu nodded. 'Of course.'

'What course was he studying again?' Indu's father asked, 'These fancy terms slip my mind.'

'Management,' Balwant uncle said proudly, 'he's studying management.'

Supriya aunty got up to hug Indu again. 'We are so thankful to have a gem like you in our family. We cannot thank the gods enough.'

Indu smiled and hugged her back, and the others got up too.

'Excellent, excellent!' Balwant uncle beamed. 'We must be going now, though.'

'*Arre*, what is this chai *pe charcha*?' her mother asked indignantly. 'You have to stay for dinner, I've already told Sunita to start preparing.'

'*Bass* Lata, thank you, but lots of pending work!'

After exchanging a few more pleasantries, Supriya aunty and Balwant uncle left. Indu told him she had, to which he nodded and retreated to his study.

Ever since Indu's grandmother had passed away, they had been trying to decide the fate of her sprawling flat in Ganpati Tower at Ferozeshah Road. After much searching, her will was discovered. They found that their grandmother had made special efforts to get her will attested by every possible government seal, leaving the flat to Indu and her sister, Amita, along with a letter. Her mother told her that the beginning of the letter contained a fair number of complaints against Indu's grandfather, before relating its contents.

'*It was in the year 1914 that I was married to your grandfather. He was just a boy of sixteen, eager to enlist, serve the British, and rise through the ranks. The freedom movement had gained momentum, but your grandfather foolishly believed that their efforts were in vain and that when war came, as he was sure it would, we would be on the right side of it. But I thought differently; I'd always believed in Kasturba bai. She would go from home to home talking to women, and told us she wanted to empower us and bring us out of our homes. But your grandfather did not let me join the women till the movement was in full force and he faced his great dilemma, that of switching sides. He often behaved foolishly, but life was kind to him, so we are where we are now. I raised my sons to be smarter, but I had decided when you two were born that if it was ever in my power, I would render to you girls some degree of independence, so that you may not be forced to give up your beliefs. To whomsoever it may concern, I leave Number 7 to Amita and Indu, and to them only.*'

When the letter was found, it was hard for Lata to hide her smile. While she had never been fond of her mother-in-law, she had redeemed herself in Lata's eyes with this final act. The four-bedroom flat was passed directly on to Indu and Amita. The house came with more than a thousand books that her grandparents had collected over the years. These books particularly delighted Indu. She couldn't wait to spend long afternoons in that house, discovering new worlds on those bookshelves.

* * *

Later that night, Indu asked her mother if it was now certain that she would marry Rajat.

Her mother spoke quietly. 'Rajat is a good man, a decent man. Much better than all the other party members who would have sent us their sons' proposals if the rumour of you marrying Rajat hadn't been floating around already. Have you seen that Hansi Lal's wrestler of a son? Imagine! I would rather you never married!'

'I agree,' Indu told her, 'but I don't know Rajat. I've seen him only occasionally and said the briefest hello, if that.'

'For sure, he is better than the rest,' her mother replied, her eyebrows knitted tightly together and her jaw set. Her father always said that Indu mirrored this look when she wanted to be stubborn. 'The good part is that he is not interested in continuing with the party. You'll have no opposition members pestering your household. But even better is that since he is going to London now, the marriage is still two years away. It gives you a lot of time to focus on yourself, do as you wish. And time is a luxury, believe me.'

Indu nodded thoughtfully.

Satisfied that she had allayed her daughter's doubts, Lata changed the subject. 'I have phoned Amita and told her to meet us at Number 7 tomorrow.'

* * *

The next morning, all three of them reached *dadiji*'s flat at almost the same time. The flat was on the first floor, but Indu took the lift because it made her feel fancy. Her sister was dressed in a sari, with her hair plaited. Amita hugged both her sister and her mother before they took a round of the house.

It was a spacious flat. Ganpati Tower was one of the few to have acquired the right permits, and the result was five sprawling, four-bedroom flats on each of the eight floors. *Dadiji* had not lived here towards the end of her life, for it was simply too big, and also because she had needed constant care.

There was a huge drawing room with large wooden windows and a little attached balcony. Mahogany chests lined the walls, atop which lay framed photos of all the weddings and babies in the family. Indu's favourite picture was of her father on his wedding, looking unsure of exactly what was happening, while her mother sat next to him, looking demure. *Dadiji's* other children—Indu's five uncles, two of them now in Canada—and their weddings and lives also found place on top of the chests. A thin coat of dust now lined the glass. Indu ran her finger along the table as she walked.

The view outside the windows was of a big *amaltas* tree, which, although green now, would turn into beautiful shades of yellow and gold come summer. Indu kept walking around the house, peeking inside the rooms, on the walls of which hung her grandfather's many laurels.

Once they'd all sat down together on the slightly dusty sofas, Amita told them how Govind, her husband, was planning to speak to their father about turning the flat into an office.

'An office?' her mother repeated in horror.

Amita nodded. 'You know how he wants to manufacture nails and screws with his Shashi uncle. He told me I can sign off on it, since I have half the stake, and Indu might anyway move to London now, so it's not a problem.'

'You will do no such thing,' her mother answered coolly.

'I won't, but what do I say to him once he's talked to daddy? I'm sure daddy will be alright with it. He won't hear a word against Shashi uncle.'

'And I am still here! I'm not moving to London,' Indu quipped.

'This flat has been left to you two,' she said. 'If someone else starts using it, you may not have the same control over it. Keep it. In case of a rainy day, you know.'

Her mother got up, deep in thought while Indu and Amita chatted. The two sisters decided to have a look at the two huge bookcases that lined the wall from top to bottom, hundreds of books on the shelves.

Indu stared at the titles behind the glass. Some of them seemed ancient, ranging from English classics to Hindu religious texts, the names of some Indu couldn't even read. There was a thick coat of dust at the edges of the shelves, and stray strands of lint covered some of the spines. Indu read the names—Robert Frost, Leo Tolstoy, Simone de Beauvoir, Jane Austen, Charles Dickens, Thomas Hardy, Charlotte Bronte, D.H. Lawrence, Virginia Woolf . . . She opened one of the cases and picked up a battered copy.

There were many Indian writers as well, Indu registered excitedly—copies of the *Mahabharata,* Tagore, Gandhi, Nehru, R.K. Narayan, Dhan Gopal Mukerji. She felt the urge to settle down in a chair right away and begin reading, but resisted.

'What will we do with so many books?' Indu asked.

Amita shrugged. 'Do as you like. Read them, take them to your college library, take them home.'

'I'm not letting these in the house, there are too many,' her mother suddenly spoke up, looking at Indu. 'I mean, you could almost stock a library out of this.'

Indu looked at the bookshelves thoughtfully and said, 'Hmm. Let's decide the next time we come here. I have to go now.'

'Where are you going?' Amita asked Indu.

'I have to go to college.'

'Why?' Amita asked.

'Just some books I have to return for the new debating president. I better get going.'

Hugging her sister again, she headed out, slinging her purse into the crook of her arm.

She thought about waiting for the lift again, but it was on the seventh floor. Natty brought the car to the gate and got out to open the door for her.

'You always remember to open the door whenever mother is around, Natty,' Indu said to him.

'I try to open it each time, madame, but it's just my poor, old memory that fails sometimes,' he replied calmly, barely containing his own laugh.

'*Chalo* college *ab*. Hope your poor, old memory still remembers the way.'

'We can always hope, madame.'

Indu looked out the window as they took the road towards Lajpat Nagar, which was quite familiar to her now. Her thoughts returned to her grandmother and how she had painstakingly collected all these books over the years. She wondered how many she had been able to read.

For each birthday, she would give Indu a book to read. For some years, Indu never bothered to open the books. But once she began reading, she couldn't wait to have her own shelves full of books and pass them on to someone younger.

As they entered the gate to the college, the red brick building shone, like it always did, for it was very new, and the manicured garden contrasted sharply with the grey sky. Indu walked in and sat on a bench next to the garden, enjoying the mild September weather. She watched a bunch of girls on the other side of the garden, huddled together over some exciting piece of news, no doubt, squealing in mirth, so that their voices were carried by the wind. She pondered about their lives, how happy they seemed. Before they knew it, this life would be behind them, and they would walk out of those gates, like Indu had done, with their lives ahead of them. Indu wondered what they'd do. She wondered what *she*'d do. It seemed certain to her that in a few years, most of them would have husbands and families, with this life a distant memory.

Indu was sure the girls would soon be admonished for being too loud. And sure enough, a security guard walked over, but not to the bunch of girls, who had gotten up to leave for a class, but to Indu, who had begun walking on the grass. He told her to stick to the path, and she rolled her eyes at him like she had done for the past three years, but she was happy to realize that nothing had changed. And so Indu slung the bag again into the crook of her arm and directed her steps towards the library, for she had two books to return.

She was about to enter the library when the guard outside stopped her and asked for her ID card. She told him it had been returned when she graduated, but she still had to return the books in her hand. He said she couldn't go in without a signed letter from the principal. Indu expressed frustration over this arbitrary new rule, but she couldn't do anything to change his mind, for the security guards in this girls' college were of a particularly stubborn nature.

Irritated, she walked across the campus, huffing, when she spotted a familiar figure in the distance.

Indu ran after her, slowing down as she approached, not wanting to scare her. 'Mrs Bala!' she called out as her old teacher stopped and looked around, her face breaking into a smile, her short hair frizzier than usual. Indu never could stop staring at Mrs Bala's hair, which was short, curly and seemed to have a mind of its own. Her own mother refused to let her cut her hair, which Indu didn't really mind, for her smooth locks were the envy of many, but she always wondered how it would be to have hair so short and wild.

'Indu, dear!' Mrs Bala exclaimed, giving her a hug. 'How are you?'

'I'm very well, Mrs Bala,' she replied. 'How's the new class?'

'Beautiful, of course. All my girls are beautiful, but no one to outdo you, don't worry.'

Indu had to laugh at that, as she had requested that answer in all future meetings with Mrs Bala, and was glad that her teacher had remembered. Yet a silence hung between them now, for it was always a sensitive subject to ask what plans young girls had, now that college was over.

'Yes, so,' Indu said, producing the books from her bag, 'I'm wondering, Mrs Bala, if it would be possible to ask a small favour? The guard wouldn't let me inside the library. I need to return these books because the new girl must need it, for the debating society, you know . . .'

'Aah, I can take them, of course, don't worry. I have to meet her after lunch anyway.'

'Thank you so much,' she said, handing over the books.

'What are you doing these days?' Mrs Bala asked after a moment's hesitation.

'I'm just thinking, you know,' Indu told her, 'about different things. What to do.'

'I'm glad you are,' Mrs Bala told her with an understanding smile.

They stared at each other for a moment. 'Well, I'll let you be on your way, then,' Indu said. 'Thanks so much for the books.'

'But wait, dear, are you free this Saturday? I was thinking, since you're not a student of the college anymore, I could invite you this Saturday evening.'

'Ah, your famous Saturday evenings with the students!'

'Precisely, but only once you graduate.'

Indu thought about it for a moment. 'Yes, I'd like to come, thank you.'

'Wonderful,' Mrs Bala said, clapping her hands and tearing off a slip of paper from a notepad she held in her hands, jotting her address down on it. She hugged Indu once again, who clutched the piece of paper in her hands, memorizing the address as she walked away.

* * *

A couple of days later, the clouds were beginning to clear up and the sun was already high in the sky. The usual heat descended on the city. At home, Indu wandered around the house, lounging on the sofa her mother loved so much, which she had had made especially after seeing something similar at Shashi uncle's house. Indu had a view of the kitchen from her seat and looked on as vegetables were chopped for the dinner tonight with Amita *didi* and Govind *bhai*.

That night, the topic of Number 7 came up when they were all seated at the table.

'Your father and I have come to a conclusion about it,' Govind *bhai* said to Amita and Indu, clearing his throat, as everyone turned to look at him. In his usual formal manner, he put his spoon on the table and took a swig of water before speaking.

'You know, this is an opportune time in the industry. We have to strike the iron now, and as your father says, a good decision at the right time can make a huge difference,' he said, smiling around the table.

Indu's father shook his head, laughing. 'Govind, you can make such a show of things.'

Indu stared at her father without blinking. 'What are you talking about?'

'Well, we've decided that Govind will set up an office there.'

Govind *bhai* nodded in agreement, turning to Amita.

Crunching on a piece of carrot, he said, 'There has never been more demand for nails and now we really need a sales office. Number 7 is in the centre of the city, it's big and it will be perfect.'

Remembering her mother's advice, Amita said, 'But it's a private flat, in a private building.'

'These things can always be sorted out,' her father said, waving a hand in dismissal.

Indu looked quickly at her parents. Her mother was staring at her husband with raised eyebrows. So he hadn't discussed it with her mother either, otherwise he would have known how she felt about the matter.

'No,' Indu said, and everyone turned towards her. Govind *bhai* looked surprised that she had uttered such a loud and clear no. Indu's heart began thumping as she was on the verge of saying what had been going on in her head for the past few days. Ever since her mother had taken her and her sister to Number 7, she could not get the image of that flat out of her head. She couldn't stop imagining what it could be. When she had walked around college the other day, it had started making even more sense.

'What do you mean, Indu?' her father asked.

Indu stared at him and then at Amita, who blinked back at her.

'I need that flat,' Indu said.

Her mother stared at her quizzically. 'What in the world for?'

Indu made her face more resolute.

'I've been thinking of doing something,' she said, ignoring the ire on Govind *bhai*'s face. 'I mean, Rajat will be away for two years. I want to make something of my time till then.'

'How about a finishing school?' Govind *bhai* suggested, and Indu threw him a look so dirty that her mother had to clear her throat loudly so she could divert her attention. 'What are you talking about, Indu?'

Indu told her father, 'I want to set up a library there.'

Govind *bhai* put his glass down noisily.

Amita turned to her sister. 'A library?'

'Like, with books?' Govind asked Indu.

'Yes, Govind *bhai*, that is the main feature of a library,' Indu said, trying to hide her testiness in her laugh.

'But why?' her father asked her.

'It's something that I really want to do,' she said. 'It will be a private library. I've been thinking about it, but I didn't know how to do it until today. Number 7 is perfect. It's empty, spacious, has the perfect energy, and all those books! I can put them to good use.'

'Indu, but, we have already decided,' Govind *bhai* said, looking at her father. 'We need it for an office. I am sure we can find another place for your, uh, library.'

Indu gave him a cold stare, avoiding looking at her sister. 'Daddy, is it set in stone? It's something that I want to do, and all those books are there already. I have an equal right to be given the chance.'

Her father pushed his plate away, scratching his head. 'I mean, of course, we didn't know that you wanted to do something with it, but Indu, it's too valuable a place. I don't know what you mean by a library . . .'

'What, is a library not a valuable place?' Indu asked. 'Come on, daddy, it'll be my own project. I want to make it a library for girls.'

Govind *bhai* sputtered as he drank water.

'Girls?' he asked her, trying not to laugh. 'What kind of girls? Like, poor, I mean, underprivileged girls? Like a charity project, you mean?'

Indu looked thunderously at her sister, who murmured to her husband not to be so crude, and he held up his hands.

'We will talk about this later,' Indu's mother said forcefully. 'Who wants ice cream, now? I found a very good brand. They import it directly from Switzerland.'

Indu gave her mother a sullen look as Amita nodded eagerly.

2

'Do you know where it is?' she asked Natty.

'Yes, madame,' he replied. 'I checked again with sahab as well to be sure.'

Indu sat back and looked at herself in the window. She had finally chosen a cream kurta with three-quarter sleeves, and a light scarf to top it off, as well as small diamond earrings. She wore her light brown sunglasses like a hairband and had done her eyes up with a light line of kohl.

She had been happy to accept Mrs Bala's invitation, of course, but was also looking forward to discussing her library plans with her. This would be the perfect setting in which to ask her.

Indu was also slightly apprehensive as she had never been to such a gathering. She had never wanted to be the sort that partied, one of those university students who ran away from home, smoked into the night and went for protests at India Gate. She had no qualms about her life and wanted it to remain the way it was; moreover, she didn't really fancy running around in the heat in unsophisticated khadi pants.

Once she rang the bell and walked in, after giving a hug to Mrs Bala, who had opened the door for her, she noticed there were about a dozen people around the dinner table, mostly men, who shifted their attention to her. Years of scrutiny had inured her to stares, though, and she walked with her chin held high, giving everyone a courteous smile, and not looking at anyone in particular. In the cursory, cool glance she allowed herself after a couple of minutes, she noticed that besides the people seated around the dining table, there were two men at another table. On this table were some drinks, including, Indu noted, alcohol. Except her, there was just another woman, also with short hair, at the other end of the dining table.

'You can take a seat over there, Indu,' Mrs Bala said, pointing to the chair next to hers, on the other side of which sat a man in a light shirt, his hands in a steeple over his plate, talking to his friend next to him. Indu gave him a perfunctory nod before hanging her scarf on the back of the chair.

Mrs Bala's house was exactly how Indu had imagined a professor's house to be—souvenirs of her travels on the walls, from paintings of cities to fancy china. A huge bookcase covered the entire wall on one side. There were wine bottles and boxes of tea in a glass cabinet, and a few plants in the corner. Stacks of magazines and newspapers were piled on a side table at the far end of the room. Her own mother would have been appalled at the bareness of the sofa, but Indu thought it quite suited Mrs Bala. She stopped looking around and focused instead on the dinner table, deciding that it had been long enough, so she could pay attention to the others around her. Mrs Bala asked Indu if she would have some wine or tea, and Indu smiled, saying, 'Thank you, tea, of course.'

Now Indu looked pointedly to her right, where the two men sat together, engaged in a conversation, who quickly broke it off when they noticed her looking at them. The one next to her took his elbows off the table and said, 'Hello, my name's Fawad.'

Indu looked at him for a second longer than she should have. He was very fair and wore glasses, and nodded at her as he smiled. The one next to him stuck his hand out towards her, saying, 'I'm Rana.' He had a light brown moustache that slanted down at both ends, and went with the stubble on the rest of his face. He wore a simply cut, half-sleeved shirt buttoned to the very top. His eyes looked right into hers, which Indu thought was a bit audacious on his part.

She ignored the hand he had extended and folded her own hands into a namaste in response, but made up for the repudiation with a wider smile, and said, 'Indu.' The one called Fawad chuckled, and Rana bowed his head in defeat.

'Are you Mrs Bala's students?' she asked them. Mrs Bala was also a visiting teacher at the college of journalism, which was a co-ed college.

'I am, she taught me a paper in journalism,' said Fawad, 'but not him, he just lives with me.'

'I do indeed,' said Rana. 'I study law.'

'Ah,' Indu said, and his eyes seemed to twinkle at her reaction.

'What, you have something against lawyers?' Rana asked her as Fawad laughed.

Indu laughed as well. 'I don't. It's better than being an accountant.'

'Of course it is!' Rana said, making a face as if she had just stated the obvious. 'We are much better built.'

Indu simply raised her eyebrows in response.

Aloud, she said, 'Tell me about one law that doesn't work in this country.'

Rana looked at Fawad before chuckling. 'Just one?' he asked.

Indu waited and stared at them without blinking.

'The land acquisition law,' Rana said. 'At any time, the government can acquire your land for official or government purposes and give you a compensation that they deem fit.'

He kept his glass down and sat back in his chair, tipping it slightly backwards, his right arm folded at the table's edge.

'I didn't know that. Anyway, my father's also a lawyer, so I'm the last person to have anything against them, don't you worry.' She turned around to accept her cup of tea from Mrs Bala.

She did not turn to them again, but heard Fawad ask her, 'How do you know Mrs Bala then?'

Indu took a sip of the tea and waited a few seconds before answering, 'She taught me as well, at college.'

'Do you mean at undergraduate college?'

'That's right. Also, she coached the debating society, and I was the president,' she told them.

'Ah, so you like to argue as well,' Rana said with a laugh, picking up a few peanuts from a bowl on the table and tossing them in his mouth.

Indu couldn't contain a smile, but then pursed her lips and raised her chin. 'That's a dangerous thing to say to a woman, mister.'

Rana leaned his head back on the chair as he chewed, while Fawad looked at them back and forth, seemingly enjoying the conversation. But Indu turned around to face Mrs Bala, who seemed to be in animated conversation with the other people at the table, among whom was also her husband.

'On the other side of the world they have reached the moon, Anil, the *moon*. Can you even imagine what that means? In the history of humankind, thousands of years, millions of people have slept every night watching the moon, but did anyone ever think we'd one day be able to visit it? No! This is the age. I've been saying it for some time now—this is the modern age. It's time to either change or burn. There, people are touching the moon and here, we are still fighting the administration to let girls wear kurtas with trousers!'

Mrs Bala looked at Indu directly when she said the last sentence and Indu nodded right on cue. 'It's true,' she said, 'they made such a *tamasha* of the whole situation, you know, just didn't understand the need to wear trousers to college. We led the movement for it! It's a girls' college, for God's sake. If there is one place we should be able to wear trousers, that is it.'

'But we aren't so far behind,' said Mrs Bala's husband. 'Our prime minister is a woman! Country only twenty-seven years young. Who else can claim that, hun?'

Indu nodded enthusiastically at that, for she herself was going to bring that point up, but the girl across the table interrupted the cheers with a disdainful 'pff'. 'She got the seat solely because she's her father's daughter, and did nothing to earn it.'

'Are you joking? After all that has happened after 1971?' Indu asked.

'1971 was a war she fought solely to consolidate her own position and change the public mood.'

'Oh, yes? She was still elected by the people of this country!' Indu spoke up, unable to stop herself.

'Yeah, because she was the First Daughter,' the girl replied in a tone so sarcastic that Indu wanted to throw her teacup across the table. 'I don't think gaining public sympathy was very hard after her father, who was also incidentally one of the founding fathers of the nation, suddenly died from a heart attack.'

'The first dissent to oppression always arises from a place of privilege,' Indu said coolly. 'Did you expect a little girl to rise from the ranks of slum dwellers, without education or opportunity, and become the prime minister?'

'That's how it should be,' Rana spoke up. 'Why is this a democracy? Where are the equal chances? There's so much corruption in the upper tiers that benefits and privileges are never dispersed enough, and so we might never have a little girl from "the ranks of slum dwellers" becoming prime minister.'

Indu shot him a look of annoyance, for she thought he'd be on her side. They had just had a nice conversation. She narrowed her eyes at him, summoning her coldest voice for the betrayal, her nostrils flaring: 'It's not a matter of how it should be,' she said, 'it's a matter of how it is.'

He again looked straight at her, and Indu stared back at him this time. He smiled slightly, the lines on his face coming alive. 'But I would disagree,' he said calmly. 'We'd never progress if it wasn't about how it should be.' Slightly taken aback, she looked at Mrs Bala, who had just guffawed.

'Don't mess with Indu over the prime minister, I'd suggest,' she told Rana with a glint in her eyes. 'She has a soft spot for her namesake.'

'So you fancy yourself a Gandhi supporter?' he asked her.

Indu shot him a look of utter contempt.

Instead of being offended, he gave another chuckle, so she gave him a fleeting, lofty look before deciding to ignore him. He was audacious and foolishly idealistic, she decided, and moreover had no courtesy. She liked Fawad much better. 'Mrs Bala,' she said to her old teacher, 'I'd like your advice on something.'

The rude girl diverted her attention and decided to listen to their conversation. Indu was sure that she had a wardrobe full of khadi pants and did all kinds of other pretentious things. Her hair was shorter than even Mrs Bala's, and she wore a nose ring.

Mrs Bala gave Indu her full attention.

'I want to open a library,' she told her. Mrs Bala seemed as if she had been expecting something else.

'Noble idea,' Mrs Bala said, nodding. 'But how do you mean? Like collect books and make them available for lending?'

Indu took a deep breath before answering, 'No, I was thinking more in terms of having a space to read and study, you know? I want to make it more about the library, the space, rather than reading itself.'

Mrs Bala waited for Indu to go on, but Indu said nothing. 'I don't think I understand exactly what you mean,' Mrs Bala then said, and Indu noticed more eyes on her.

She ignored everyone and said, 'I wonder what it would be like if all the areas that we live in, like Civil Lines, where I am, had a library, and people actually used it. If there were a dedicated space to study, to read, a place where we may spend two hours training the mind, as part of a larger community, where everyone does the same. As a . . . as a focused effort, not a distracted whim.'

Mrs Bala nodded, 'But what gave you the idea?'

'I was thinking about having your own space, you know,' Indu replied, watching from the corner of her eyes that Fawad and Rana were listening intently to her, which somehow gave her more confidence. 'My sister and I used to share a room. Now she is married and it's my room. I feel my thoughts go wider. I read more, because I am alone in that space, and I think more about what I read. I would like to create that space for others, but also make it one where they can come together to discuss and grow.'

'But there are libraries,' Mrs Bala said. 'There are public libraries, and college libraries for students.'

'But I'm talking about a local library, where women who stay at home could come. The public ones are too crowded, the college ones too academic.'

Indu paused for breath, and felt the room go quieter and listen more intently. 'Women?' Mrs Bala asked.

'Yes. I want to set up a library, but just for girls.'

Mrs Bala took a swig from her glass of wine and spoke to her husband, 'You see, Anil? People coming from affirmative spaces always want to enlarge that space.' She turned to Indu and added, 'He says there is no point of women-only spaces, that they create greater inequality.'

Indu wasn't sure what she was supposed to say, but Fawad broke in, 'I don't know how exactly that would help the situation. A library for whom? The poor don't have time to sit in libraries and train their minds.'

Some of the hurt of the instant rebuttal must have shown on her face as the girl across the table 'hmmed' in agreement.

'You don't have to listen to him,' Rana said, lighting a cigarette. 'He's just a commie.' Everybody laughed. Much to Indu's chagrin, she didn't understand what the laughter was aimed at.

'I don't know what to say to you, Indu,' Mrs Bala said. 'Of course, it's an idea worth looking into; slightly unusual, but I'd hold on to it. I'll of course be happy to help and advise in whichever way, but have you thought of the practical considerations? There are so many things—who would visit, and why would they visit? What do you offer them? How do you intend to explain the concept? Someone might consider just sitting on a chair for two hours a waste of time. And more importantly, where on earth would you find such a place?'

Indu stared at her and gulped before answering, her head still held high, 'I have a place in mind. All I'd need you to do is spread the word in your network.'

Mrs Bala nodded thoughtfully. The girl across the table turned away and began speaking to the others beside her, not wanting to give Indu the courtesy of her attention. Fawad looked at her curiously; Rana took another drag of his cigarette and extended her a smile, which Indu did not return.

* * *

'Indu madame, hold *dum laga ke*—yes, like this!'

She stood surrounded by professional lights and reflectors, being ordered around by a photographer whom she obeyed only reluctantly. The cheap material of the salwar-kameez made her sweat more than usual, but more than anything else, the ribbons in her hair increased her irritation by the minute. She had hated tying her hair with ribbons all throughout school, and this ad campaign was making her revisit that feeling. To be fair, it had come at an opportune time: Shashi uncle had suggested her name for the spokesperson of the '*Beti hee jaan hai, Beti hee shaan hai*' campaign, and when Lata had heard that it was about education for girls, she had encouraged Indu to go for it. 'It will give you greater credibility if you are already speaking for the education of girls, for the library.'

It was the perfect arrangement. The daughter of one of the Chief Advocates of the Cabinet, whose name was incidentally also Indira, setting up a library for girls, a champion for the cause of education for girls under the Prime Minister's special campaign, who understood the injustices felt by women . . . except for the hideous, red hair ribbons.

'Smile, please, Indu madame, but not too much! You have to look happy, but also not too happy. You have the burden of making your family proud!'

The photographer took pictures from various angles of Indu holding a set of books in her arms, and when he was finally done, she asked him what processing he would do on the pictures.

'I'm an expert, don't you worry, madame,' he replied smugly, packing his camera into the bag with care.

'I hope you are,' Indu said to him with a dangerous smile. 'If I don't come out looking good, you, sadly, won't have many chances to make your family proud.'

He had nodded with a nervous gulp as Indu packed up and left for home.

Diwali was around the corner, and most places they passed in the car were lit up with yellow string lights. Often, they had to stop and wait as firecrackers were set off on the road. Indu thought about the girl at Mrs Bala's party who was intent on arguing, ready to prove that the government did nothing. Typical of a girl who wore khadi pants, Indu couldn't help but think—a proper rebel without a cause. She thought of Rana and how he had spoken of his friend, 'He's just a commie.' She thought of Rajat, and, despite not knowing him at all, was sure he would never say something like that. She knew him to be poised.

Her mother was waiting for Indu when she returned and promptly took a seat at the dining table to ask about the shoot. Indu told her it was fine except that she had to spend six hours holding a bunch of books while they took the same picture over and over.

'See how hard it is to be a Salome Roy, now?' her mother asked. 'And you had dreams of being a Bollywood queen!'

Indu pursed her lips primly. 'I still maintain that I could have been where Sharmila Tagore is right now if it weren't too tacky a profession for you and father.'

'But now you will be standing up for something even better—the education of girls!'

'Will this campaign work?'

'It should; they are putting in lakhs of rupees,' her mother replied vaguely.

On the table, Indu spotted a letter addressed to herself and took it in her hand, her thumb running across the dry, starched envelope. She opened it swiftly and pulled out the letter. Her mother cringed. 'What?' Indu asked, noticing the expression.

'How can you handle it so crudely?' she asked Indu. 'When I used to write to your father, it would take me five minutes to be able to unfold the precious paper.'

'Because there wasn't that much to do in those times,' Indu told her. 'Today, things move too fast to spend five minutes staring at an envelope.'

Her mother shook her head at her. 'Don't you want to go to your room while you read it?'

'What? No,' Indu almost laughed out loud. 'You think I'll cry or something?'

Her mother gave a long sigh and muttered something that sounded very much like 'May God bless the man marrying you'.

My dearest Indu,
23 August 1974

I hope you are ever so well. I am alright, but had a terrible cold last weekend. I am told that these are probably the last few summer days, so I better strengthen myself for the upcoming winter.

I can certainly smell a change in the air; the leaves have lost their lushness, and the sky is greyer than it has been in the last few weeks. While I miss India and its rain, I do not look forward to the rain here! Other than that, I think I like this country, although it's been only a few days. One can understand why London is considered the centre of the world, for it really charges towards modernity in every aspect. The underground trains are absolutely spectacular and transport you with perfect ease, while the trams glide across the roads carefully and without any accidents. It actually makes me laugh sometimes, because, my father had told me once, around Independence Day, of when he took the tram in Delhi, the electrical wires had got tangled so badly with the kite strings that the poor operator had to stop the tram, untangle the wires and then continue.

I am still adjusting to the food here; did you know they eat peas and potatoes plain and just boiled? I find it so strange. There are a few Indian restaurants, but it's not economical to eat at those places every day. Yet, I really do love this city, its pace, its discipline and its neatness. They seem to be very fixed about their meal timings, which is certainly something we can pick up.

At the moment I have a lot to study, but I do certainly miss you, and hope that you are having a relaxing time. Give my greetings to your parents, and to Amita and Govind, of course.

Yours,
Rajat

When Indu was done reading, she got up from her chair and her mother again let out an exaggerated sigh. 'Indu! Are you really leaving the letter here?' she asked, outraged.

'Oh God,' Indu turned around and picked it up from the table. 'I'll go put it somewhere safe in my room. Happy?'

'Thank God Rajat isn't here to see you throw it across the table.'

'I didn't throw it!' Indu yelled back, and then put it in a drawer in her dressing table.

'This magazine is what should be thrown!' her father said from across the room. 'I don't know what journalists these days are writing, imagining themselves the kings of the world, writing as if public officers are their servants.'

'What are they writing now?'

'Same old—government is inept, trains are late, food prices rising . . . *arre,* tell that to all the opposition party protestors who sit in a *dharna* on the tracks every day! How is it our fault if these people make the trains late and stop the movement of grains for their unreasonable demands?'

'Nobody even reads these, father, don't worry about it,' Indu said, waving her hand, but her father seemed troubled all the same. Indu walked out of the room before her mother could admonish her further about the letter.

* * *

Two days later, Amita called Indu and told her that Govind was meeting their father at Number 7.

'What for?' Indu asked immediately.

'I'm not sure,' Amita replied quietly, 'but I think to see what they will do with Number 7 together.'

'Oh my God,' Indu said. 'I'm going to go and see what.' She hung up and rushed to get her *dupatta* and bag.

Indu went straight to the car, telling Natty to drive her to Number 7. When they reached, she quickly went up the stairs, ignoring the lift, and stopped outside to find the door ajar and a bunch of men inside, moving furniture.

'What is happening here?' Indu asked loudly, and the command in her voice made the workers stop what they were doing and glance at each other doubtfully. When nobody replied,

Indu asked again, this time more forcefully, and so one of them replied that 'sir' had instructed them to take things away.

'Which *sir*?' Indu asked. They all looked at each other, wondering which one of them would be impudent enough to take his name, when the person in question emerged from behind them. Govind *bhai* was leading two workers, one of whom carried a huge alcove, and the other a stack of files. Her brother-in-law smiled and put an arm around Indu's shoulders. 'Anything wrong, Indu?'

Indu stepped away and asked him sternly, 'What's going on here?'

Govind *bhai* looked around nonchalantly, as if he had just noticed the flurry of activity. 'This? Nothing, we are just getting the place ready, moving in stuff. We have to start as soon as possible.'

'Ready for what?' she asked, infuriated.

'Ready for the office. I'm thinking of getting pest control done, you know, there could be bugs—'

'Did you speak to daddy about this?'

'Of course, my dear. He said we should get it ready as soon as we can. In fact, he should be coming up in a few minutes.' Indu gave him a suspicious stare and went around the room angrily, checking what had been moved. The workers were afraid to look at her.

'How can you just—just presume? It's not your flat!' she hissed at him.

'Indu, the matter is already closed,' Govind *bhai* said with forced patience. 'Your father decides what happens to it, and we agreed we aren't going to pander to your fanciful—'

'My father didn't say anything to me,' she cut him off, clapping her hands to gather every worker's attention. 'Everyone, stop what you're doing—this work will continue some other time, but at the moment, you all have to leave!'

'What? No!' Govind *bhai* said, alarmed, standing next to Indu and waving his hand at the others. 'Go back to what you're doing, nobody has to leave!'

The workers looked confused, not knowing whom to obey.

'Do you even know what you're implying?' Govind *bhai* barked, losing his cool. 'This property, this flat—it's worth so much!'

'I know exactly what I'm doing, thank you,' Indu said. 'No, I won't be bossed over, I'm not like—'

She broke off when she heard footsteps as her father entered the room, followed by Sharma*ji,* bumbling behind as always, carrying a little brown briefcase under his arm.

'Daddy,' Indu said, rushing to him, immediately trying to gain his support. Her father looked at her but ignored her appeal, hissing something to Sharma*ji.*

'Daddy, look what's happening here! Did you tell Govind *bhai* that he could make this an office already?' Indu asked.

'Yes, I did,' he replied.

'I can't believe you aren't willing to give me this one chance! It's not like I've asked for something crazy, I want to do something good, and my own father won't—'

Her father held up a hand, pressing his ear as if the shrillness in his daughter's voice had hurt his eardrums. His pained expression made Indu stop.

'There's no need to look so fierce, dear,' her father told her.

'Indu,' Govind began in a patronizing tone again, 'I really don't want to spoil any of your plans. But you know that we have put up a unit, and to make it grow in any way, we need a proper office now. Every day they say the economy is slowing, people don't have jobs, there is drought, flood, famine. But it's not true! The industry is there, and anyway nails are something that people always need, slow economy or not. We are one of the few who have begun to manufacture, and it's the right time. If we strike now, in a few years, we could be the leaders.'

'Govind *bhai*, I fully respect your ambition, and if you ask, I will offer you any help in my capacity; but this flat is not the right place for the office! I know you don't understand what I want from it, but it is something valuable as well, and I know that my grandmother would have appreciated it.'

Govind *bhai* waved a hand in impatience. 'How can we say now what your grandmother would have wanted or not?'

'Even so, as I told you before, this flat is perfect for what I want, and I think that I should be given a chance to prove myself—especially since it belongs to me!'

'And to Amita!' Govind *bhai* retorted.

'Indu . . .' her father began.

'Daddy, I mean it, you know I am serious about it. It won't be a waste!'

'But a *library*?' he asked her. 'I don't understand the purpose. What do you want from it? What you want people to do there?'

Indu took a deep breath. 'I want women to come and study there.'

'Study what?' he asked, confused.

'Anything they want!'

'But there has to be a purpose to the studying—do you mean college students? Is it for your college?'

'No,' she said through gritted teeth, 'it's like, I want women of different ages to come and spend time here to educate themselves.'

'But who goes to a library for leisure? I mean, I don't think your mother or sister would just go and hang around in a library. It's a different matter with you—'

'That's the whole point,' Indu said. 'You need to take time out to read and do things you want. And only when you have a space where you feel comfortable can you do that. I want this library to be a place like that. I see it as a spot for women to come together, exchanging ideas and growing. Women who have already passed school, living their day-to-day life—they don't have the time to think beyond their chores. I want this space to help them do that.'

'But to what end?' Govind *bhai* asked, exasperated. 'Why do you need a special place for it? Why can't they do it at home?'

'I'm still not convinced,' her father said.

'Fine, give me a chance to convince you, then.'

Her father couldn't argue with that, and so he looked painfully from his daughter to his son-in-law. 'Alright, we'll talk about this further. At home.'

'So can you stop this now?' she asked.

'No!' Govind *bhai* said, and her father put a hand on his head. 'Indu, go home and you'll get a fair chance, but stand here and argue and I will make sure—'

'Alright, alright,' Indu said, flinging her bag over her shoulder, and gave Govind *bhai* a triumphant look before walking out of Number 7.

3

Dear Rajat,
25 September 1974

Thank you for your letter. Happy to know you have adjusted well. The food problem can be easily solved if you learn to cook a little. Moreover, it will be good practice for the future (ha ha).

The other day, I made a joke about Govind bhai when he gobbled up three bananas in a minute. After he finished, he said, 'Goodness, I'm such a monkey.' And then I said, 'Yes, and you just finished three bananas so quickly.' He didn't get it at all. That's a pitiable sense of humour.

You know that Shashi uncle suggested me for the spokesperson of a kind of 'education for girls' campaign. I think it should be interesting, and I've always wanted to do something to bring about change. Good that you're away from all the mess here (strikes and protests everywhere all the time), although I'm enjoying the drama.

Keep me updated.

Love,
Indu

She watched the other cars pass by as she sat in her own, with Natty patiently behind the wheel as usual. She had had a long conversation with her father this morning about the library at number 7. Though Govind *bhai* was still miffed at not being allowed to use a flat half owned by his wife, her father was coming around to it for a completely different reason. 'It also looks good on the whole family,' he said, 'with your *beti hee jaan hai* campaign. Especially because we have two daughters, it really draws the focus to the good things we do, unlike those magazine people always trying to write ill about us.'

'It's not you that these articles personally point at, they're talking about the government,' Indu said. 'Don't take it to heart, daddy, it's not your fault.'

'Any finger raised at the government is a finger raised at us,' her father said, shaking his head. 'Of course, there is a division of responsibilities, but I am one of the chief advisors to the PM.'

She nodded sympathetically but was glad her father now approved of the plan, and hoped fervently that the whole mess with Govind *bhai* would be sorted out soon as well. She tried to think of how she would explain to Rajat in the letter why she wanted to start the library, but decided she would elaborate it in her next correspondence. In her own head, it was quite clear. The sky today was cloudy and the sun hid behind the white fluff in the sky. She imagined how the library would look on such a day. In her mind, a cold, gentle breeze would drive away the heat that day, and the windows would be open so you could breathe in the air. The wind would be delicious and would ruffle the corners of the pages, so one would keep a finger or two at the edges, feel the rustle of the paper beneath their skin. In one of the rooms, one would hear the music, because there'd be a record playing. In the mornings and evenings, there would be a dedicated news hour so that one could be informed about what was happening in the country, so nobody could say women didn't know anything about politics, that they couldn't understand economics.

There would be a few copies of the newspaper delivered every morning, and displayed so prominently that one would naturally pick it up, not just to read what was screamed out in bold letters, but also talk about it with each other, to understand that there were things that had not been reported. The books that *dadiji* had left behind would be available to everyone. One might read some good fiction, delve into distant, famous lives, escape from the monotony and demands of the husband and the child. One might read some history so that when it is said, this is not the way it's done, this is not the way of our life, one could have an answer ready. Most importantly, one might sit and indulge herself with a magazine or two, idle the time away in beauty tips and little jokes, day-dream a while and find some time to think about irrelevant things, to dream of holidays that may never be, to think of another life.

In the winters, the cold rooms would be bathed in sunshine, so that all women may sit together, shelling peanuts, peeling oranges and building bonds. One might find strength in this refuge, and think that if nothing else, they have some time in the day to lose themselves, find a willing ear.

One might find a room for herself.

* * *

Since it was another pleasant day, Indu decided to search for him first on the terrace rather than indoors. The walls had been muddied and neglected by time, overlooking the growing city centre, which was lined by trees lush and proud in the rain, interspersed with parked cars and people on the road. Waiters, dressed in their classic white uniforms with Nehru topis, bustled about, serving the flurry of guests seated at the tables—young students finishing college homework, men off on their lunch breaks, mostly in twos and threes, a couple of larger groups. She saw him sitting in the corner in clean-cut trousers and a half-sleeved shirt buttoned to the top, stroking the side of his face where the stubble had grown thicker, right hand holding a cigarette to the mouth.

Indu walked towards him with measured strides, her *dupatta* trailing in the breeze, arms swinging slightly. Her lips pouted slightly as she walked up to him. Noticing her, he immediately stubbed out his cigarette in the ashtray and got up from his chair. This time, he remembered; he did not offer her his hand.

'Hello, Indu,' he said, and Indu noticed how he didn't attach the *ji* at the end, how he addressed her in intimacy. She said hello and gave a non-committal nod, sitting on the chair that he had pulled out for her.

They sat opposite each other and as before, he looked straight at her without hesitation. She averted her gaze, folding her arms in front of her, looking around the terrace in interest. 'I used to come here a lot while in college,' she mused.

'I still come here a lot,' replied Rana, his arms resting on the edge of the table, leaning towards her. 'Tell me, what would you like to have?'

'Nothing, thank you.'

He raised his eyebrows at her, but did not insist and ordered a coffee for himself. She stared at him as he lit another cigarette. He noticed her looking at him. 'Do you mind?' he asked, holding up the lighter and the cigarette, and Indu shook her head in dismissal.

'So, Mr Rana,' she said, adding the 'mister' to re-establish the distance he had sought to dissolve, 'what is it you want?'

Rana looked at her and smiled, 'The question is not what I want, the question is what do you want?'

'What do you mean? Mrs Bala called me and said that you had a very specific interest in meeting me, and it is only on her insistence that I am here.'

'Yes, but I am here to do whatever you want, so really, this is about what you want from me.'

Indu narrowed her eyes and gave him a long stare before replying, 'Please explain what you mean clearly, I have no patience for guesswork.'

He held up his hands in surrender, and then put them on the table. 'Okay, you said that you wanted to open a library for girls, right? I want to help you do it.'

She looked at him, confused. 'Why?'

'It's a noble cause, I'd be glad to be a part of it.'

'Oh, sure,' Indu scoffed. 'I don't think you believe in it.'

'What? Why not? What's not to believe in? Education, women's empowerment . . . I'm all for it.'

'You don't sound very serious about it.'

'Well, maybe I don't know all the details yet, but I still like the basic plan, and I am sure you can do with some help. Everyone can do with some help. And I've seen you on that poster, *beti hee jaan hai, beti hee shaan hai*. Nice braids.'

Indu stared at him, for the first time returning his audacious gaze. She noticed his chiselled face, the edges of his beard that weren't very closely trimmed and grew naturally. His oval eyes had tints of light brown, and his hair was longer on the sides. Even his hairstyle was audacious, Indu couldn't help thinking. He had the kind of face that looked grumpy except when he smiled. He raised his eyebrows at her and Indu continued to glare at him.

'Very funny,' she replied coolly. 'How many people have *you* helped educate, hun?'

'None, and that's why I want to join you.'

'What can you do for me?' she asked him.

'Whatever you'd like.'

'For example, *what*?' she asked him again with emphasis.

'I can crack some jokes to try and make you laugh; you seem to need it . . .'

Indu continued staring at him.

'*Uff!* I'm sorry I haven't set up a library before, but I'm sure there's lots of work. Acquiring the books, setting up the place, advertising your library—whatever you need.'

Indu wanted to laugh, but held herself back, pursing her lips to restrain herself.

'I cannot pay you,' she said flatly.

'I don't want to be paid.'

'What's in it for you, then?'

'The pleasure of your company?'

Indu noticed the lack of hesitation in his answer and gave him a cold stare.

'You sound exactly like Fawad when I offer to do something for him—*what's in it for you?*' he imitated in a sing-song voice. When she didn't laugh, he put his hands up. 'Alright, I am not going to lie. I know that your father is a well-connected lawyer, and I wouldn't mind being in his good graces . . . for a job, you know. If you find me useful, you could recommend me.'

Indu sat back in her chair and crossed one leg over the other. 'Okay, I want a coffee too,' she said.

Rana looked at her, bemused, and then signalled to one of the waiters to bring another coffee. He then looked at Indu expectantly, waiting for her to explain, but she simply sat there staring at him.

'Have you watched it yet?' he finally asked, pointing a finger at something behind Indu—a huge poster outside Regal Cinema, which they could see from where they were sitting.

Indu turned in her chair and saw a poster of Rajesh Khanna and Mumtaz; *Aap Ki Kasam*. It had been released a while ago but she still had not found the time to watch it, and felt ashamed.

'No! I am dying to watch it, I think it will be the best one this year.'

'Don't be too sure, Rajesh Khanna has a few more coming this year.'

'Rajesh Khanna is my absolute favourite,' Indu said, her hands over her heart, her eyes dreamy. 'I think there is no man like him.'

Rana laughed, and then contorted his lips as if in contemplation. 'People have often told me I resemble him.'

Indu shot him an exasperated look, and he laughed some more. 'Do you want to watch it? We can go tomorrow, or the day after that.'

'No, thank you,' Indu said, her voice turning cold again, and sipped her coffee, which had arrived while she had been gushing over Rajesh Khanna. Rana stared at her but looked away when she glanced at him.

After a while, she got up, arranging her *dupatta* and swinging her bag over her shoulder. 'Thank you for the coffee. I will consider your offer.'

'What? Come on!' He got up from his chair as well. 'I can really be of help, you know. I'll be a lawyer soon.'

Indu just smiled at him.

'Can I walk you downstairs, at least?' he asked her.

'No, that's fine,' she told him with a wave of her hand. As she went downstairs, she looked for Natty, leaving Rana gazing at her in chagrin.

* * *

Amita said she would get ready for the wedding with them. 'I want to wear mumma's *kundan* set, the one she bought last year, and it will be too much trouble to first bring it home. Anyway, Govind wants to be there *throughout* to help his Shashi uncle. If I go with him, I will be far too tired by the time of the ceremony,' she had remarked nonchalantly.

Amita was the taller and fairer of the two, with full lips and a huge smile that lit her face up, contrasting sharply with Indu, whose smile usually remained measured and contained.

Indu gushed over Amita's *sari,* which was all pink but without being startlingly so, and had a light blue border with embellished handwork that made for a beautiful drape. She watched her sister put her hair up in a tiny beehive, and then asked her to do her eyeliner.

'Do it like you do yours, with the wings,' Indu insisted and Amita laughed, asking Indu to shut her eyes.

'Did you fight with Govind *bhai*?' Indu asked her sister, her eyes still closed.

'You figured it out?'

'Of course. What is it? Because of Number 7?'

'Yes. I mean, that's just on the surface. There are other things too.'

When Indu didn't say anything, Amita went on. 'Okay, so tell me exactly what you have in mind for Number 7.'

Indu sat down on the seat with a sigh, patting down her *sari* neatly beneath her. 'I know it seems to have come out of the blue. But you know I have some time now, until Rajat comes back, and well—I want to make something of it. I want to open this library, just for girls, and I wish you would support me in this.'

'But why a library? And aren't you already doing that *beti* campaign?'

'For which I am just posing and getting clicked! No, I want to make it a place where women can use their time for themselves—a place where you could go every day and nurse a passion, something beyond everyday life. You of all people will understand,' Indu said to her. 'You say you want to finish your medicine degree. Are you able to find time at home to study?'

When Amita didn't respond, Indu knew she had her thinking.

'Think of most women,' Indu said to her, appealing earnestly. 'They must have a passion, something they want to spend time on, learning, reading. I want to create this place so they can go there every day to spend time with themselves.'

When Amita didn't say anything but seemed to be thinking, Indu continued.

'It's solitude, it's your space! Something which you, of all people, need so desperately, *didi*. You are stuck at home all day doing the same work, talking about the same things, waiting for Govind *bhai*.'

Amita walked around the room, picking up the earrings from the set that lay in the velvet case on the dresser.

'You started studying again, *didi,*' Indu said, 'but you always say you never get time, you never get space, that you'll never be able to finish it at this rate. Think—what if you have a place to go to every afternoon after lunch, where nobody can disturb you? Nobody can ask you what you've made for dinner, nobody to tell you to pick out a dress. Four hours every day just to yourself, studying with other women and discussing things with them. Wouldn't it change a lot?'

For a while, her sister said nothing except put on the jewellery, and Indu fell quiet as well. Then they waited for their parents on the sofa in the living room. Indu went out to check on Natty and told him they would be out soon.

When she returned, Amita looked Indu in the eye and said, 'If you want to do this, I'm with you.'

Indu felt a rush of affection for her sister and hugged her. 'Really?'

'Yes. Govind can find another place.'

'Someone offered their help, you know. I think I should accept the offer.'

'Really? Who?'

Indu paused before saying, 'Do you remember my debating teacher?'

'Yes . . .'

'One of Mrs Bala's favourite university students. She recommended him,' Indu didn't know why she lied. He had recommended himself. 'He seems capable, and he is a lawyer.'

Her sister nodded nonchalantly, not looking at her. 'Good, go ahead. Have you told Rajat about it?'

Indu realized she had still not posted the letter. 'Yes,' she said again. 'I haven't heard from him yet, but he should be fine with it. He is very busy with his studies, you know. So . . . will you talk to Govind *bhai*?'

Amita nodded, but looked grave. 'I will, but he seems really set on Number 7, Indu.'

In the car, Amita stared outside the window, and Indu knew she was thinking. Indu couldn't help but remember Amita's wedding picture, for it seemed to her the happiest picture she had ever seen. She wasn't alone in thinking that, for the picture was greatly reproduced and shown to everyone who might have ever known the Narayans. Look at the bride, they all said, 'doesn't the bride look simply radiant?', 'see how her face glows', and 'how beautiful they look together'. Amita had her head tilted, resting on Govind's right shoulder, and she smiled her widest smile, her eyes twinkling. Govind stood upright, sincere and radiant; he was tall, with a neat moustache and a round, shiny face. This picture had probably played a part in cementing the idea that Amita and Govind were the perfect couple.

Indu remembered how they had learnt slowly, as each month went by, that everything wasn't as rosy as it seemed. They had been trying to conceive for a while now. They had gone to doctor after doctor, and each one suggested something different: get this test done, and we will give you a prescription, the latest one from Europe. Parsley and pineapple juice under the full moon, all the women had insisted, that will definitely work. Homoeopathic medicine every day for six months, but for it to work, tea must be given up. Nothing changed, however, and life remained as it was—underwhelming.

As Indu had observed, something else had caught Amita's fancy along the way, though, an old dream; she wanted to be a doctor again. She had given it up in a hurry for the perfect husband, the perfect family and the perfect life. Amita had realized how quickly that hope had come and gone, how transient that feeling was, and how fragile the threads on which relationships were sustained. She felt that old ambition again, but quickly realized that for others everything had changed. 'Is this the time for you to try and begin a family or to sit in a college classroom reading books?' they had asked.

Indu knew that as the months passed and nothing seemed to be right in their lives, Amita caught herself thinking about it again and again, and when she couldn't contain it any longer, she brought it up again. Her husband wasn't impressed: he didn't understand the cause, or the need, for this new obsession, and neither did his parents. They found it unbecoming in a woman to suddenly want to give precedence to an apparently strange dream over her married life. Studying medicine might require her to live elsewhere, spend long hours buried in books and have new priorities.

Yet, Amita couldn't let the idea go, and despite all the sniping and disapproval, she found a way to study. It was far more difficult to do that than she had predicted while also taking care of the household—there were people to attend to, meals to arrange, elders to take care of. There was household shopping, the garden to maintain, and domestic help to manage, so much so that even stealing a couple of hours in the day was a big feat.

Add to that all the gossip in the community; the Narayans' older daughter, happily married for three years, instead of seeking solutions for her infertility, was focusing her energy on a distant dream. What was the meaning of this now? How on earth did it make any sense? Of course, the family was too highly respected to be openly questioned about it, but there were private sniggers, hidden jeers and whispered taunts. The same people were now at the wedding, giving the sisters patronizing looks; one, too headstrong, and the other, too naïve.

It wasn't cool enough yet for an outdoor wedding, and so the ballroom had been chosen. Indu had to concede that Shashi uncle had outdone himself. The expansive chandeliers glittered on the ceiling, shedding hues of golden light on the tables decorated with roses and lilies in extravagant flourishes on table runners. People milled around the hall, where dinner was laid out. Shashi uncle stood by his son up on the stage, his chest puffed out proudly, beaming at all the people that had arrived in their finery.

Indu looked around, knowing it was a while before the bride arrived. The usual groups had formed quickly: her father had gone to lounge around with the other men, her mother had greeted her own friends, with whom Indu had lingered for an appropriate amount of time, allowing them to ask her a little about her life. She had then slinked away to Amita, who also sought out Indu once Govind *bhai* headed to the bar. Indu needed to speak to her sister.

The sisters greeted people around the room as they circled, briefly stopping for whomever they met along the way: 'Rajat is well, missing India a little bit but enjoying London immensely,' Indu would recite the standard answer. 'No, there's still time, it's a full two years, this course.' With Amita, they would approach with more caution, restricting the questions to how Govind's business was going and if her mother-in-law was better now. Most of these people had also come to Amita's wedding. Indu spotted Govind *bhai* in the distance and turned away.

'Look at Aggarwal aunty over there,' Amita said to her sister. 'When I came in, she asked me if I would now start working at the government hospital. Said the people camped outside the hospital always took up all the parking spots there, so I must put in a word to ensure a smoother parking system.'

'Typical,' Indu said, rolling her eyes. 'If only there were no cobra protecting their lockers and safes thirty feet under their house, they could have donated some of that money to the hospital for the parking she so desires.'

'Ha ha ha, how did you come up with a cobra?'

'Didn't you hear? When the government threatened a crackdown on defaulters some time ago, they panicked and got a cobra and his charmer to sit guard outside their hoards.'

Amita sniggered, 'As if the government could touch them anyway. All they need to do is offer them a piece of it.'

'She's changing everything, though, how systems work,' Indu said. 'I knew it from the start, *didi*, she's not one to take things as they are. Have you seen how quickly banks are cropping up now in every town? After nationalization? I mean, I haven't seen it, of course, but I've read about it.'

'Are you talking about Indira Gandhi?' Shashi uncle said to the sisters, coming up from behind them with their father, giving them both a one-armed hug.

'Congratulations again, uncle,' Indu said, and both she and Amita smiled. 'Let us know if we can do something to help you tonight.'

'Of course, my dears, but you don't have to do anything except be the beautiful girls you are,' he said, turning to her father. 'Ajit, your Indira seems to want to follow in the footsteps of Indira Gandhi, eh?'

'It is in her blood, of course,' her father said, laughing.

'What about the Prime Minister, then?' Shashi uncle asked Indu. 'What do you think will happen now?'

'Do you mean with all the trouble going on?' Indu asked. 'Yes.'

'I believe in her,' Indu said. 'She's done more for this country than anyone else. She is the future.'

'You've taught her well, eh, Ajit?' Shashi uncle said, looking at her father, as Indu beamed in response. 'But not even she can predict the future.'

* * *

'Esha, *paani pilao, didi* is tired, get her some water,' Sunita told her daughter, who generally trailed her mother around. Esha immediately ran off to bring water and Indu realized that her mother wasn't home.

Indu smiled at Sunita and asked, '*Theek ho*? Everything okay?'

'*Bass*, it's okay, same old routine, same old life,' Sunita answered as Indu nodded distractedly. There was a chill in the air now, and Indu would have to get her winter clothes unpacked soon. She was about to ask Sunita when she could do it when Esha handed her a glass of water and smiled.

The phone rang and Indu walked over to pick it up.

'Hello?' she said carefully into the receiver.

'May I speak to Miss Indu Narayan, please?'

'You may. Is that Mr Rana?'

'Yes, I just wanted to hear how you respond to me saying your name.'

'What?'

'What?'

'What do you mean?

'Nothing. Did I call on time? You said you hoped I wouldn't be late.'

'Yes, you did,' she said, smiling, looking at the clock on the opposite wall. 'A little early, actually. A couple of minutes earlier and you would have missed me.'

'Sorry, but I just couldn't wait.' Indu found that his voice sounded deeper on the phone.

She forced herself to stop smiling, for she knew that some people could tell over the phone when the other person was smiling. Summoning her strictest voice, she said, 'Do I have to remind you that the purpose of this phone call was only work and not idle chatter?'

'I meant the work! That I couldn't wait to begin work! You're the one who's delaying it . . . *uff*, women.'

'We can try to work together on this,' she pressed on, 'but we have a lot to plan.'

'I agree. I think we should meet every day till we have some clear idea of how to go about it. Chalk it out, you know.'

'Yes, but I'll have to think of where, what all we need . . .'

'We can meet at my house, if you want.'

'Of course not,' Indu said sharply, and heard him laugh.

'Where, then?'

Indu didn't have an answer. As inappropriate as it would be to meet at his house, it would be even more so to meet him at Number 7, which remained empty all day long, or even at her own house.

'Maybe again at Indian Coffee House. Is that okay for you?'

'As long as you make up your mind about whether or not you want coffee . . .'

This time, Indu couldn't suppress her laughter. 'Okay, after lunch? 2.30?'

'Fine by me,' he said briskly.

'Don't you have classes or anything?'

'Not too many, and the classes that I have are not very important right now.'

'Compared with me, you mean?' Indu asked.

She heard him chuckle before he said, 'How important is someone feeling today? I didn't think there was any scope for improvement.'

'The work that I have, mister. I meant the work.'

'Ah, just like I meant the work before?' he asked her, still laughing.

Before she could answer, Indu heard the front door open. She hurriedly told him she would see him later and hung up.

4

'. . . it lets her do something with her time, occupies her mind. I don't know what mischief this girl will get up to if she has free time on her hands,' her mother was saying.

'It's true, but this changes things. I mean, Govind—I don't know how to explain it to him.'

'Should we talk to them about it?'

'I don't know,' her father said in contemplation. 'Govind has his mind absolutely set on it, it will create a problem for Amita . . .'

'Poor Amita. As if she doesn't have enough problems . . . but I do want Indu to have something these two years, or everyday will be a new surprise. I don't know if I could handle it.'

Indu waited until she heard the scrape of the chair and the sound of her father's footsteps receding.

Sunlight cascaded over the little garden in the front, with its charming perimeter of bushes. Three white chairs sat around a table in the middle of the manicured lawn that morning. Sunita picked up the remnants of last night's celebrations, singing '*Mere sapno ki rani kab aayegi tu*' to herself, swaying to the beat, with the end of her *sari* tied around her waist for easy movement. Indu lounged in one of the chairs, enjoying the sun, which had begun to feel nice as the weather became cooler every day.

She held a notebook on her thigh, the end of the pen in her mouth, thinking. She shut her eyes, for the sun always made her sleepy. Clouds covered the sky as the day progressed, so that by the time afternoon arrived, Indu found the perfect opportunity to wear her new coat, which Rajat had sent her from London. In the car, Natty asked her if they were going to meet the young, handsome man again.

'You find him very handsome, do you, Natty?' Indu asked him.

'How does my opinion matter, madame?' he replied with a dramatic sigh.

'For someone who doesn't think their opinions matter, you sure voice them a lot, Natty.'

Natty acknowledged her reply with a grunt of laughter and honked at the bicycles in front of him.

Rana wasn't that bad, Indu had decided, and it could be useful to have him around. He was well-spoken and smart enough to get things done, but more importantly, he wanted to do them. He had been pretty honest about why, and Indu would be sure to put in a good word about him if things worked out.

Indu walked inside to the usual din at Indian Coffee House, assuming he would be inside because it was windy. This time, he saw her first and nodded in greeting. Indu raised her eyebrows in acknowledgement, looking away purposely as she walked towards him. He noticed her averted gaze and grinned in response, getting up from his chair when she reached him. She sat down on hers, removed her coat and hung it on the back of her chair, adjusting the *dupatta* on her shoulder.

He was wearing a round-necked shirt today and his hair stood straight instead of falling neatly on his forehead. He was still unshaven, so when he smiled, his teeth looked whiter against the dark hair on his face.

'How are you?' he asked, smiling, his eyes looking straight at hers. He sat down again with his forearms on the table, leaning towards her.

'Fine,' Indu said, looking away. 'But it's getting cold and I don't like it.'

'Good thing you have such a fancy coat, then,' he said, eyeing it with exasperation. 'Why do you need this thick thing?'

'I prefer to wear more than just a thin layer,' she said, with a glance at his windcheater, and he shrugged. 'Plus, it was a gift.'

'For?'

'It was my birthday yesterday,' she said to him with narrowed eyes.

'Really? Why didn't you invite me?'

She pouted at him. 'You could wish me, you know, before expecting an invitation like that.'

Instead of replying, he stared at her, grinning even more widely. Indu could not believe the audacity of this man. She looked away, flustered by his scrutiny.

'What do you want from me, then? For your birthday,' he asked, and now she had to look straight at him.

'Just for you to stop talking nonsense,' she said.

'Would you prefer it in a poem? I like poetry, you know.'

Indu ignored him and took out a notebook and a pen.

'Let's start,' she said. He steepled his fingers and looked at her with his full attention.

'Your test begins now. How do you suggest we start?' she said.

In response, Rana looked at her for a few seconds and then turned to signal to one of the waiters. Indu thought Rana had a lot of nerve when he looked at her cheekily and asked if she wanted coffee. She continued staring at him with her eyebrows raised and when she didn't reply, he turned to the waiter and ordered two coffees.

'Okay, to the basics first, then,' he said. 'Where is all the action taking place?'

She noted it down as she spoke, 'There is a flat that will be used solely for the library.'

'What is this flat like? May I see it?'

'In some time, maybe,' Indu replied.

'What are the main things you need there?'

Indu slapped her hands on the table and leant forward. 'I thought I was asking the questions.'

He shook his head. 'Well, first we need to examine what you want out of this. Only then will we know what we need.'

'I don't know how to explain it exactly,' she said. 'I want it to be a place where women would be able to read, write, study, the things they want to but which they cannot accomplish at home because of their other responsibilities.'

'I don't understand that,' he said. 'If someone can take the time out to come here, they could take the same time out at home.'

'You're such a man,' Indu said, shaking her head. 'Do you live with your mother?'

'Fawad does like to act like a mother sometimes,' he replied, pouting as if in contemplation.

'So you don't. But think—when you go to visit her, think of her routine in the day, and think of what time she is able to spare for herself.'

'I don't know, I guess in the afternoons. After lunch or something.'

'But then maybe you need something from her. Or there are extra chores to do. A cupboard to be cleaned. Some guests who have come over. Rations to be bought. Do you have any siblings?'

'Well, yes, two brothers.'

'There you go. One day, it's one son, the next day, another one. Household chores, kids to raise, to educate, make sure they aren't running wild, get them married, grandchildren, neighbours, her husband's work . . . if there is ever a spare moment, it's spent recovering from the exhaustion.'

Rana kept staring at her but didn't say anything, so she went on.

'But if this effort to spare time was an everyday thing, a part of the routine like everything else, if she came to a place each day to read, just for the sake of it, if nothing else, or to learn a new language, or tutor someone else, or to work on something she always dreamt of, without distraction or household worries . . . it could really make life different for her.'

The coffees had arrived by this time and Rana sipped on his without replying, deep in thought. Indu was happy to see that he was trying to imagine what she had just described, and so she didn't interrupt him. Finally, he put his hands on the table.

'I think I see what you mean now. It'll take me a little more time to realize its significance, but I get your point. So we need to start working on a few basic points.'

'Which are?' Indu asked, leaning forward again.

'Let's start from the things we need: books. Different kinds, fiction, language . . . you are the best judge. Books are expensive, but we'll acquire those slowly. We need to catalogue these books, get bookcases for them. We can build some. The next important point is how we get people to come here. Do you have any ideas?'

Indu said, 'My grandmother left me many books which are all lying, dusty and neglected, in bookcases in the house. I agree that we will need to catalogue them. As for getting people to the library, we can always hold events.'

'What kind of events?' Rana asked.

'Something that would attract people—performances, entertainment, talks, discussions.'

'And how do you want it to be—free or for a membership fee?'

'It has to be free in the beginning. Nobody would pay for something that they don't yet understand,' Indu replied.

He didn't reply, and Indu looked at him for some time. He seemed smarter than she gave him credit for, and she found herself more receptive.

'So what's this about you and poetry?' she asked him. 'You fancy yourself a poet now?'

He grinned at her sudden change of topic, his eyes laughing at her question. Indu noticed that the lines on his face made it crinkle when he smiled, and that he had to only smile and nod once for you to believe the sincerity of his words. She pushed away these thoughts as he replied, 'I actually write for a weekly magazine Fawad runs. He has a special poetry page for me,' he said proudly.

'Do you also read poetry?'

'Yes, I feel inspired by Ghalib.'

'Ghalib? Really?'

'No, *Ghalib*. You have to say it like you're drunk.'

Indu laughed, and he joined her.

'God, your laugh is so abnormal.'

'What do you mean, "abnormal"?' Indu asked, suddenly conscious.

'It increases with every breath, getting bigger and bigger. You could do sound for a horror story.'

Indu made the meanest face she could muster and said, 'What about your laugh, hun? You laugh like such a sheep!'

That made him guffaw again, and he slapped the table, laughing.

'See?' Indu said, laughing at the way he laughed. 'If you could hear yourself . . . people are starting to stare, you know . . .'

'This morning I heard a song on the radio,' Rana said, '"*Tumne mujhe dekha*", do you know that one?'

'Of course!' she replied, a pfff escaping her lips. 'I've seen that movie so many times. We used to watch them all together.'

'Who?'

'In college, I mean. We had a screening one day of each week. It was the only day everybody turned up,' she said with a laugh.

'Yeah?'

'It's one of the only times you don't have to think of life and its worries—'

'Wait,' he said suddenly, staring at her, straightening himself up from the chair he sat back on, 'we could start by organizing a screening. That will draw people to the library, right?'

Indu looked at him for a few seconds, realizing that it was actually a good idea. 'You're not so bad after all,' she told him, nodding.

'Once women turn up, we could tell them about the library, how they can be members etc.'

'Which movie, though?' Indu asked.

'Has to be one with Rajesh Khanna, obviously,' Rana said, laughing as he watched her smile at his name. 'What are you doing now? Do you want to take a walk?'

'A walk?' she asked him, taken aback.

'Yes, unless it's too cold for you.'

Indu considered it for a few seconds and then got up and put on her coat, saying it was fine.

The grubby stairs led them out on to the road, and the breeze, which had been light earlier, had become stronger. Indu was careful to stay clear of the cars that drove through puddles, for nothing enraged her more than being splashed by dirty water. She buttoned up her coat as the cloudy sky rumbled slightly. Hawkers lined the streets around the circle, which was thronged by customers now, crowding around the warmth of the food, looking forward to *bhel puri, matar kulche* and especially chai. Rana walked ahead and looked back at her, wondering if she would follow him. Indu dug her hands into the pockets of her coat, raised her chin and looked everywhere but at him, and in a few seconds she spotted Natty standing outside the Ambassador, watching her.

Indu narrowed her eyes and walked towards him, making sure Rana noticed this change of direction and followed her.

'Good evening, *madame*,' Natty said, blinking innocently.

She smiled and said, 'I will return in some time. Please just wait here.'

'Good evening, sir,' Natty said, bowing slightly as Rana reached them.

Rana looked behind him to see who Natty was talking to, and then realized it was him.

'A very good evening,' he finally replied, his face showing that he was impressed.

'If you want, I can bring the car behind wherever you are going, *madame,* so you wouldn't have to walk all the way back to me,' Natty said.

Indu smiled dangerously and replied, 'I think I am fine, Natty.'

'Also, there is some kind of strike on at Janpath,' Rana said. 'You'll get stuck if you take the car out to the circle.'

Natty gave a long, dramatic sigh and leant against the car. 'Someone strikes for sugar, someone else for salt . . . these problems never end. So I say eat your *samosa* and forget about it.'

They strolled for a while; there was less pressure to say something. Here and there, they would point out things to each other. Indu saw that he liked to walk with his hands in his pockets and constantly looked around, his neck turning often, drinking in the sights, watching the people who caught his fancy.

It started drizzling soon, getting even colder. 'Ha! Aren't you regretting your thin jacket now?' Indu asked Rana with a smirk, fingering her coat.

'At least I have a hood, but you . . .' he said laughing, pulling her hair up from the back to indicate the absence of the hood, his finger brushing her neck. Indu laughed as well, noticing his intimate movement. 'I like Delhi best in February, when the *simal* blossoms on the trees,' Indu said.

Rana smiled. 'I like living here. I don't want to return to Lucknow; life is good there, of course, but people think of different things. The world seems smaller there and I want to be able to broaden my life.'

Indu heard him talk of his life like he could do whatever he wanted, go wherever he wanted, without obligation. They walked together, and she sometimes felt like bumping her shoulder against his, but contained herself, lest he began thinking she liked him.

'When do I see you next?' he asked her, the sound of his voice warming her in the rain.

'Call my house at 11 tomorrow morning,' she told him, hoisting her purse up, 'and maybe you'll get a chance to make yourself useful again.'

He nodded, grinning.

'I'll think about the things we talked about in the meanwhile,' she said.

'Your laugh? Yes, better change it while you still can,' he said.

She gave him a scathing look one last time and walked towards Natty and the Ambassador in a huff. He yelled out 'goodbye, Indu' from behind her, his own sheep-like laugh still booming in her ears.

* * *

A few days later, Amita arrived with a bag full of clothes, her face aggrieved. She banged the door shut and walked straight inside, past her mother, to what used to be her bedroom. Her mother called out to her and then followed. Indu made her way to the bedroom on hearing the commotion, throwing a quizzical look at her mother.

She had never seen Amita fume this way. She paced the room, hands on her waist, and Esha watched them from afar, too scared to ask her if she wanted any tea or water at this apparently sensitive time. Indu and her mother stared at each other, at a loss for words, but they didn't have to wait long; Amita seemed to tower over them both as she finally spoke loudly in anger.

'That man,' she said, her voice almost shaking, 'deserves not a minute of the time that I've given him.'

'What did he say?' her mother asked immediately, moving towards her, placing a hand on her shoulder to pacify her.

Amita paced around some more before answering, 'We had a huge fight. It had been going on for some time, but this morning . . . This morning he said that I wanted him to lead a lonely life.'

'What? Why?' Indu asked.

'He said that he sought to fill the emptiness in his life by dedicating himself to his work, and that I was trying to prevent him from doing so.'

'What emptiness? How does that even—'

'The emptiness of not having children.'

Indu stared at her sister, aghast, for it was one of those unspoken things, things that people might dare to think but never say aloud.

'He said that he had emptiness in his life because you don't have children?' Indu asked her sister incredulously as her mother's face turned to stone.

'He wants to fill that hole by trying to expand his business,' Amita said, 'and that I was actively trying to prevent him from doing so.'

'How?!'

'Number 7,' Indu's mother said with a sigh.

Indu stared at her sister.

'That I was actively creating hurdles in his life—as if I want this! That I don't want him to succeed, because I cannot. That it was my revenge because I don't have the "skill or willingness it takes to study medicine".'

'Let me go and give him a piece of my mind—skills my foot!' Indu said, flaring up. Her mother told her to calm down.

They sat together for some time, and once both Amita and Indu had settled down, they discussed men and their insecurities. Indu insisted that Govind was trying to mask his own incompetence by projecting his problems onto Amita. Her mother, however, advised that they resolve their problems in a more appropriate manner, and that fights between a couple were part and parcel of married life. But Amita refused to go back to the man who was quick to blame the slightest hurdle in life on a biological issue. Indu supported her, which annoyed her mother even more.

Amita shook her head. 'This I cannot forget. I am done. I gave up a lot for him, but I'm not going to do it anymore.'

'What will you do?' Indu asked her.

'I will resume studying.'

5

'I can cook bhindi, *bharta, rajma,* pulao and *anda.* But I don't eat it. Oh, and also *khichdi.*'

'Nobody likes to eat *khichdi,*' Indu said, making a face at Esha, 'so it's fine if you don't mention that.'

Esha nodded at Indu, staring at her admiringly. It always made her uncomfortable whenever Esha looked at her like that, like she looked up to her.

'You can say *malai kofta* also, everyone likes that,' Indu told her. 'And you can easily learn how to make it later.'

Esha had told Indu that that evening, she was going to meet a boy, and if everything went well, she'd be married to him. When Indu had questioned her about the hurry, she had told her it was because of her stepfather, that she couldn't be home alone with him, because her mother said he was a drunk and not trustworthy. It was easier for everyone that Esha be married so Sunita wouldn't have to take her along everywhere she went to work.

'That must be Amita *didi,* go open the door,' Indu told Esha when she heard the doorbell ring.

Indu hugged her sister as she walked inside, and Esha automatically headed to the kitchen to fetch her a glass of water.

'At first I thought I overreacted, but now I am even more sure that I don't want to see him,' Amita said. Indu looked at her mother; she didn't seem surprised.

'He can set up his office thing anywhere,' Indu said. 'Why is he so bent on Number 7?'

'That's exactly what he said about you,' Amita replied.

'You cannot dismiss his feelings so easily, Indu,' their mother said.

'He's posing an unnecessary problem in something so straightforward—'

'He's Amita's husband, and what he wants is also important.'

'Well, she's made her decision, hasn't she?'

'That doesn't mean it's going to be easy to stick to it,' her mother replied.

Amita got up and walked around, hands on her waist, not saying anything that would allow her mother to launch another attack at Indu.

'Indu, you are so stubborn. If you don't get the flat, it's not like your life will stop,' their mother began.

'What do you mean? Of course life won't stop; life won't stop without so many things. That doesn't mean we shouldn't try. And you're the one who actually told us that we must remain in control of the flat!' Indu retorted.

'I'm not really liking your behaviour. That day, you threw such a tantrum—'

'Well, it was needed—'

'You threw up your hands and started yelling, I won't eat, I won't drink, I'll die!' her mother said, mimicking her in a way that Indu thought was a very unfair and inaccurate depiction.

'I may have been a bit melodramatic, but I did what I had to,' Indu said, raising her chin and closing her eyes in dignity.

They both glanced at Amita, who was still pacing around the room.

'Govind doesn't understand Indu. He's always grumbling, "Why do you always let her have her way? She's immature." What he actually cannot stand is that I chose to support you over him. But how could I not, after he basically never supported me? And so . . . he stopped talking to me when I tried to sort things out with him today. I shouldn't have gone, it was a moment of weakness. He says I'm afraid to say things that I should. But when I did, today, he launched the attack on me, took out his frustration, said that things weren't going his way. It's weak behaviour, is what it is.'

Her mother put her head in her hands.

'I'm moving back here,' Amita announced, and Indu tried not to look too delighted in front of her mother; she was glad not because she wanted her sister's marriage to be in trouble, but because it would be nice to have her around.

* * *

She found him leaning against a pole, his hands in the pockets of his trousers, looking around as people went by. She watched him for a few seconds from inside the car as his hair blew in the light breeze, the bristles of his beard glistening under the sun. He held his jacket on his arm and was soaking in the sunshine. She saw him spot the Ambassador as they pulled over to where he was standing, and he straightened up and nodded at the car in greeting. She asked Natty to stop and got out of the car. Wearing her *dupatta* elegantly, she gave him a cursory look before putting on her sunglasses.

He smiled at her as they approached each other, and Indu watched the corners of his eyes crinkle. She looked away, as she always did, when she saw him looking at her, her sunglasses making her seem even more pompous, but she couldn't restrain her lips from curving upwards as he grinned broadly at her.

'Ah, you're smiling,' he said. 'Did the sun come out right today?'

She made a face at him, her smile disappeared, and she took off her sunglasses and gave him an icy stare. That didn't deter him, though, as he went on grinning.

'Come on, let's go,' she told him, turning around and indicating the Ambassador.

'Are you excited?' he asked, adding, 'about our Indu-Rana day out?'

'Yes, but it's not just a day out, we also have to get some work done.'

'Of course,' he said and cheerfully took a seat at the back.

She got in from the other side, sitting as far away from him as possible, and found him already in conversation with Natty.

'You have to drive her everywhere, huh?' he was asking.

'It is the will of God,' Natty said in an exaggerated tone, starting the car, but then, noticing Indu's expression, added, 'and my utmost pleasure, of course.'

Rana chuckled, sitting lazily with his arms behind his head, looking out the window. Indu stared at him, but he didn't turn towards her.

'Do you eat non-vegetarian food?' Rana had asked her.

'I've had some,' Indu admitted, 'and I would like to try some more, but most people I know don't eat it very often.'

Rana put a hand on his mouth and snorted. 'Thank your gods you've met me, then! I may be a Rajput, but kebabs are my first love.'

When Indu laughed, he said they would go to Karim's.

Indu was watching him when he turned to her and asked, 'Why don't you drive yourself?'

'Me?'

'Yeah,' he said.

'Why should I?' she said.

'Seriously, why don't you drive?' he asked her.

She looked at him derisively for a few seconds and then finally admitted, 'I'm scared.'

He shrugged without judgement. 'We can teach you. Right, Natty?'

Natty gave a thumbs-up from the front.

In a rare display of amiability, Indu gave a slight smile. They slowed as they passed a market with stationery shops, and Indu suggested they buy some.

Walking on the side of the road, Rana let out a loud noise of contempt when he saw a large hoarding that said 'Progress through Congress', next to which were a calf and cow in a nurturing embrace. 'What?' Indu asked him sharply.

'*Progress* through Congress,' he scoffed.

'Well, who else?' she said.

He looked at her strangely. 'Oh, yes. You support Indira Gandhi, right?'

'Yes,' Indu said loyally, at which Rana shook his head, which incensed her, but she said nothing and they continued in silence.

It was wintry but warm that day, and she and Rana scoured the Nai Sarak market, passing newspaper vendors and booksellers who had their wares spread out on mats, sitting at their head like custodians. Indu subscribed to a few magazines and newspapers using the address of Number 7. They reached the shop where Indu wanted to get some chairs. They spent a while there, taking their time picking them out. When they got one for free in the end, Rana smugly insisted that they had got it free because of the great conversation he initiated. They walked through various markets, musing over what they might need, ending up with a bunch of homely stuff for the library: a rug, stationery holders, utensils for the pantry.

'*Ishq ne Ghalib nikamma kar dia*,' he said, as if he'd just remembered it, '*varna hum bhi aadmi the kaam ke* (Love has made me useless now, though I was once quite the man to know).'

'Sounds like you,' Indu remarked snidely.

'You know, I dreamt of you yesterday,' Rana told her as they began walking again, his hands in his pockets. Indu looked behind her to make sure nobody could overhear.

'Really,' she said, raising her eyebrows sceptically.

'Yeah,' he looked ahead of him in contemplation, twisting his lips into a pout. 'You told me that you were in love with me.'

Indu snorted, looking at him in exasperation. 'Even dreams need to have boundaries, mister. Remember the bird that soared too high?'

Rana couldn't help laughing. Indu watched his hair blow in the wind again, and tugged at her braid.

'I think I'll write you one,' he said, more to himself than to her.

'Write me what?'

'A poem, of course.'

Indu merely smiled at that.

When they reached the car, Rana directed Natty through the lanes of old Delhi, where the Ambassador could go only up to a point. There was the usual chaos outside, people hurrying past, selling everything on the streets—wares, snacks, shoes of the latest fashion. When Natty stopped the car, Rana caught Indu staring doubtfully at the streets.

'Come on,' he said, leading the way, as Natty said, 'Enjoy, madame,' from behind them.

Rana walked briskly ahead of her, parting the crowd easily, not looking back to see if she followed. Indu didn't mind very much; she wanted to feel as if she was going through it on her own. She tightened her hold on her bag and saw from behind her sunglasses the unceremonious stares that were thrown her way. The street was lined with little eateries, outside which people huddled, waiting to get inside. Meat was being smoked on skewers over trays of coal, and Indu saw a large board for Karim Hotels Pvt Ltd. When they reached, Rana led her to a seat in the corner and sat down happily. 'Food fit for a king,' he said, laughing.

Waiters bustled around, serving each table with speed and precision, signalling with their eyes, serving one place but looking somewhere else. She held the laminated menu in her hands as Rana sat back and relaxed, watching everyone eating, looking around as if he had never seen anything like this before. He grinned at Indu as he caught her looking at him, and she went back to the menu with an exaggerated sigh.

'So what should I have?' she asked him.

'*Burra,*' he replied without even glancing at the menu, his hands folded behind his head against the seat. 'Mutton *burra.*'

'I've never had mutton,' she said, making a face at him.

He shook his head with certainty. 'It's the only thing in which you get the purest flavour.'

She ignored what he said and scanned the menu again, meanwhile asking him when he had first arrived in Delhi. It helped reduce the pressure to make a quick choice. He told her how he had arrived three years ago, that he was completely taken by the liveliness of the city and wanted to make it as a lawyer here. He said his father owned a bit of land in Lucknow, but that he had given up farming to become a police inspector. Being an inspector in UP was no joke, he told Indu, talking of the harsh realities his father faced every day.

'Ready to order?' the waiter asked, coming up to them.

Rana looked at Indu, who had indecision writ large across her face. 'Two mutton *burra*,' he said to the waiter. She was relieved he ordered so she could be saved the trouble, although she didn't show it.

'I thought about the movie,' Rana told her as they waited for their food to arrive. 'I think we should screen *Mughal-e-Azam* for the opening.'

'Ooh,' Indu said, impressed. 'I like that idea. Good choice.'

Rana nodded. 'There never was another movie like that and there never will be.' Just then, the mutton *burra* arrived. Indu held her thumb up to Rana, telling him that she liked it.

'*Ek berehem shehenshah ke khaane mein Salim ki Anarkali dam nahi todegi, nahi todegi!*' Indu said between bites.

'I don't think he says it twice.'

'Shut up, it's more fun to say it twice.'

Rana laughed, and when he didn't say anything more, Indu went on, 'I think Salim is the most real character of the lot.'

'Why so?'

'His dilemma! Love versus duty, the struggle of his life. It seeps into every part of his body, into his acting.'

'*Salim ki* Anarkali,' Rana said.

'Who do you identify with the most?' she asked him.

'The *shehenshah*,' Rana said with a wink. 'Do you think it's better if we show another love story for the opening? To attract more people?'

'Come on, it's the best love story of all time,' she said.

'After ours, you mean?' he said with a laugh.

Indu snorted loudly and went back to her food.

* * *

As the days went by, they did little things every day and built up the library. Rana seemed only too happy to spend time with her. She found him and his company more and more pleasant, as he questioned curiously, laughed sincerely, and said what he thought. She knew he liked her, for he never really missed the chance to express it, overtly or otherwise, and she lost no opportunity to spurn his trifling, which he took with spirit. He talked to her ardently of things he liked, of cricket and music, never hesitant in his thoughts. But mostly he spoke about her, as if he had known her all his life.

'You may pretend to have your nose all up in the air, Indu Narayan,' he said to her, 'but I know you love all our quips just as much as I do.' They met mostly in Natty's presence, who had also developed an easy rapport with Rana.

One day, as they were setting up two additional bookcases, Rana said, 'Remember, I told you my friend Fawad has this magazine?'

'Yes.'

'Well, I was thinking, could he sometimes also come and work at Number 7? He has lots of work to do, compiling the various stories that are posted, editing them, putting it all together before sending the final version to print. Could he do some of that work here?'

Indu thought about it; she wouldn't mind him doing the work at Number 7, that is what it was meant for—but for women. But what if the women visitors felt discomfited by his presence? So she suggested to Rana that he work in the fourth room, the empty one. And that he would have to set it up himself. Rana beamed even more widely at that.

For the books, they settled on the most basic cataloguing system. Her *dadiji's* collection included mainly religious texts and spiritual books, some encyclopaedic volumes, and books on housekeeping and embroidery. Rana obtained a few books related to law from his college and some on politics and history from his seniors. Indu picked out the English classics and some contemporary writers, mostly books about the freedom struggle, besides multiple copies of the works of Nehru and Gandhi.

They went by genre and then author names, numbering them from the outside in. Keeping track of the books was a whole other matter. The most important feature of any library was that the right book must be at the right spot at any given time, and once read, should go back to the very same spot. They debated for a long time on the best system, and finally decided that instead of requesting people to keep the book back on the right spot, they would collect all books taken from the shelves at the front desk and place them correctly every evening.

They also agreed that Rana would be the custodian, for as long as he could be there, and the rest of the time, Indu would carry out the job. Rana told her that he did not mind spending his days at Number 7, managing the library with her, as long as Indu could give him space to write for Fawad's magazine and study for his exam. 'Do you have classes as well?' she asked him. 'Not often; I mean, it's my second-to-last year, so we're mostly supposed to study at the library ourselves. Which is exactly what I'll be doing.' Indu was happy to oblige. At the front desk, they would keep a logbook, where each borrowed title would be recorded when issued and returned. Indu would write letters to the weeklies and periodicals of which she wanted subscriptions for the library; she assigned a week to collection for the common fund every month, when donations could be made on a voluntary basis.

Now that the days were getting slightly longer and it was not as cold, sometimes they took walks in the late afternoons and evenings. Indu told Rana about Govind *bhai* and her sister, how she felt that their relationship had soured because of her, and that it was weighing her down.

Rana began whistling as they fell quiet. Indu shouldered her coat, which she had gotten along just in case it was cold, but it had proved totally unnecessary. Rana looked at her as she moved the coat from arm to arm and chuckled.

'People must be thinking, look at this strange girl with the strange coat, how fancy does she think she is?'

Indu looked at him, not laughing only because she had an answer, 'No, they must be thinking, look at this strange boy with the girl, does he sometimes think how lucky he is?'

He laughed loudly and Indu laughed with him, so that the people around them really did begin to stare at them. Indu threw her coat at him to carry, and he shouldered it with a sigh.

* * *

Different troubles brewed at home, and the dining table became a battlefield. Her parents blamed Indu for the recent rift between Govind and Amita. They didn't miss any opportunity to attack Indu and got even more annoyed when Amita supported her sister. Indu, on the other hand, was totally unimpressed by their show, wondering why they couldn't support her daughter in her decision.

'Of course we support her,' her mother replied, stung. 'If she wishes to study, she will. But this is not the way, to leave your house and fight with your husband.'

'Well, if the husband is so—'

'Not another word, Indu,' her mother warned.

Lohri came and went as bonfires cropped up all about the city, the popcorn crackling in the fire. Yet, at the Narayan residence, a grim mood prevailed.

If her parents thought the problem would simply go away, they were wrong. Amita was resolute in her decision, and Govind made no attempt to take back what he had said. But Indu understood—not only had Govind practically told her sister that it was because of her that he felt his life was empty and bereft, he had also insulted her abilities. Her mother might not understand it, but that was what hurt most of all.

Every morning, then, Amita bathed and dressed early, sitting at her desk with her books. Sunita served her breakfast and lunch so that she could study. Amita seemed determined to show her husband the skills and willingness that he claimed she lacked. Her parents had no idea how to deal with the situation as Amita, up till then, had been the more peaceful of the two children in the family. It annoyed them even more when Indu merrily declared, 'Wait till the library is completed, *didi,* you can sit and study there in peace all day and show him what you're capable of.' They thought that it was unnecessary encouragement for more strife in their marriage.

For Indu, it was exciting to have her sister back in her life, especially at a time when things were happening for her. She looked forward to introducing her to Rana, and the three of them working together in the library. She thought about it for some time and then wondered if it was a thought too naïve; they all had very different lives and would have to go back to them eventually. Yet, the more she thought about it, Rana seemed the only one who was free to fashion his life any way he chose, to do whatever he wished, live and breathe as per his will.

6

April rolled into May, bringing the dry, enervating heat typical of that month in Delhi—relentless sunshine provided by the sun, which seemed to rise higher in the sky each hour. The city stretched in sunlight like someone waking up after a satisfying slumber, relishing the kind of repose that comes with the cracking of knuckles after a long rest. Rana rued the summer. When Indu asked why, he looked at her like she should already know; 'the best food is in the winter, of course.'

As all the supplies for the library started coming together, Indu turned her attention to sprucing up the house. She asked Sunita to come with her to Number 7 so the house could be properly cleaned. Sunita went about the flat, cursing its deplorable condition, with Esha trailing behind her, handing her the necessary equipment. Indu imagined how it would look once it was a library, with rows of chairs and tables, women browsing the bookshelves, with maybe a huge pinboard at the entrance displaying announcements and advertisements for events happening around the city.

Indu had also invited Rana and Fawad to come to Number 7 that day. As Sunita and Esha were there, she wouldn't be alone in the house with two men. Indu noticed that Rana hadn't gotten his hair cut, and it curled slightly at the edges. His narrow face tapered towards his chin, and his beard covered the sides of his face. He seemed even taller than usual today in his buttoned shirt and trousers. When he entered, he looked questioningly at Sunita and Esha, who had both stopped working to look at the young man. Indu made sure he stood a little way away from her.

'How are you?' he asked, his voice deep and smiling, looking over at Sunita and Esha again. 'And who are they? What are they doing?'

'I'm getting the house cleaned, obviously,' Indu said, raising her eyebrows at him, like it wasn't that hard to deduce. 'And they are Sunita and Esha.'

He nodded tersely, moving a step closer to her and grinning again. 'So what do you want to do today?'

She narrowed her eyes at him. 'Nothing that you want to,' and moved away to tell Sunita to clean the tops of the bookshelves as well. He sighed and followed her around the house, bending down to say hello to Esha, who giggled. Her mother sharply reminded her to pay attention to the job at hand, and Rana walked about, picking up and inspecting various knick-knacks.

Later, Rana and Indu sat outside in the balcony.

'What about the screen and the projector for the movie?' she asked him.

'It's all sorted. I've already arranged for it.'

'Good,' she said, putting one hand on top of the other. 'I thought you were bluffing about taking care of it, as usual. I should probably trust you more.'

Rana looked at her in exasperation. 'You should trust me on everything!'

Indu made her most sarcastic face, just managing to hold her laughter.

Rana remarked that the women would have a lot to gossip and giggle about once they started coming to the library, and it would become a place where they had fun.

'And why is that?' Indu asked him.

'Come on, look at our chemistry here,' he said, putting his arms behind his head, against the chair. 'With your snootiness and my dazzling humour, we make for a deadly duo.'

When she giggled, he added, staring at her intently, 'You have these little things when you smile.'

Indu blinked innocently. 'Teeth?'

He acknowledged her joke with a pout.

'No, these, beneath your lips. I think . . . little dimples. Doesn't she?' he added to Esha, who had appeared in the balcony, and who nodded vigorously. Indu smiled at her, feeling a bit self-conscious, and got up from her seat to have a look at what Sunita was doing.

The most important task now was the seating plan. The seating had to be arranged in a way—she had discussed it with Rana—so that it would facilitate quiet, group study. For that, they needed new furniture, apart from the chairs they had already bought. Indu was glad that her sister was now in it with her, as she could help with a lot of this planning.

Indu knew that her parents held her partly responsible for Amita having returned home and for all that had gone wrong between Amita and Govind, but if they believed it, they had to be fooling themselves. Discord had been sown into their relationship long before they found out that Amita couldn't have children. According to her, it had begun when the match had been arranged, when Amita was still studying and had cleared the initial examinations for a degree in medicine. She had to leave it mid-way as Govind *bhai*'s parents wanted the wedding to take place as soon as possible.

Amita had tried to get over the disappointment, but it must have been deep, so she resolved to resume her studies one day. Indu was happy that she had been the one to trigger it. But now, as a result, whenever Indu announced anything new that they might be planning for Number 7 to her mother, she turned a deaf ear.

'This one,' she told Amita, 'she will make life hell for any man. Poor Rajat, uff, poor, little Rajat . . .'

Indu had made a face, but still told both her parents that they should prepare for the big launch. Her mother now looked worriedly at her husband. 'But there are so many things. That house has to be made hospitable. Every day, it has to be cleaned, swept, taken care of, dusted . . .'

Indu glanced at Sunita, who had gone into the kitchen, anticipating the demands of dinner.

'What about Esha?' she asked her mother suddenly.

'What about her?'

'Is she getting married?'

'No,' her mother replied with a sigh. 'He turned out to be a *maanglik*. It would have been too much of a risk.'

Indu looked at Sunita again. 'Well,' she asked, 'why can't Esha work there?'

'Where?'

'At Number 7! That will also help her stay out of the house while her mother is away.'

Her mother considered the proposal, looking at her husband, who was now engaged in a conversation with Amita.

'I think it is perfect,' Indu said excitedly. 'Don't you think so? She would be earning a bit of money as well; I mean, we can pay her. It will be so helpful to have her there, that flat is a *chidiya ka ghosla* right now, dust everywhere . . .'

'I'll talk to Sunita,' her mother replied, and Indu squeezed her hand in excitement. Amita put the radio on. At the first beat, Indu recognized the music.

'What? Is this another Rajesh Khanna song?' her mother asked.

'Yes,' Indu replied dreamily as Mohammad Rafi's voice floated through the room, singing '*Gulaabi aankhein jo teri dekhi*'.

'I don't know how many women have fallen in love with this man,' her mother said, getting up from her chair as if with a heavy heart.

'*Yeh bhi koi gaane hain!* These are not songs,' her father said over Indu's singing. 'The real songs were the good, old songs; these days, it's all about love and dancing around trees!'

Indu wanted to tell him that Rana felt the same way, that his favourite movie was *Mughal-e-Azam*, but chose to focus on the song instead. She then wondered what he would have to say about the fact that she was learning how to drive from Rana and Natty.

It had started off as a joke, of course, but Rana kept asking her. 'What if Natty is not there, or what if he's sick and you have to take him to the hospital?'

'Then I'll ask you,' Indu had immediately replied, suddenly realizing what she had done, implying that he would be there in her future. 'I mean, if it happens one of these days, since you're always following me like a bee. Or anyone else who's around, honestly.'

'Alright, what if you have to escape, and you can't really ask for someone's help?'

'I'd never put myself in such a situation,' she said, 'but okay, whatever, let's try it.'

More than anything else, it ended up being great fun for all three of them. But when Indu finally begun to get the hang of it, Natty grew morose, thinking he wouldn't be needed any longer. So Indu had to assure him that she would always need him, because she would never drive on her own.

'Why not?' Rana had asked her, laughing.

'Why would I if I can loll in the back and read a book?'

'You'll be driving for your life one day, Indu Narayaan, I can tell you that much,' he said as she stuck her tongue out at him.

* * *

They created a membership application and discussed how they could go about getting women to sign up. Signing up wouldn't be a problem, Rana told Indu, it's free. It's the following up, the coming here every day, that will be tougher. They decided to focus on the movie screening as much as they could and put up flyers. Rana put up some in his university, and Indu met Mrs Bala again to update her and ask her to spread the word among the girls in college. It was important, Rana noted, that women who lived nearby know about it, since they would be the most likely to sign up.

But what really helped, of course, was her campaign—people were more open to the idea because they had seen her on all the posters for the *beti hee jaan hai, beti hee shaan hai* campaign. Indu's excitement was contagious, so much so that it managed to distract her parents from Amita and Govind's problems as well.

After a few weeks of cold-shouldering, Govind had tried to talk to Amita and persuade her, but she had not relented despite her parents' insistence. The matter was put aside for some time, and Amita stayed on at her parents' house. Govind resented Indu more and more with each passing day.

With Esha coming to work at Number 7, another problem was solved. All of thirteen years old, she happily agreed to spend her time at the flat for she had always liked Indu *didi*. Each morning, she would go with Indu and Natty to Number 7 and begin cleaning, sweeping the whole flat, dusting the surfaces and wiping the floor clean. Indu showed her how to set up the chairs every day and to make sure that no books were moved from their positions.

Together with Esha, they designed the membership cards, signage, posters and leaflets. Rana had taken a fancy to Esha, teaching her all the latest songs and watching her side with her Indu *didi* whenever he made fun of her. When Indu told him that Esha's stepfather could not be trusted and that's why she had to be married off soon, he looked dejected and promised her that things would turn out fine.

'Ah, but you are the Champion of the Minorities, I forgot,' Indu told Rana, remembering his comment.

'You can say only "champion", that fits fine,' he said, grinning at her. 'And so is your favourite politician. At least that's what she claims to be.'

Indu shook her head at him. 'Only "champion" for her is also fine.'

With Esha always at Number 7, Rana could walk in and out more freely and stay for as long as was required. Sometimes, he'd get his books and study there, and Indu would sit and read from her *dadiji's* collection. They prepared the kitchen as well, making basic tea and coffee arrangements, and decided to let everyone use it as they wanted. Indu suggested that later, they could consider getting a cook and have set meals every day of the week, so women needn't think of how to arrange for lunch.

One day, Rana pointed at one of the cabinets and said, 'Whoa!' Indu looked where he was pointing.

He said, 'Your *dadiji* liked her alcohol, hun?'

Behind the glass cabinet were glass bottles in all sorts of shapes and sizes, holding dark and transparent liquids, none of which Indu knew or recognized.

'Must be my grandfather's,' she said, touching the window glass with her fingers. 'They moved all his stuff here. They used to live in Civil Lines with us.'

Rana opened the cabinet slowly and took out a seemingly heavy glass bottle, filled with a golden substance. He opened the cap and smelt it, and must have found it strong, for his eyes opened wide.

'Strong stuff. Have you ever tried it? Alcohol, I mean?' he asked her curiously.

She shook her head.

'Do you want to?'

Indu stared at the bottle, narrowing her eyes. 'What will happen if I do?'

'If you have it, you mean?' he asked, amused.

She nodded.

'I don't know. You might want to kiss me,' he said with a casual shrug.

'Stop dreaming, mister,' she said, taking the bottle from him to put it back. 'It's not yet late enough in the night for that.'

* * *

The park was starting to dry up. Frayed, parched grass began to lose its colour and freshness in the sun, but as long as they walked in the shade on the paths, it was not very bad. The weather was more still now, less people out in the early evenings, most waiting for the sun to go down before they ventured outside their homes. Rana walked slightly ahead, but stopping for her by a bench. She paused as they crossed a jasmine bush, plucked a big, bright flower and sniffed. It reminded her of evening walks with her sister. She took the jasmine and handed it to Rana when she reached him.

He accepted it with a smile, looking at her in surprise. 'What?' she asked him.

'It's a very human thing to do. I didn't know you had it in you,' he said.

'Oh, shut up,' she said, spotting a small jasmine bush nearby and picking another one for herself. He looked at the new flower and scrunched up his face.

'That is the worst-looking jasmine. I'm going to pick you a better one,' he said, going off to search another bush. Indu stared at his back as he looked, separating the branches to find the perfect flower. He walked over to her after a couple of minutes, handing her one. 'I'll wear it,' she said, putting the little flower in her braid.

'Wait,' he said, extending his hand, adjusting the flower and pushing a strand behind her ear. He smiled. 'There you go.'

She stared at him and said after a moment, 'You do it too.'

He put the flower behind his right ear with a shrug.

'My jasmine is still prettier than yours,' she told him.

'Well, you need it more than I do,' he said, and she punched him lightly on the shoulder as they started walking forward.

Outside the park, there was a stream of tourists, and in front of them a photographer with a camera on a tripod, asking each of them if they would like a photograph. Indu stopped in her tracks, and he looked back at her, a step ahead.

'What?' he asked.

'Let's get one,' she said. He looked at the photographer, then at her, and with a smile, called over the photographer.

He trotted over to them happily, blessing them, saying they looked just like Rajesh Khanna and Sharmila Tagore, and that they would have four fat, happy children. When the time came to stand next to Rana, Indu shuffled her feet awkwardly, but when she saw him scratching his head in the same confusion, she leant towards him with a smile, their jasmines close together. They wore careful smiles, and the photographer readied his camera.

'Please try to look good, although I know it's hard for you,' Rana muttered to her and she turned her face to him with an expression of indignation just as the camera snapped.

'*Arre* madame,' the photographer said, 'please try to take your eyes off sahab for a moment!'

Rana sniggered as Indu fumed and crossed her arms in front of her chest while the photographer readied the camera again. 'Smile!'

Indu smiled widely this time, looking straight ahead, and the photographer took another snap. 'You can take these from me tomorrow, madame,' he said happily. 'They will be first-class.'

The next day, when Indu brought the pictures around, Rana gazed at the one where they were both smiling at the camera. He looked neat, with this buttoned shirt and clean-shaven face, a new look for him, except for his hair, which had been ruffled by the wind. Indu's flying *dupatta* and hair created a flurry in the picture. Both wore happy smiles.

'Very impressive picture,' Rana remarked, 'considering your face.'

She pushed him lightly as he laughed.

7

'Could you maybe, for two seconds, not look like you'll bludgeon someone to death?' Rana asked Indu as she stared around her at the transforming Number 7, her eyes narrowed. A flurry of activities was taking place inside the flat on that hot Saturday morning, in preparation for its inauguration the next day. Indu's father had sent Tinka Ram and Nathu Ram, two peons from his office, to help them set up for tomorrow, the day of the big screening. They moved about taking instructions from Natty, who seemed to be enjoying every minute of it, asking them to set up the chairs one way, and after a few minutes, another way, unnecessarily. Esha went about dusting the whole house, singing to herself, apparently having inherited her mother's love for the latest songs.

'You think it's going okay?' she asked Rana, her arms folded.

'Yeah. Everything will be finished by tonight, don't worry. Once Fawad arrives, I'll set up the projector and screen with him, he knows better how it goes.'

The screen would be set up right opposite the main door, against the balcony door, where all the furniture would be placed for the day. A huge standee saying 'The Library at No. 7—India's First Local Library For Women—Become a member today!' graced the entrance, along with a reception desk, where

Rana would take his place. They were yet to collect the little map-and-facilities pamphlet they had had printed. With *dadiji's* old furniture moved out and the new, identical chairs and tables moved in and set up, it definitely looked more like a library. They had labelled the bookshelves and put up some posters of past Indian leaders.

In the adjacent room, the tables still had to be set up for the snacks and drinks. Another room had been set up as the music room, where one could work while a record played in the background on *dadiji's* old player. In her old bedroom, her bed and belongings still remained. The spare room had been turned into a group study/conference room.

Esha walked up to Indu and Rana, her cotton *salwar-kameez* bouncing along with her braid, little hoops in her ears and nose, smiling like a little girl who's just finished her homework. 'I've finished, Indu *didi*,' she announced.

'You're finished, hun?' Rana asked her in an affectionate, mocking tone.

Indu nodded distractedly. 'Good, now go eat something. There is a banana for you in the packet I got from home. And tell Natty to hurry up and bring up the lunch for everyone. For Tinku Ram and Nathu Ram also.'

Esha nodded happily and scampered off. Indu sat down for a few minutes, watching Rana move about the house, till she heard a knock on the door, which was ajar, and saw Fawad there.

'Hello,' Fawad said to Indu, sticking a hand out, his glasses glinting with the sweat on his face.

Indu smiled back sweetly, having completely forgotten how much more awkward he seemed next to Rana, who could talk easily to anyone.

'I'll get the screen and other things from the next room,' Rana said and walked away, leaving Indu to ask Fawad how he was doing.

'Good, good,' Fawad replied. 'How have you been dealing with Rana's company?'

Indu snorted, 'You know my pain best, hun?'

Fawad laughed. 'But he's a brilliant guy, you know. Best in his class, very responsible, always locks the doors and windows at night . . . he's also very strong. You should see the weights in his room.'

She raised her eyebrows and gave him a doubtful look. 'Did he tell you to say this?'

His face fell. 'Is it that obvious?'

'Yes, you idiot,' Rana said as he walked up to them, having overheard a bit of their conversation. He handed Fawad the extension cord and said to Indu, 'Ignore him,' as if he hadn't himself asked his roommate to talk him up.

'So what kind of things do you write?' Indu asked Fawad as Rana bustled away.

'Ah', Fawad said, 'you know *Goonj*, our magazine, is independent? We don't report just the news the government wants people to read.'

'The government wants you to read news that's different from real news?'

'There comes the question—what is the real news?'

'And what would you say it is?'

'Nothing! Just the spirit of the publication and the effort of the journalist. Here, have a look.'

Indu took the magazine from him. It was just a few pages thick. On the cover was a picture of two little girls sitting on a pile of rubble, with the caption, 'The Aftermath of a War Won'.

'Interesting,' Indu said. 'What is it about?'

'Just some stories about how the war didn't really help solve the crisis as it was in East Pakistan anyway, and instead, the retaliatory atrocities, and those by the Army as well, were completely ignored.'

'Is it true?' Indu asked.

'These people say it is,' he replied.

'How can you trust them?'

'How can you not?'

At that moment, Rana came in and announced that it was time to test the projector. Indu watched them fiddle with the screen for some time, and then connect the player to the projector to test the cassette. After a few minutes, the opening credits of the movie rang out in the house, and Rana looked triumphantly at Indu, who smiled in appreciation as Natty, Esha, Tinku Ram and Nathu Ram stared at the screen in amazement.

'I feel like watching it now,' Indu said.

'Tell you what,' Rana said, looking at Indu and Fawad, 'let's get the work done, and then we can actually sit down to watch a bit of it. I doubt we'll be able to catch much of it tomorrow, there will be so much running around to do.'

Indu considered it and decided there wasn't any harm in the proposition, and Fawad shrugged. 'What are we left with now?'

'We have to pick up those pamphlets . . . wait, maybe I should send Natty for that, yes? Okay, then we have to arrange for the water . . . yes, that's about it . . .'

Rana set the projector aside as Indu went to give Natty instructions. He got the last bit of work done by Tinku Ram and Nathu Ram, so they could leave. Then they decided to get water from Sharmaji ki Shop. They stopped by a *shikanji* stand nearby on their way, and Rana ordered three glasses.

'I'm very excited about tomorrow,' Indu told Fawad.

'Are you expecting many people?' he asked her, taking his glass from Rana.

'I don't know. I hope there are enough people. I've already told Mrs Bala to ask her students to come, so I'm sure some of them will be there, especially because it's only for girls. That should fill it up. Some of my sister's friends, some people I know . . .'

'Can anyone come to the screening tomorrow, or is it just for women?'

'Anyone can come tomorrow, of course. Just later on, it's women-only.'

'That's why Rana fits in well, eh?' Fawad asked, and Rana accepted the jibe with a grin.

'I really hope that lots of young girls join, you know. The younger, the better; they'll get into the habit at a formative age,' Indu said. She took a sip and added thoughtfully, 'I've already picked out the sari I'm going to wear.'

'I have to say, I am quite envious now,' Fawad said.

'Come on, I don't mind lending you another sari,' Indu suggested innocently, breaking into a laugh with Rana.

Rana looked at Fawad sympathetically. 'Yes, she has a weird laugh. Surprised me the first time as well.'

Indu walked away in a huff, refusing to look back despite their half-hearted sorrys between snorts of laughter. She reached Sharmaji ki Shop to order the water, and asked him to send extra glasses to the flat the next day.

'Let's play the movie from the main song,' Rana suggested after they returned to Number 7, 'the one in colour.' Indu agreed, drawing a couple of curtains to make sure it wasn't too bright but not completely dark, and took a spot on one of the chairs. Rana sat on a chair away from her and Fawad in the row in front of her.

They began from somewhere in the middle of the movie and the familiar vision of Madhubala dancing to '*Pyaar kiya toh darna kya*' appeared on screen. Indu stared at the screen and eventually realized that Rana was repeating all the dialogues passionately. Indu joined him wherever she could. Half an hour later, she felt a touch on her arm and saw Rana leaning towards her, realizing a few seconds later that he was handing her a note.

'What is this?' she asked him in a low voice, not wanting to alert Fawad.

'I told you I'd write you a poem,' he whispered.

She unfolded the crushed bit of paper slowly.

Salim ne Anarkali ko marne nahi diya
Shehenshah ne use jeene nahi diya
Ek din mai bhi baitha aur socha
Ki uparwaale se maine ab tak kya liya?

Khoobsurat banaya, dilkash banaya
Phir bhi Anarkali ko pasand nahi aaya
Aur phir ek andheri sham
Sab samajh mein aaya

Rajesh Khanna se Rana bana diya
Superstar se waqil bana diya
Anarkali ki ajeeb hassi sunkar
Ek darpok Salim bana diya

Indu clutched the piece of paper in her hand, shaking because she couldn't stop giggling. She looked directly into Rana's eyes;

he had an arm behind the extra chair and seemed to be enjoying her amusement. She was still chuckling when she leaned forward and said, 'I'll get back to you with one of mine on this.'

Rana stuck out his lower lip and said to her, '*Woh shayari hee kya jo sochne pe aaye?*'

She stuck her arm out for the little notebook in his hands, and he gladly handed it to her with a pen. She thought about it for a couple of minutes, and then scribbled, handing it to him. It said,

> *Shayari hai,*
> *Hazir-jawaabi nahi*
> *Pratiyogita hai,*
> *Pyaar nahi*

He sniggered when he read it, conceding by raising his hands. The movie went on without further interruptions, with the Shehenshah declaring to Anarkali the price of Salim's life: being buried alive in the wall. '*Kaneez Jalal-uddin Mohammad Akbar ko apna khoon maaf karti hai!*' Rana shouted at the screen along with Madhubala as Indu exchanged a giggle with Fawad, who, though used to such displays of enthusiasm from his roommate, was still amused. The loudest cheer, though, came when Prithviraj Kapoor released Anarkali at the end, and Rana yelled out along with the Shehenshah's booming voice, '*Hum mohabbat ke dushman nahi, apne usolon ke gulaam hain!*'

Indu hit him lightly on the shoulder, got up and walked to the switchboard to switch on the light. The sun had set by this time and the room was dark. 'Alright, calm down there, *shehenshah*,' she said.

'Come on, we need to go downstairs now, Natty will be back any minute,' she told them. After checking that everything was in order, they locked the flat carefully and took the stairs down. Indu handed Rana her bag, which he took with an exaggerated sigh.

'This is how you treat Salim, hun?' he asked.

'Depends on the kind of Salim I'm dealing with,' Indu said, shaking her head. 'That Salim offered to make Anarkali his *mallika*, the queen of the whole kingdom. What do you offer me, hun? Just your witty little jokes.'

'As if you don't feel like enough of a queen already,' Rana said, yawning.

There was an evening lull in the air, and traffic moved slowly outside the gates of Ganpati Tower. Inside, a few kids went around on a bicycle.

'You can go on,' Indu heard Rana tell Fawad meaningfully. 'I'll wait here with Indu till her driver comes.'

She pretended not to have heard him, and Fawad said a short goodbye to her, walking out of the gates. She and Rana chatted for a few minutes till she saw Natty glide over in the Ambassador, parking outside the gates. 'I am back, madame,' Natty said. He held the pamphlets in his hand.

'You can put the pamphlets upstairs,' she told him, 'and then we can leave.' He nodded courteously and headed upstairs, leaving her alone with Rana at the gate. Rana looked at her directly and Indu looked away.

'A bit of a cool summer night, eh?' she asked him, stroking both her arms with her hands.

'I have a solution for that,' he said, laughing, opening his arms wide, facing her. Indu folded her arms and turned the other way, but couldn't help laughing as well. Rana saw Natty's silhouette heading towards them from the building.

'So I'll see you tomorrow? Big day,' he said to Indu, and she nodded.

'Well, goodbye,' she said to Rana, wondering what else she could add, as Natty came up and went to the driver's side of the car.

Rana gave a slight nod and then turned to Natty. 'Goodbye,' he said, and then with added emotion, 'I'll miss you, Natty!' Indu smiled and got into the back of the car.

She was looking forward to tomorrow, although she was a bit nervous. She would definitely wear her sea-green sari, the one with the brocade border, which she had gotten from Jaipur a couple of years ago but had not yet had the chance to wear. This was something that she could wear it to with pride, something of her own doing—the woman in the sea-green sari who was in charge there. Along with Rana.

She wondered what he would wear, and how they'd look standing together. She decided that she'd glance at him a few times while making the speech so everyone would know that he had an important role. His stupid, wavy hair would lie perfectly on his stupid, little head, and the stubble on his face would make his smile stand out even more.

He was always ready for anything—to take up responsibility, walk with her, eat a mutton *burra*, build a bookcase, make a stupid joke, and bring up Rajesh Khanna. Her mind went back to him constantly, imagining him telling Fawad to say to her, 'Tell her I'm very responsible, that I lock all the doors and windows at night', and shrugging off Fawad's incredulous look, bribing him with a night's dinner in exchange. She thought of him running his hand through his hair, asking her why she needed that thick coat, of sitting back in the chair and talking about their chemistry.

She reached home with Rana still on her mind, only to find people sitting inside her drawing room, all looking up in delight as she appeared before them with a tired face.

Supriya aunty stood up first. In her head, Indu still called her that, although she had insisted Indu call her 'mummy'. 'Just like you address your own mother,' but there was still so much time, and besides, it didn't come naturally to Indu.

'Indu,' she beamed. Indu gulped as she remembered that she was her future daughter-in-law. 'How are you?' she asked as Indu bent to touch her feet, and murmured that she was fine.

Then Balwant uncle got up from the sofa, and Indu bent again. He blessed her and put his arm on her shoulder.

Her own parents nodded at her smilingly, motioning that she join them, and Amita waved and poured her a cup of tea.

'We just couldn't help dropping by,' said Supriya aunty directly to Indu. 'We were coming back from a friend's and then we thought, let's say hi to our daughter.'

Indu listened carefully, nodding and chewing a biscuit she picked up from a plate on the table, which gave her time to think. 'I was just coming back from the library. Tomorrow is the movie screening, as you know. I am very excited to have you there!' she added, looking meaningfully at her mother, who, she was sure, would have invited them. Supriya aunty's laugh confirmed her assumption.

'This girl is just too talented,' said Balwant uncle, looking at Indu and then at her parents. 'I tell Rajat to count his lucky stars all the time.' Everyone else laughed while Indu gave a weak smile. A wave of guilt washed over her as she watched her mother's smiling face, her sister arranging things, and her father looking proudly back and forth between her and Rajat's parents.

They spoke about her and Rajat and looking forward to having her around more. They mentioned that Rajat had settled quite well in London and was now considering a few possibilities, but they would be quite happy to have him living wherever he deemed fit. At first, Indu stared blankly at them all, but slowly gathered herself and entered the conversation.

She told them about her correspondence with Rajat and about all that she had been up to in setting up the library. They listened interestedly, but the conversation kept going back to Rajat and Indu, and behind the clatter of plates and spoons, Indu hid her quietness, this reality reminding her of a direction in life she had completely forgotten about.

* * *

The bright morning brought with itself a stillness that only comes with the assurance of summer, that it is here, and here to stay. Indu awoke before it was time. Her mind was clear and purposeful. She dressed with care, folding all the pleats of her sari with precision. One by one, she asked Natty to carry out each task she had allocated for him, coordinating with her sister. She reassured her mother that she didn't need more help. It was one of those times that the extra reservoir of confidence in your being opens up, at the right time, right when it's needed.

When she got into the car with her sister, she felt slightly nervous, but she chatted as if it was just another day. She smiled at Amita, staring at the mole on her chin, her face worn down by the past couple of years but still shining with interest, especially when she looked at her sister.

'Are you excited?' she asked Indu.

'Yes . . . I really am.'

Upon reaching, she saw that Esha was already waiting outside Ganpati Tower, standing a little way off from Tinku Ram and Nathu Ram. Indu nodded at them all, giving an extra smile to Esha, and led the way up the stairs. Unlocking Number 7, she immediately set them to work. The next hour was spent getting everything arranged, only briefly interrupted by Rana's arrival, who also immediately went about setting up the mic and his desk. She introduced her sister to him, and Amita smiled kindly at his enthusiastic hello, complimenting him on his shirt. Only then did Indu notice what he was wearing.

She went up to him, deliberately looking him up and down, arms folded, contorting her face in contemplation as he waited. He wore a white shirt with trousers and a blazer, which she presumed was his lawyer get-up, his hair combed neatly to one side. The blazer prevented him looking tall and lanky, and he gave her a pompous nod before smiling. A thin moustache would have completed his lawyerly look, but Indu had only ever seen him at extremes: either with a beard or shaved clean.

'You pass,' she said, and his face broke into a grin. She stared at him, waiting for him to say something back.

'And?' she said, her voice threatening.

'Eh,' he said, moving his hands to say 'so-so'. She knew he was pulling her leg, but she still narrowed her eyes at him and turned away.

'Come on,' he said laughing. 'Are your parents coming as well?'

'Yes,' she said, remembering last night, 'they will be here.'

'Uff,' he said, rubbing his forehead as if in tension, 'I hope they don't ask about how much I'll be earning in the future.'

Indu stared at him for a few seconds, unable to say anything. Finally, she said she had to check something in the kitchen. She told Esha how much tea to put in each cup, where to place the empty cups and how to arrange the food. 'Make sure all used plates and cups are removed as soon as they are set down. You have to serve everyone, and make sure there are no dirty things on the table.'

Amita went up and down the flat as her friends began arriving, showing them the way, and Rana took his place by the front desk, talking to whoever came in, explaining about the library, its facilities, its membership and planned activities. Indu looked at him proudly before entering the conversation to explain the concept.

More people began filing in, and Indu grew more and more nervous by the minute. Finally, her parents entered with Rajat's parents, and Indu went to greet them, uttering pleasantries. When she saw that Rana was nearby, she introduced them to him, hoping that he would behave himself.

'Rana is Mrs Bala's student,' she told them and he gave an earnest nod. 'He's helping me with the project.'

Her father patted him on the shoulder in response, and her mother asked him a couple of questions before others came up to them and started a conversation. There were many women, most of them Amita's friends, of various ages, dressed in saris and suits, and a few in trousers. Indu spotted Mrs Bala, who had just come in followed by a bunch of girls, and both she and Rana went to greet them. They directed them to where each kind of books was kept, and where they would screen the movie.

A few minutes after the official time, Rana was urging Indu to begin when Supriya aunty and Balwant uncle came up to them.

She stared at Rana, who was smiling, and said, 'Rana, meet Supriya aunty and Balwant uncle, my future parents-in-law.' She saw the smile fade from his face slowly, and then reappear as he responded to their 'namaste *ji*'. She walked away after that, her heart heavy. But the need to take the stage made her collect herself. She clutched the paper with her speech on it and went to the mic as Rana and Amita asked everyone to settle down. Her parents sat at the back in a corner, and she could see them looking at her attentively. She also spotted Fawad in the seats, and about fifty more people staring up at her. It felt like she was at one of the debates at her college, especially with Mrs Bala and the girls from her college in the audience.

Now that the room had quieted and people seemed to be waiting only for her, Indu felt a pang of nervousness in her stomach. She began the speech she had prepared. Her throat felt dry. She saw Rana staring at her from the desk and took a deep breath.

'Good morning, everyone, and many thanks to all of you who took the time to wake up early on the weekend and made an effort to be here today,' she began. 'I'd like to talk for a bit and explain what this place, this library and its set-up, is about before we go on to screen the movie. I am sure all of you have seen *Mughal-e-Azam*, but a classic like that needs to be watched again and again until we know it well enough to scream out the lines to each other, even better than the characters themselves.'

She looked at Rana, and he nodded once, smiling.

'Everyone asks me—asks us—what is it, this library, and what do we aim to achieve with it? In its basic form, we have books here left by my grandmother, who passed away.

'We really hope that we'll get donations to keep adding new reads very, very frequently. If you have books lying around at home that you don't think you'll read, we would be glad to house them. The idea as such is that we have a variety of books here, and anyone who is a member can borrow and issue them to read as per their need. But behind this is also a larger aim, a larger idea, one that we hope will convey itself without too much trouble and best be understood in practice. Yet, I will try to explain.

'It has been almost twenty-seven years since we got Independence, yet, in the building and progress of a young and free India, among those who have been left behind are women. Nowhere in the world is a woman so truly worshipped, so greatly idolized, yet so pathetically deplored. While the literacy rate for the male population in the country is slightly short of forty per cent, for the women, it's just eighteen per cent, less than even half that of men. While men get countless chances, time after time, to educate and train themselves, to stand on their own two feet, to maintain and support a family, to feel able and in control, the women have to simply stand by and surrender their fate to the forces of society that govern their lives at every point.

'In that situation, it is important to sit and just think for some time, what is it that holds us back? Why don't we have jobs that bring home money, and why aren't there more of us in the Parliament, elected and voted, to formulate laws and policies? What is it that keeps us from achieving and being something that comes so easily to the other sex, but is rare and exemplary for us? Where does it all begin to go wrong? We have the same faculties. The Prime Minister is a woman, and the roads haven't collapsed, the railways haven't stopped working! In fact, we are making progress.'

Indu paused to take a sip of water from the bottle in front of her and was suddenly aware that each and every pair of eyes was on her, each person listening in singular attention. Somehow, the thought gave her more confidence. She went back to her paper.

'I don't believe it's because we are born less intelligent or are in any way less capable, but we are still not equal when the statistics reveal themselves. It is because we are not given a fair chance, a fair opportunity; that we are given a few things, the scraps and the leftovers, simply because the law says we must. We are given the right to education, but not the conditions that facilitate the smooth functioning of this process—clean public toilets, the transport required to reach the educational institute, the safety that needs to be assured to a marginalized group. Are we given the time to bloom and flourish, or the encouragement needed to move forward and chase the goal we set for ourselves in life? Are we given a quiet room of our own and three hours a day to study in peace, to take time out for ourselves, to train our minds to be better every day?

'The Library at No. 7 is an attempt to create an alternative space that might have been denied to you in your life, denied to the extent that you don't even realize that it must exist in the first place. In your daily humdrum routine, we provide you with a space where you can find time for yourself. We encourage you to spend at least a few hours every day to sit and read here. To pick up a book that you have been meaning to read but haven't gotten around to. To flip through a magazine or cookbook without your kids running about. To find the space and time to study for that teaching diploma.

'Most of all, we hope that you will come here to engage and relate with other women who think like you, who will laugh in your company, give you a little tip that might prove useful. So that together we might form a community that will raise each other, for when we have been put down for so long, a little support can go a long way. We ask that you register to become a member. Membership is absolutely free and will give you access to a large number of books. We will organize activities and workshops, little courses that you can take to learn something new, and a movie screening every week. Most of all, you get a space of your own, one absolutely free from any diversions, to use your free time as you want. We hope that you will join us in this room.'

A slow clap from the corner of the room was followed by decorous applause, and Indu smiled and bowed. She announced that they would collect the membership forms now, and after a tea break, the movie would begin. People got up to head to the front desk, where Rana sat ready to register, and then towards the room with the drinks and snacks. Indu moved around greeting more people, switching from namaste to shaking hands. 'Indu, dear,' someone called out, and Indu turned around to see a woman with a large *bindi* and a sugary, sweet voice, standing beside a girl who seemed to be her daughter.

'Namaste, namaste, I am Kamla, a friend of your mother. She invited me, and this is my daughter, of course,' she said to Indu.

'Hi, I'm Enakshi,' the girl replied, sticking her hand out to Indu. She had a broad forehead and had her hair in a beautiful ponytail. 'I really want to be a member here! I like to read classics and I'm learning the *sitar* as well, I would really like to put up a concert for everyone.'

Indu looked at them, nodding in admiration, and then said that was wonderful, and that they could certainly arrange something like that.

'I really want to go to your college once I finish school,' Enakshi told Indu breathlessly.

'Then you should meet my teacher there—see that lady? Mrs Bala; go say hi to her,' Indu said, moving away to other people. Her parents patted her on the back as she approached them, and Rajat's mother too said something she did not hear. A babble had broken out and suddenly, Indu realized how many people there really were inside. She greeted them, answering questions, constantly looking over her shoulder at Rana, who too was answering questions, laughing and talking.

After it seemed like most people had enquired about memberships and submitted their forms, Indu asked Fawad to begin the movie. By the time the credits began rolling, most people had settled down. They pulled down the blinds, which made it sufficiently dark to watch the film. She went to the back and watched the stragglers settling down as the voiceover floated through the room. Rana came and stood next to her, his arms folded against his chest, smiling at her. She returned his smile and went to check on Esha, but he followed her.

'It went well!' he said to her, excited. 'There are forty-five registrations!'

'What?' Indu asked, stunned; it was much more than she had expected. 'That's crazy!'

'It is. I mean, yeah, it's free, so everyone will register, it's not a big deal to fill out a form. But still, it means most women who came here registered, except a few, and that's great!'

She felt like jumping, but her sari wouldn't allow it, so she just gave him the widest possible grin.

'You were very good on the mic,' he said.

She nodded and said thanks, telling him he wasn't too bad either. She looked up at him, and his eyes looked directly into hers as they always did.

'Are you really—was that them?' he asked her. She knew he was talking about Supriya aunty and Balwant uncle.

The world seemed to stop. The hundred people inside the flat seemed to disappear. The rest of her life felt like a mirage.

She nodded quietly, and he lowered his head.

Even in the dark, she saw his face change; his eyes widened, and his eyebrows were raised.

'What do you mean? Engaged to marry?'

She nodded with her eyes lowered, but then looked up.

'To whom?' he asked quizzically.

'I have known him a long time . . . and our families are friends.'

He stared at her for what felt like a long time, with only Akbar's voice ringing out from the room outside.

'So . . . there is no—no way, that we can . . .'

She found it hard to look up at him but did it anyway; it was hard to read him, so she appeared stony too. 'No.'

She put her hand on his shoulder lightly and walked out before anything else could be said.

The movie went on in the other room. Indu found a chair to sit on, Rana's poem going on in her head. She wondered if she would see him anymore, if he would still like to come to the library. She regretted it, but she knew there wasn't any other way.

She didn't see him come out but heard him talking to Esha in the same affectionate tone he always used. She contained her smile and walked inside to tell them to begin laying out the snacks.

END OF PART 1

8

Six months later

Breakfast outdoors in the morning sunshine was the only thing Indu looked forward to when it was really cold, as it was in Delhi in January. Her favourite iron chairs and table were spread out in the garden, the sun's rays casting a glow over the white marble tabletop. Her father had his nose buried in the newspaper and her mother murmured instructions to Sunita, who was serving them.

'Are these the earrings that Supriya gave you?' her mother asked her, peering at Indu as she served herself some *poha*.

'Yes, these are Supriya aunty's,' Indu replied, touching her earrings.

Indu noticed her mother's sharp glance when she said 'Supriya aunty'. She knew that her mother was both uncomfortable and glad that she didn't yet consider Rajat's mother her own.

Her father shook his head over the newspaper and Indu immediately asked him what was going on.

'Things are starting to get out of hand,' he mused.

'What is it now?' Indu asked him.

'Same old thing. Strikes all the time, this bandh, that protest . . . everything is going wrong, it seems.'

Indu exchanged a look with her mother.

'And does it affect us greatly?'

'The other parties are starting to join hands, even those who would never imagine doing so before now. It can only lead to problems.'

'But how?'

Indu buttered another slice of bread, sipping her tea before taking a bite.

'They can't win,' she said confidently. 'There is no way.'

'Send Natty to get the lunch at 12.30, it won't be ready before that,' her mother said, and Indu nodded without listening.

'Maybe, but you never know. It's too early to tell. Shashi and I have a meeting this evening.'

'What for?'

'How to run the campaigns. How to fund the campaigns, more like.'

'And how is that?' Indu asked as she wiped her mouth with a tissue napkin.

'Of course, we all have to contribute whatever we can. This time it's essential, we don't want to lose our offices. But Shashi depends too much on goons, I can't stand it.'

'To get the votes, you mean?'

Her father nodded, glancing at her mother.

'But I thought goons were used more by hardcore right-wingers,' Indu said.

Her mother shook her head, calling out to Sunita to clear the table. 'Goons belong to whoever pays them. Anyway, I expect Amita will come later, she's still sleeping.' Living at home with her parents and seeing Govind *bhai* only on the weekends had been working well for Amita for the past few months. To Indu's delight, she and Amita generally came back home together in the evening, even though they arrived at Number 7 at different times in the morning. Indu checked the letterbox and found a letter from Rajat in it.

She said goodbye to her parents, ripping the letter open, and headed to the car, where Natty gave her a cheery good morning.

'What's making you so happy this morning?' she asked him, taking a seat.

'Just the thought of serving you, madame. And also, there is a new *vada-pav* corner down the road.'

Indu looked, and sure enough, there was a *vada-pav* stall on the street. It looked quite busy. Their car glided by, leaving behind a cloud of dust.

'Some people started shouting at him when he took up that spot,' Natty said. 'But when they tasted his *vada-pav, uff,* everything was forgotten.'

'Yes, but what does one do?' Indu said. 'You can't let just anyone come in and take over a spot—what is yours is yours, and you have to protect it.'

Natty shrugged. 'I say it doesn't matter where someone is from, as long as the *vada-pav* is good.'

Indu didn't want to argue with the logic of the *vada-pav* and chose to read the letter instead. Rajat had written to her with news of the weather, how he was always overloaded with work, and the quiet way of life he had learnt to appreciate. Indu made a mental note to ask him in her next letter how he spent his weekends, realizing that she didn't know. She wondered if Rana would already be at Number 7 today. He had started off with such a bang, setting everything in order perfectly, but since returning from Lucknow, he had been in and out as he deemed fit. Indu decided that it was obviously not for herself that she wished him to come, but for the sake of the library.

The women were used to his idiotic jokes. In that sense, it was better that he turned up some days and remained absent on others, since it created curiosity and excitement. But Indu still felt it would be much better if he were there every day to smooth everything over, since some women had never warmed up to her. Especially Mrs Leela, who took every opportunity to chat with him. Shameless woman, Indu muttered, shaking her head, flirting with a man fifteen years her junior, in front of her daughter, sometimes while her husband waited outside to pick them up!

Rana was in this morning, arranging the books behind his desk when Indu walked into Number 7. The curtains had been drawn back and sunlight was streaming in, falling on the few plants they had added in the corners and the chest of drawers they had arranged to serve as lockers where personal books could be left. The pinboard at the entrance saw more and more notices added each day as posters of events around the city were put up, most of them brought by Rana.

He was humming a song as he sat at the desk, and Indu could hear Esha sweeping the floor in the other room.

'Damn,' said Indu, 'I would have gotten my earplugs if I knew you were going to be here and in the mood to sing.'

He chuckled, and Indu saw his bright eyes light up as he walked up to her, leaned close in to her ear, and then suddenly sang out in his deep, booming voice, '*Zindagi ka safar, hai yeh kaisa safar!*' Indu moved away, covering her ears.

'Esha, did you do the drawing room already?' Indu called out and heard the young girl reply, 'Yes, *didi*'. Indu walked around the house, setting things right, getting into the endless cycle of putting things back in their place. She heard Rana go to the music room and set up the recorder. He put on one of his classical records, which Indu had earlier been completely unfamiliar with, but could now hum along to.

He scanned the shelves, replacing some books that were out of place and still humming. She hoped he would engage her in conversation, but he seemed absorbed in the task, so she moved on to counting the issue cards. There was one less than there had been yesterday, and she jotted down the number in the pad. When she looked up, she saw that Rana was flipping through a book. She was about to ask him what he was reading when she glanced at the door and found a head peeking inside.

'What do you want now?' she said roughly to the little Sardar boy peeking through the door. She wouldn't be fooled again by his wide eyes and innocent face. She had found him staring inside multiple times.

The little boy scampered off along the corridor, his *joodi* bouncing on top of his head, as Indu shut the door loudly and then opened it again to make sure that he had left. Now she could feel Rana's attention on her.

'What is up with that?'

'This stupid, little *Sardar*,' she said, flipping her hair over her shoulder, looking to see if his eyes followed her actions, feeling a twinge of disappointment when he continued to stare at the door confusedly. 'He's always trying to spy, have a look at the girls.'

Rana raised his eyebrows in response, his mouth forming the upside-down U of surprise that was so characteristic of him. 'He's a neighbour?'

'Yeah, they live on the other side of the corridor. No control over the kids, pathetic. Twelve years old and staring at girls all day long!'

'Well, with a girl like you in here . . .' Rana blinked and gave a small shrug, 'he must be slightly blind.' Indu threw the wiping cloth in her hands at him, which he caught with ease and walked away, laughing.

Once everything seemed more settled, Indu took her usual seat near the balcony, which had a small table by the side. Esha would generally hang around there, running from there to the front desk, where Rana sat now, his books spread out around him. Indu took out the inventory book and asked Esha to total up everything. Like other days, nobody came in for the first hour or so, but later, there was more activity. A couple of women from the sixth floor walked in to return their books and had a chat with both Rana and Indu. They could talk loudly, since nobody else was there.

Amita was late, but when she finally arrived, she looked happy to see Rana as well. He told her he had had some classes and other appointments that he could not miss. 'He's been very irregular, *didi*,' Indu told her sister.

'You missed me that much?' he asked her, sticking his lower lip out, and Indu gave a disparaging laugh, going back to her seat. Esha asked Amita if she wanted tea, while Rana went over to the pile of recently returned books, taking out a title that Amita had asked for a while ago.

More women began filing in and greeted Rana in delight. Indu's favourite member of the library, Divina, all of sixteen years old, with wide eyes and dreams of being a famous surgeon, almost squealed in mirth at the sight of Rana. She always rooted for the two of them to be together, to which Indu loved to reply that it would happen if only Rana's kismet shone golden one day.

'What did you learn today?' Rana asked her. Divina's parents had told her they would allow her to spend time at the library only if she learnt to cook one new thing every day.

'*Chana masala,*' Divina said, yawning, 'but that is the easiest thing to make.'

'We wouldn't mind tasting some of it, would we?' Rana asked Indu rhetorically, and Divina smiled radiantly.

After lunch, it filled up a little more. Mrs Leela walked in and straightaway went to Rana, her daughter trotting behind her. Indu watched them with narrowed eyes as Rana stood up while he spoke, his hands in his pockets, leaning forward slightly, running his hand through his stubborn hair. A few minutes later, they all looked over at her, and Indu looked away quickly. When she could still feel them staring, she looked up, and they signalled for her to join them there.

'Yes?' she asked them purposefully, as if disturbed during a very important meeting.

'Mrs Leela wants to conduct a needlework course here,' Rana said.

'Needlework?'

'Yes, and some embroidery,' Mrs Leela answered. 'I was taught from a very young age and I would hate not to pass on the skill. All girls should know it. I taught my daughter when she was seven.'

Indu looked at Rana, who stared back at her.

'It's an essential skill for anybody,' Indu said, after a pause. 'And yes, why not? Sounds like a good activity. Do you also want to charge for it?'

'Definitely.'

'Okay, why don't you give the proposal to us in a letter? We'll try to arrange it. Right, Rana?'

'Anything for Mrs Leela,' he said, grinning. Mrs Leela looked so flattered that Indu looked away. Once she had walked away with her daughter, Indu turned to Rana indignantly.

'What?'

'Could you maybe not flirt with someone old enough to be your mother?'

'She likes it. I'm doing us a favour; she wants to spend more time here only because of me.'

'What a generous soul you are,' Indu hissed at him. 'You might also want to think about her daughter.'

'What? She'll pick up some good tips?'

When Indu continued glaring at him, he said that at least he wasn't like Fawad, who was always looking for chances to talk to Sangeeta. 'Women come to me, not the other way around,' Rana said.

Indu glowered at him for a few seconds more, hoping that he'd take back what he had just said. When he didn't, Indu went on, 'Listen, mister, if you intend to abuse your position at the library and treat it like—oh hello, Kittu!'

Kittu had the most beautiful hair, and it swayed behind her as she walked into the library every afternoon. Both Indu and Rana would ogle at her luscious curls. She had told them that she was growing it out for her wedding next year. She lived close by as well, and her parents had been only too happy to send Kittu to a girls' library every evening on the neighbour's recommendation, instead of having her strolling in the gardens and attracting unruly boys. Kittu had been delighted to find an array of fashion books there. As it wasn't considered a respectable enough professional field to pursue seriously, and she had no other chance to indulge her interest, she gazed at these books whenever she came in.

'Hello!' she exclaimed, hugging Indu and Rana both. She then looked at Rana and asked, 'So you are back, hun?'

'Yes, Kittuji,' Rana said, giving a guilty smile and scratching his head. She was one of the few people he called ji, despite her being only as old as Indu.

Indu then took Kittu to show her the new books they had procured over the weekend, which a friend of Amita had sent— glossy black-and-white hardcover collections of the fashion of yesteryears—which made Kittu exclaim in glee. 'I will try to sketch all these designs,' she said to Indu, 'and actually, I was thinking, I also want to sketch you.'

'Me?' Indu asked, surprised.

'Yes. One day, when I have my exhibition, I would like your portrait there.'

'Why?' Rana asked, walking up from behind them. 'We don't want to scare people now, do we—ow!'

He massaged his ribs where Indu had elbowed him.

When they had finished talking to Kittu, he followed her into the kitchen, still chuckling. The cupboards inside the kitchen were nearly empty and Indu stared at them, wondering if they could store other stuff there.

'Do you want some tea now? I'm asking Esha to make some,' she asked Rana.

'Yes, thank you, but where is she?'

'Must be around here somewhere . . .'

They walked around to find her in the other room, her hair falling over her face as she bent over the notebook.

'How many times have I told you to braid your hair, hun?' Indu told her in a disapproving tone. 'Do you want to be a *chashmish,* working with your hair all over your face like that?'

Rana uttered a *tch-tch* and said, 'Better listen to her,' as Esha giggled. He picked up the book she had written the numbers in and Indu asked her to boil some water for tea, for them and for whoever else wanted it. 'But first, eat your banana, it's in the kitchen,' Indu said, and Esha sprang up instantly.

'How does she do this accounting so well?' Rana asked, stunned when he saw Esha's calculations in the book.

'Oh, she's brilliant,' Indu said, taking the book from him to glance at it herself. 'When she was a child, her mother taught her tables when she couldn't sleep at night. She's so precise, I never even double-check.'

'This is crazy.'

'I know. What do we have to order from the grocers, do you remember?'

'Well, we could do something for her, right?'

'I suppose we can.'

Indu smiled in satisfaction, wondering if she could dare to imagine that it could actually change lives, this library. Wasn't that the aim? It was going quite well, even beyond Indu's expectations. Granted, it wasn't a big venture that needed a lot of care and coordination, and Rana's presence definitely helped. But things remained under control; only a few books had been lost, and most of them were usually returned on time. They personally got to know each member who came in and learnt quite a bit about their lives. Some women did not find themselves benefitting in any way, so they never returned, but quite a few of them turned up almost every day.

They weren't always good days, but there were enough of them. There were many empty days, especially in the beginning, when they just sat and talked, wondering if anything would come of it. But people did trickle in, one by one, and at first Indu couldn't stop engaging with them. Apart from managing the library, each day, she decided to meet more and more people, to spread the word as far as possible. With the help of Mrs Bala, she spoke to several girls. 'Put it out there,' Mrs Bala told her. 'Show them what you have.'

Rana then went on a letter writing rampage before leaving for Lucknow, where he would spend his summer. He wrote to every newspaper and publication, drafting a press release about the library, inviting them to have a look. When one newspaper picked it up and wanted to do a story on Delhi's first library 'by a woman, for a woman', the rest picked it up as well. The results were little mentions in city newspapers, and free subscription to newspapers, periodicals and journals. Eventually, they had a stream of people lining up for membership.

'But we don't even have the space for so many,' Indu had said to Rana.

He had pffed in response. 'Do you think all of them will come every day? If fifty sign up, only one of them will likely be a regular.'

But then he left for Lucknow for the summer, and Indu felt the difference. They were closer than Indu had thought they were, more than she cared to admit, and she realized she looked forward to seeing him every day. Before leaving, Rana had laughed and told her reassuringly not to worry, that they would spend time together when he came back.

But he was essential. Whenever there were holidays, to Indu's delight and distress, it started to get busy. Girls streamed in from everywhere, having all that free time on their hands, especially the younger ones. Parents felt comfortable allowing them to engage in something academic and safe. But Indu had to organize a range of activities to keep them interested, and found it more difficult to do it single-handedly. Rana's easy manner always lightened things up. When he returned, Indu was more grateful than she let show, and more annoyed when he didn't show up sometimes. But he already gave so much of himself to it without expecting anything that she could never utter a word of complaint.

That evening, Fawad turned up, and he and Rana stood outside, sniggering.

Indu walked up to them and asked, 'What are you two giggling about?'

'Indu,' Fawad gushed, 'how goes life?'

'It would go a lot better if you didn't watch my girls all the time,' she told him.

'Me? Come on, it's your boy here who's the danger,' he pointed towards Rana, who tried to look as though he had never been subjected to worse slander.

'Yes, because I'm the one with Sangeeta on my mind.'

'For me, at least, it's just one. A library full of them aren't enough for you.'

'Good point, Fawad,' Indu said, looking at Rana with mock disgust. 'You are no better than that little Sardar.'

'I wish someone wouldn't be so jealous of my charm, you know,' Rana told Fawad, nodding.

'Jealous, me?' Indu laughed with contempt.

'You've begun challenging the authority, hun?' Fawad asked Rana, grinning at Indu.

'It's my favourite thing,' Rana replied as Indu raised her eyebrows.

'Don't mind it, Indu,' Fawad said. 'Authority is meant to be challenged. Just like I love challenging the authority of our other Indu here.'

Indu shook her head. 'I'm glad you feel enough familiarity with her to address her by a nickname, but I'm sure it's harder to challenge her authority.'

'There's where the fun is,' he said.

'We'll have this debate again,' Indu said.

Rana pretended to bite his nails in fear. 'I'd be scared if I were you, Fawad. It's a good thing you have Sangeeta, hun?' he asked him, patting him on the back, looking at her bent over her books at the far end of Number 7. 'Just that she doesn't know it.'

'Yet,' Fawad said with a grin.

Thankfully for Indu, Fawad's confidence would plummet when he was around Sangeeta, and he would retreat into the room allotted to the boys.

* * *

A week later, Rana came in late and they didn't get the chance to speak very much; Mrs Leela had multiple concerns about her needlework course, and Indu could hardly bear her overenthusiastic manner, so she left Rana to deal with it.

After a while, Natty turned up.

'When do I have to take Amita madame home?' he asked Indu, who looked over at her sister and then at the clock.

'Another half hour. But wait,' she said as he turned around to walk away. 'Bring the books from the car, the ones you picked up from Shashi uncle's last week. But leave the other package there, we don't have space for it.'

'She's not easy,' Natty said to Rana, looking at him tiredly.

'Tell me about it,' Rana replied, shaking his head in mock exasperation.

'*Uff*, I'll come downstairs, nothing gets done till I do it myself . . . now come, what are you sniggering at with him?' she said to Natty.

When they returned with the books in their arms, Indu noticed Rana wasn't standing alone. She walked over to them and almost dropped the books.

Fawad and Rana stood next to a woman who looked familiar. Within a couple of seconds, it hit Indu as she looked at the short, wispy hair that reminded her of that party at Mrs

Bala's. She looked slightly different now. She wore a small, stylish nose ring, loose beige pants and a sleeveless black blouse. Indu observed the way she was leaning towards Rana.

Fawad was in the middle of saying something when they noticed Indu. When nobody said anything, Rana broke in.

'Indu, do you remember Runjhun? She was at Mrs Bala's that time when we met?'

Indu gave a tight smile and narrowed her eyes. Of course she remembered her.

Runjhun stuck her hand out to Indu and she took it, touching as little of it as she could without breaking the handshake.

'Runjhun also wants to be a member here,' Rana said, looking at all three of them. 'She has many plans. We met a few weeks ago and she was totally blown away by me.'

Runjhun laughed and hit him on the shoulder, shaking her head at Fawad as if she couldn't believe this guy. 'You're the one who kept sending me notes, asking me if I would go out with you.'

Indu stared at Rana, her fake smile slipping off her face, her chest knotting up.

'Well, you are my girlfriend now, aren't you?' Rana said to her.

Indu shot Rana a hard look, her eyes blazing; she thought she saw something rueful in the way Fawad looked at her, but she couldn't be sure, so she adjusted the *dupatta* on her shoulder and walked away towards the bookshelves, leaving them mid-conversation, her head held high.

9

Indu had not been the most well-behaved child, and for some time, Amita had been the target of her mischief. The phase had lasted only a couple of years, but those years had been long and tough for Amita. Indu had begun doing exceedingly well at school, especially at sports. She had held the title of the fastest runner in her year for a long time, something that made her proud even now, for a good student wasn't rare—that was something all girls were taught to be—but excelling at a sport was more special.

Indu would show off her skill and subject Amita to her taunting, despite being much younger. She would pull her sister's braids whenever she came upon her in the corridors, darting off to giggle with the other little girls at her sister's slow reactions. At home, she lobbed slingshots at her at the dining table, tripped her up at every possible opportunity, and made up lies about Amita's non-existent boyfriends to her parents. 'You were a horrible sister,' Amita often reminded Indu later in life, 'but I wanted to be your friend so badly, and it crazed me that you wouldn't give me the chance.'

Indu was quick, outspoken and determined, insisting to everyone she knew for many years that she would be a great Bollywood actress one day. Her parents laughed away this childish fantasy, but for Indu, it had been a very real aim until she grew up to realize that most actresses had to follow a debauched path to get to where they were. It was the profession of women without families, of those who had to make it in the world on their own, and not of girls hailing from respectable, educated backgrounds, she was told.

Yet, for a long time, Indu believed she would rule Bombay, and that belief only strengthened when Simmi became her new best friend. She had recently joined school because her father had been stationed in Delhi for a few years. The girls instantly got along, for both of them were like each other, strutting around the school like they owned it. 'It's not like we seek attention,' Indu and Simmi would say, blinking their eyes innocently when the teachers confronted them about the boys lining up outside the school asking the guard to call them out, 'it's just that we get it.'

Indu felt betrayed when Simmi actually heeded the attention and went out with one of the boys from the boys' school. To Indu, at the time, it appeared tasteless and forward, for she considered herself too superior to actually accept the attention that was bestowed. Its acceptance by Simmi was the ultimate form of treachery, especially because it was something they didn't do together. After a very public fight that provided the school much gossip, the girls bitterly parted ways and Simmi joined hands with a new group of girls who were fascinated by the fact that she had a boyfriend.

Indu never forgave Simmi, and as competition became more intense in each successive year, they resented each other even more. When the time came to go to university and Simmi never took the exams, Indu decided that in the larger scheme of things, she had won, and bid goodbye to school in peace.

Moreover, the rift with Simmi grounded her and brought her closer to Amita, and so Indu decided that it was all for the best.

Indu had thought she would never again harbour feelings of hostility equal in intensity to those she had for Simmi. But now, she was proven wrong. Each time she saw Runjhun, with her nose ring and her short hair, both of which she considered exceedingly stupid, Indu gritted her teeth and looked the other way, almost as if it caused her physical pain to even see the other girl. She did everything she could to be as different as possible from Runjhun, whether it was brushing her hair diligently in contrast to Runjhun's unruly curls or wearing the most ethnic of her clothes while Runjhun dressed in everything western.

When Runjhun came to the library for the first time as a member and Rana greeted her earnestly at the door, Indu forced a smile and asked her in her most contemptuous voice possible, 'Wait, what's your name again?'

Rana, at first embarrassed by Indu's malice, eased the mood by taping a small piece of paper to the hem of Runjhun's blouse with her name on it, saying loudly, 'Just so everyone knows everyone's name,' and Indu gave a weak laugh.

The more time Runjhun spent at the library, the more Indu distanced herself from her and Rana, preferring to work on her own or sit with her sister, concentrating entirely on the affairs of the library, running about the flat as if she had absolutely no time to spare. Annoyingly for Indu, Runjhun had an opinion about everything, right from the functioning of the library to what the hero should have done in the latest movie, and always felt free to voice it. Indu increasingly found herself taking up the opposite view, even if she did not believe it wholly. She'd raise her eyebrows at Runjhun's opinion like it was the most preposterous thing she had ever heard, looking at

Rana in utter exasperation, telling them that she didn't think so at all.

Indu could bear it even less that Runjhun seemed to live as freely as Rana. One day she wanted to do a job, the next, study further. She didn't seem tied down at all by the same constraints that brought them all together at the library. As much as her being present in the library was a nuisance, Indu still preferred it to her not turning up at all, because most of the time, when she was absent, Rana would be too. Indu didn't want to think at all about what they might be up to together.

Indu couldn't help feeling a sharp stab of jealousy whenever she saw Runjhun, even though she knew it wasn't right. Once, when she was sure that Runjhun was within earshot, she couldn't help saying loudly to her sister, 'It's fine if they want to protest at India Gate. Why do they have to wear those ugly khadi *kurtas*?'

Earlier, she felt like she understood Rana, but now she felt completely misled. She had thought that certain things he did were just for her, that she brought them out in him. She missed how he would tell her that she behaved like a queen, and speak of them as if they were one entity. When she saw him behaving the same way with Runjhun, extending to her the same courtesies that Indu thought were reserved solely for her, she didn't know what to be think.

Yet, she felt strongly that there had been something between them that defied understanding, and felt pleased and vindicated when, at first, most of the girls in the library were shocked to learn that *Runjhun* was his girlfriend, not her.

'What? No, no,' Indu said, overly casual, peeking over her shoulder to see if Rana was listening, when Sangeeta said she saw only the two of them together. Divina was completely aghast and asked Rana if it was a joke, and when he said that it wasn't, she refused to speak to him for two days, which amused him very much.

Yet, when Indu felt the wave of surprise turn into a wave of pity, she laughed away the whole thing, saying Rana's stars were not shining that brightly yet. She added that she had a fiancé in London, and was looking forward to even maybe moving there with him. She found her sister staring at her at moments like these, but Indu would look away like nothing was amiss.

Sometimes, Runjhun didn't turn up but Rana did, and Indu liked those days the best, for she had his absolute, undivided attention and didn't have to play silly power games with her to emerge as the cooler girl. Rana had, in fact, arrived early that morning, whistling and smiling at her when she nodded in acknowledgment of his arrival. It was much colder today than it had been the past few days, and Indu wondered whether if it would be too much to wear her coat indoors. She chuckled to herself as she remembered the last winter, when Rana had eyed her coat with exasperation, asking her why she needed such a thick one anyway, and she had been eager to wear it just because it had newly arrived from London. Then she remembered how he had opened his arms wide, telling her he had another solution for the cold.

'Indu, do you mind putting these books back?' Rana asked her as she walked by. 'Up there, on the top shelf, under P-Q.'

Indu hmmed at him and picked them up. She thought of how they had set up the entire place from scratch, adding bits and pieces so that now it all came together like a strange kind of patchwork quilt that somehow worked. She thought of how he had approached her honestly and confidently, saying outright, 'I want to help you, I want to set it up with you'. She wondered now what had made him come to her, whether it was the connections he would make or the chance to spend time with her.

She decided it was the latter, considering he hadn't yet asked to be connected to anybody.

Evening rolled around and found her, Amita and Rana sitting together at a desk. Indu slid a few pens down the table and nudged Rana's arm, prompting him to pick them up. When he didn't respond, she nudged him again, laughing.

He gave her an expression of mock exasperation and picked the pens up with a sigh.

Rana closed his book and said, 'I wanted to ask you two something. It is Fawad's birthday on Saturday and we are inviting our friends home in the evening. Will you come? I was really hoping you would.' He looked at Indu particularly.

Indu exchanged a long look with her sister. 'Can we?' she asked her. Amita nodded slowly, considering it.

Indu gave Rana a plain, poker-faced look. 'Yes, I guess we . . . might show up.'

She saw that he was about to say something, but then changed his mind and nodded with a smile, telling them he looked forward to having them there.

* * *

Indu and Amita had always agreed that white was the colour of grace and that nothing could take its place. But for an impact, black always takes centre stage. It didn't escape Amita's eye that Indu emerged from her room wearing a black *multani kurta* with intricate Kashmiri embroidery at the neck and chest, buttoned up to the collarbone. She wore bigger earrings than was her usual style, and high heels.

Amita said, 'Are you sure we shouldn't wear saris?'

'Yes, I'm sure,' Indu said. 'It's just at his house, it's no big deal.'

Indu wanted to look beautiful for this party and for everything to go well. Their parents had already given instructions to Natty about which route to take and not to bring them back too late, while Amita decided to spend only the Sunday with Govind.

In the car, she asked Natty if he had managed to find out anything about the little Sardar boy who would still creep up to the flat.

'Nothing new, madame,' Natty reported. 'I did see that his mother was not surprised to see him coming from the direction of Number 7 yesterday. Very smart, that little *chhichhora*.'

'Maybe the mother is in on it,' Indu said darkly.

There was very little traffic and they found his flat easily. They could see the lights on and people moving about inside as the curtains weren't drawn closed. Indu could even hear Rana's laugh from the staircase, and unconsciously smoothened her *kurta* with her hand, placing the pashmina delicately to the side. She went up the stairs carefully, slowed down by her heels, with Amita following her.

He came to the door even before she could ring the bell, and she saw him take in the sight of her as she smiled at him. His warm brown eyes shone in the light. Whatever he had been about to say seemed to have evaporated in the air, and Indu looked away from his uninterrupted gaze, assuming an air of obliviousness.

'Hi,' she finally said to him. He shook his head slightly, and his face broke into a smile. He wore a shirt but had kept the top button open today.

'How are you?' he asked her, holding out his arms, and Indu couldn't decide whether it was for a hug or to simply take the things she had in her hands. She was spared the trouble of deciding when he noticed Amita behind her.

He greeted her loudly, asking her if they had found the way easily. Indu walked inside.

There were a few people inside, but Indu couldn't recognize any of them, so she stood at the door, gazing through the gallery, which opened out into a bigger room. From the door, Indu could see a carved wooden table in the centre, the room illuminated by a lamp in the corner. A couple of bags and jackets hung from a hook in the gallery, and next to it was a painting of a small boy in a field. As Indu looked around, she realized there were quite a few paintings on the walls, as well as a canvas on a stand at the far end of the room. She could hear a record player humming inside. As she walked in, she noticed the room had minimal furniture: a sofa by the wall, two or three chairs lying about, and a few foldable ones against the wall. The windows were shut and the number of people inside made it quite warm, so Indu held her pashmina in her hands. She saw a few figures huddled by the kitchen table, where there were drinks. She had already scanned the room for Runjhun and realized she wasn't there, which cheered her up.

'Who made all these paintings?' she asked as she heard Rana and Amita come up behind her.

'That's our sensitive little artist, Fawad,' Rana said, taking Indu's pashmina and purse from her hands and placing them on the table. He then led the way inside.

Indu and Amita followed to where everyone was gathered. Indu was surprised to see there were quite a few women as well. She hoped they were Fawad's friends, for Rana had never mentioned other women friends.

'He always helps me paint them,' Fawad walked up to them, having overheard what Rana said. Indu and Amita wished him a happy birthday, not knowing how to greet him at first, until Indu gave him a one-sided hug with an awkward laugh.

'These paintings are amazing,' Indu said to him, looking around. There was one with a wide blue lake full of lilies and boats, and another one of a valley filled with flowers.

'Thank you,' he said, looking pleased. 'They are all scenes of Kashmir.'

'Is it really so beautiful there?' Amita asked, looking at the paintings interestedly.

'Even more so.'

'Now that you like them, you should know that it's true, I did help him,' Rana said, and Amita laughed.

'Why don't you make one for me?' Indu asked.

'He wouldn't be able to do justice to you,' Fawad answered for him. 'A painting can only bring out so much.'

Indu acknowledged the compliment with a gracious nod and saw Rana nodding enthusiastically as well.

'It's true, actually. It would be impossible to capture that nose and that grimace on paint,' he said, and then began imitating her in an exaggerated, high-pitched voice, 'Natty, you better not be late today! Natty, bring the books from the car. Natty, why is Rajesh Khanna not mine?'

As Fawad and Amita burst out laughing, Indu successfully managed to stop herself expressing any hilarity at his impression, and gave him a dangerous stare.

'You know I'm joking,' he said, putting his hand on her arm when she gave no indication of relenting. 'Come on, what will you have to drink?'

'Just a Campa for me, please,' Amita said, and Indu walked to the table with Rana, saying hello to people she didn't know.

'Oh wait, we have to bring out more glasses,' he said, and Indu followed him into the kitchen, where he took out a few and began rinsing them.

'Are you thirsty?' he asked her.

'Oh, yes, a little bit.'

He flicked his fingers so that the water running from the tap sprinkled all over her face, and she gasped.

'You are dead, mister,' she said, raising her voice over his laughter. He handed her a towel and she wiped herself with it. She handed it back to him and he dried the glasses.

'Why are you trying to ruin my face?' she asked him as he handed her a couple of glasses to carry.

'I'd say it's a little too late for that,' he said with a sad pout.

For some time, it seemed like there never was a Runjhun; he introduced her and Amita to his and Fawad's friends, and they all seemed to happily accept the sisters, asking them questions about themselves, doubly fascinated when Indu told them about the library and how she worked there with Rana. She felt proud of the library and sensed the same in her sister, who narrated excitedly how she was finding studying again, which speciality she would aim for and what kind of work it would require.

'I'm actually thinking of starting a formal book club from next month onwards,' Indu told two men and a woman who were speaking to her and Rana, asking them about their future plans.

'Really?' Rana asked her, taking a sip of his drink, one hand in his pocket.

'Yeah, don't you think it would be good? We could have a book of the week to discuss, and hold talks on it. I'd wanted to initiate discussions anyway, maybe some debates . . .'

He shrugged, finishing his drink. 'Yeah, sounds good. Make sure you clash with Mrs Leela's needlework course.'

Indu laughed, shaking her head, telling the others about her and how Rana shamelessly responded to her flirtations.

He was defending himself when Indu spotted a large device near the window and asked, 'What's that?'

'Oh, that's a telescope.'

'A telescope?' Indu asked in surprise. 'I've never seen one like this. I mean, I've seen some in pictures, but this one looks different. Wherever did you get it?'

'Fawad got it from some uncle of his. I couldn't afford one, it's too expensive.'

Indu walked over to it, looking at it and then back at Rana in amazement. 'Could I try it?'

'No, of course not.'

She gave him a reproachful look. He cleaned the lens with a small wipe that lay next to it and rotated the plates around it. 'It's quite a clear night,' he murmured, 'go for it.'

He gently placed a hand on the back of her neck to make her position her head properly, his fingers going through her hair, lightly brushing the bones at the back of her neck. She could hear the sound of his breathing and he told her to focus and look to the top and right.

The moon, which always seemed dull and grey, unremarkable in the humdrum of daily life, suddenly looked bright and exceedingly white. Indu could see the craters on it, smudges of black on a sparkling white surface. He adjusted it for her a little bit, and she saw stars, glittering and magnified.

'It's beautiful,' she murmured.

'It is, but here it's still quite limited. Some weekends, Fawad and I take it out away from the city; it's much better there, the view. You can see so many constellations, so many stars . . .'

'I wonder why you need to look for stars in the sky,' Indu said, straightening up and stepping away from the telescope, 'when the biggest star is me?'

Rana laughed and was about to speak again when she saw him look at the door and his face break into a smile. Runjhun had just entered wearing a knee-length green dress, waving at him while greeting others who were in the way. Rana immediately went to the door, leaving Indu standing beside the telescope. She watched Runjhun hug Fawad. She and Rana then moved to a corner. She began narrating something animatedly and he listened with interest, leaning toward her.

Indu took a deep breath and walked over to her sister, who was chatting with Fawad, and turned her back to Rana and Runjhun.

'It's always a bit delicate there, you can never say,' Fawad was saying. 'It's a total mess. My father always says don't trust anyone. Not the Army, not the government, not anyone who says "*azad* Kashmir". And you can see why it's so hard, for each of them wants to take over for their own benefit. They don't care if a few hundred of us die as long as the land acts as an obstacle for the *Chini*.'

Amita was nodding sympathetically, asking him, 'Did you really write all this in the magazine?'

Fawad nodded proudly as Amita told him he was very brave. Indu thought about what he said.

'What do you think should be done?' Indu asked him.

'Leave us alone,' Fawad said simply.

'To what end? Even if the government leaves Kashmir alone, calls the Army back, you can be sure that Pakistan won't. They will send their army the very next day!'

'They consider us as much a part of their country as India does.'

'Exactly,' Indu said, looking at him and then at her sister. 'Should we just leave it for militants to take over?'

'But they don't think they are militants, do they? They think they are reclaiming their territory. Anyway, what can I say? We are just stuck in the middle. Actually, now you have put me in the mood to listen to the Beatles, do you know them? They always take me back home.'

'I don't listen to English music,' Indu said.

'Why not? You have to now,' Fawad said, heading to the record player.

'Can you believe him?' she asked Amita. 'That's not a solution—"what can I do, we're stuck in the middle". That doesn't lead anyone anywhere.'

Amita pursed her lips. Just then, Indu saw Runjhun walk up to them with Rana by her side.

'Hello,' Indu replied stiffly to her greeting when she smiled brightly and said hi to them.

'I had a great idea, Indu, while Rana was telling me something,' she said.

Indu looked at Rana sharply, and Rana nodded earnestly; she didn't want to hear what they were up to now, but clearly had no other option.

'Yes?'

'Well, I was thinking we could have some discussions next month at the library on the theme of Partition,' she said.

'What do you mean, a discussion?'

'Maybe a talk, a moderated debate—to bring the issue into the public discourse, you know.'

Indu looked at her sister and then replied, 'What do you mean?'

'Lots of people have begun to think that maybe it was for the best,' Runjhun said. 'The Partition, you know.'

'Thousands of people were raped, brutalized and killed,' Indu said coldly.

'Perhaps it would be better if people were invited to share their stories, you know,' Rana said. 'I think it would be good for the library. We could announce it in advance so people could come prepared.'

'I'll think about it,' Indu said, looking at Runjhun, asserting the I; Runjhun looked taken aback for a second, and then nodded, turning towards Rana.

'Where's my drink?' she asked him, and he laughed and went into the kitchen.

From the other end of the flat they heard Fawad's shout, and Rana came out again to see what was going on.

'Listen to this,' Fawad emerged, holding the transistor radio in his hands and bringing it over to where everyone stood, placing it in the centre of the table.

A radio feed announced that the Prime Minister had to appear in a court today to testify against charges of electoral malpractice.

'What?' Amita asked Indu quietly. 'Who filed the case?'

Indu wasn't sure either, but had vaguely remembered reading about this.

Runjhun seemed completely aghast at the news, while Rana nodded. Fawad moved his hand, catching the transistor accidentally, almost making it slide across the table, and Rana reprimanded him in anger.

'If anything happens to my Bush . . .' he warned. Runjhun put an arm around him to calm him down.

Indu took a deep breath and turned towards her sister. 'Okay, time to go home.' They said a quick goodbye and walked back to the Ambassador. Indu was glad to see Natty by the car.

'How much do you hate her?' Amita asked Indu when Natty began driving.

Indu turned her head towards her sister, tired. 'Is it that obvious?'

'Yes.'

'Good, I mean it to be,' she replied, her face resolute.

When Amita didn't say anything further, Indu gave in. 'I know it's not fair, but . . . I can't watch it. Watch her, like this, with . . . with him.'

'But it would have happened anyway,' Amita said softly. 'If not her, then someone else.'

'I know.'

Amita took her hand. 'I am with you.'

Indu laughed. 'In what?'

'He dared to move on and parade a girlfriend in your face,' her sister said. 'We'll make him pay.' Indu laughed loudly, squeezing her sister's hand in gratitude for her unquestioning loyalty.

10

'What are you staring at so intensely?' Indu asked Natty.

His failure to reply made Indu follow the direction of his gaze, and she saw a cow standing in the middle of the road. The cow held up the traffic behind it, but Indu didn't find anything remarkable about this; it happened every day. She went on watching the cow, who coolly chewed the *chapattis* that someone had given her. Occasionally, the cow flipped her tail, trying to swat away the flies that hovered at her back. She moved her head lazily, seemingly oblivious to the surrounding cacophony.

'*Arre chalo chalo!*' someone yelled from the driver's seat of the car stuck behind a *tonga* stuck behind the cow.

'Remove it from there *yaar,* stupid cow!' a man on a motorbike yelled.

'Show some respect,' the woman sitting on a rickshaw told the motorbiker, throwing him a strict look. 'She's like your mother.'

The biker started laughing and slapped his thigh. '*Arre* aunty, I know they look the same. But my mother at least listens when I yell at her.'

The woman looked at him, aghast, and turned her face away, hiding her pained expression by asking the rickshawallah to hurry up.

After a couple more minutes of chewing, the cow seemed to throw an irritated glance at the people yelling behind her and heaved forward. She turned slowly, and Indu understood why Natty was staring at this particular cow.

Written in red paint across the cow's massive body was 'Indira *hatao*'.

* * *

That evening, Rana watched Indu as she scanned the roads where they walked, a fierce expression on her face.

'Why do you seem so angry? Can't spot any *simal* trees?' Rana asked her. She barely heard him as she continued scrutinizing the lanes, and replied after a pause.

'I'm not looking for the *simal* trees,' she said, looking left and right again. 'I'm looking for hooligans who might attempt to throw Holi colours on us.'

'What, already? It's still a few days away.'

She didn't reply as he looked at her amusedly.

'Oh, relax, no one's going to throw colour or water on you as long as I'm around,' he said, suddenly gripping her by the shoulders and tipping her towards a puddle of water. He pulled her back at the last second, making her gasp. He laughed, 'Except for me.'

She hit him on the shoulder and walked away, and he followed her on the pavement. It had rained all of last night, and while the roads were wet and dirty, the trees smelt fresh and new. Indu walked resolutely. She could still feel his touch on her arms.

'Come on now, don't be angry,' he said, and she could still hear the laughter in his voice, 'or I might have to trouble the other Indira here.' She looked slightly to the left, where the walls next to the pavement were all papered with Indira Gandhi's face, looking decisive, asking for a vote with the slogan of '*garibi hatao*'.

'You couldn't handle the likes of her,' she said without turning around.

'After dealing with this Indira here? She'd be a piece of cake.'

* * *

Amita was back from the weekend with Govind *bhai*. She was ranting to her mother that she couldn't stand the party workers walking in and out of her house like they owned it, while Govind threw open the drawing room for them. 'Uncouth, absolutely no etiquette,' she said to Indu and her mother in disgust.

'What do you expect?' her mother asked. 'You don't live there any longer, and without a woman, of course he will turn it into a bachelor's house.'

It had been most conducive to have Amita stay with them till she finished studying for her medical degree. There had been a huge hue and cry from her family and everyone around her: no one believed that the husband and wife would live apart, until it happened. But Amita was by now too used to the gossip to care, and, in fact, found a friend in distance, as things started to become easier between her and Govind and they began spending the weekends together again.

On this particular day, they were stretched out on reclining chairs in the garden—Indu, Amita and their mother—eyes shut while the warmth of the sun lulled them to sleep. The trees around their garden managed to partially shut out the noises from the street, and sometimes, they could even hear the birds. When Indu opened her eyes, she didn't know how many minutes had passed, but her mother was gone while her sister was scratching away with a pen on a notebook.

'What's going on?' Indu said, covering her mouth as she yawned.

'I'm trying to study,' Amita said.

'Keep it up. May you study all your life.'

Amita nodded, staring at her notebook, and then looked up at Indu.

'It was pretty intense yesterday, hun? When Runjhun brought in that boy?'

Indu shook her head—the memory of it still made her angry. Runjhun had befriended the little Sardar and welcomed him into the library. Indu had had to remind her that it was a library for girls. 'He's just a little boy,' she had protested. Indu went up to Rana and told him to control his girlfriend.

'What do you mean?' he had asked her.

When Indu explained to Rana what Runjhun wanted, to her annoyance, he agreed with Runjhun. Neither Rana nor Indu had spoken to each other the rest of the day.

Indu admitted to Amita that she might have overreacted, but that she couldn't help it, that Runjhun made her blood boil.

'We used to have a nice time,' Indu said, 'before she came.'

Amita stared at her closely for a few seconds. 'What about Rajat?'

Indu held her head in her hands, shaking it. 'What about him? I'm still going to marry him. I don't know what else to do.'

Amita said, 'Not the right way to approach a lifelong commitment, you know. Not quite as enthusiastic as one would expect.'

Indu sighed. 'I don't know. I don't love him. I don't even know him well. I've never loved him.'

'And you love Rana?' Amita asked, surprised.

'Of course I don't love him!' Indu reacted. 'How can you love someone who—who—never mind. And if I don't marry Rajat, what will I do?'

Amita put her books down on the grass and leant back in the chair, shutting her eyes. 'How can I say? I just know that I'm glad I'm not you. Somehow, it's harder having a choice than not having one.'

* * *

'Hand me those one by one,' Indu told Esha in a voice that was sterner than necessary. Esha nodded meekly behind her braids, which she had made hurriedly, realizing that Indu *didi* was in a bad mood. If she had seen Esha with her hair all over her face, she would have been furious. Indu had decided to rearrange some of the books. Rana and Runjhun stood outside in the balcony, talking about something, and Indu had half a mind to tell him off for wasting his time, but she suppressed that instinct and decided to ignore them.

'Next,' she told Esha as the young girl handed her another book. Indu noted the name, author, publisher, number of pages and the ISBN. It was the translation of *Pinjar* by Amrita Pritam. Indu made a mental note to read that one, taking the next one from Esha. She sensed Rosie walk up to them and didn't look up until she had absolutely had to.

'Yes, Rosie,' Indu said tiredly.

'Indu *di*,' Rosie began, her great chest heaving, and Indu had a hard time looking at her face, for Rosie was just nineteen but had the breasts of a forty-year-old, 'I have a problem, Indu *di*.'

Indu went back to the books, and indicated that Esha should continue handing them to her. She knew it would be a long discussion.

'*Di*, I've really started to doubt if my life is going in the right direction,' she told Indu. 'In another year, my parents will start looking for a boy for me. I told my parents I would finish my teaching diploma, but I know they will tell me to get a government job. It's safe and secure and what not, but if the job transfers me to some godforsaken village, or somewhere in the south, I swear upon my chicken *tangri*, I will raise the kind of hell the world has never seen!'

Indu nodded sympathetically and advised Rosie that she should calm down and wait till something actually happened before worrying about it.

Indu was interrupted when Rana called her from across the room. And although she wanted to appear cool and distant to him, she responded.

'Yes?' she asked, walking over to him, her arms folded across her chest.

He raised his eyebrows at her tone, and then crossed his own arms with a sigh.

'What is it?'

'What?' she asked him, feigning innocence.

'Don't play your games now.'

'Games?! What *games* have I played with you?'

He gave a long and, Indu thought, rather dramatic sigh, and then shook his head.

'Whatever. I wanted to talk to you about something important.'

'What?'

'Well, I've been thinking for some time, and I think we should do something about Esha.'

'What do you mean?'

'Tutor her. You see, her skill—with a little bit of tutoring, we can get her to pass her grade exams, and then she could really study further, make a life of her own.'

Indu stared at him. 'But how—how do we . . .'

'I was talking about it with Runjhun and she reckons that Sangeeta might do it, she's also doing a diploma in teaching. It'll be good practice for her as well.'

Indu clutched her arms tighter at the mention of Runjhun's name, and raised her head. So he had spoken about it to Runjhun before he spoke to her. She felt the bitter tang of betrayal.

'So . . . what do you want me to do?'

He looked up sharply at her curt question, and then pursed his lips.

'Get it arranged.'

She looked at him for a long time, and then at Esha, who sat arranging the books, while Runjhun stood a little way behind him, still giving her cold looks, pretending she was not trying to overhear.

'I'll think about it,' Indu said, and Rana stared at her as if he couldn't believe what she had just said.

For the rest of the day, Indu went about her work with a formal, curt manner, but finally collapsed on a chair, her head in her hands, when Rana left in the evening without saying anything to her. Eventually, Amita nudged her to get up. She spent the night miserable.

When morning came, she spoke to her mother about Esha being tutored.

'But who will do the work in the library?' her mother asked.

'I'm sure it won't take her all day. I mean, she could maybe help out for two hours and study for the rest of the day.'

Her mother again didn't say anything for a while and then finally asked, 'And how does Esha feel about it?'

'We haven't yet spoken to her about it.'

'How do you know she would agree to this?' her mother asked, shaking her head.

'Of course she would,' Indu waved her hand. 'Who would mind some free tutoring?'

Her mother shrugged. 'But why would you decide something for her when you don't like things being decided for you?'

Indu ignored her mother, sure that she was posing unnecessary complications in a matter so obvious, and decided to speak to Sangeeta herself, for no matter what her problems with Rana, the suggestion held merit, and why deprive poor Esha?

She expected another cold day with Rana at the library but he greeted her cheerfully the next morning, as if nothing had happened. When she walked away without making an attempt to talk, he reached out and lightly held her arm.

'Hey,' he said softly, and she turned around, disengaging her arm, and stared at him and the audacity in his grin.

He held out his palm, and on top lay a couple of jasmines, slightly crushed by his touch, but otherwise fresh. She gave him a long look before accepting the flowers and kept them in her hands, which didn't seem enough for him. He kept looking at her till she put them in her braid and then folded her arms. 'Happy?'

He nodded happily and spoke up before she could turn around again. 'What are you doing today?'

'Guess,' she said, and he laughed, acknowledging the stupidity of his own question.

'I wanted to take you somewhere,' he said.

'Where?'

'Have you watched it yet? *Kati Patang?* It's back up at Regal and I thought I would watch it.'

'I've already seen it,' she said.

'Yes, but this one you have to watch with me again. I told you I wanted to see a Rajesh Khanna movie with you. And you promised me a movie.'

Runjhun hadn't come in yet and probably wasn't planning to. Maybe that's why he asked her. She found him staring at her determinedly.

'Fine,' she told him briskly and walked away.

The afternoon rolled around. 'Come on, let's go,' he said to Indu, standing at the door as she quickly asked her sister to take over for some time, and told her she was going to watch *Kati Patang* with Rana.

She wrapped her coat around herself, buttoning it up slowly while Rana stared at her, impatient.

'What are you wearing this stupid coat for? It's sunny right now, it'll be cold later in the evening!'

She narrowed her eyes at him and buttoned it up even more slowly, making him grit his teeth.

Indu was sure they wouldn't get tickets, but Rana had gone out earlier and bought them before even asking her. 'And what if I hadn't said yes?' she asked him. 'I guess I'd have had to take Mrs Leela,' he replied with a grin.

Indu started out a little stiff, but they soon broke into their usual banter after she had elaborated on the many merits and qualities of Rajesh Khanna.

'Show me your wrist,' Rana asked her.

Indu clutched the sleeves of her coat tightly. 'What? Why?'

'I knew it was you.'

'Who was me?'

'I read in the paper yesterday that some woman sent Rajesh Khanna a letter written in blood.'

She laughed despite herself, but tried not to speak to him the rest of the way. She forgot all about their conversation when they reached the theatre and saw the posters. Arriving just in time, they quickly took their seats. Thankfully, it was a new movie for Rana so he couldn't recite the dialogue from memory, but Indu watched him as he reacted to the scenes, completely engrossed, turning to Indu to comment on something or the other. He laughed when he saw her eyes following Rajesh Khanna on the screen, and they both hummed along to the songs.

'Why doesn't Madhuri finally jump off the cliff, then?' Rana asked Indu as the credits rolled down.

'Because he sang her a song.'

'So you wouldn't jump off the cliff if I sang a song for you?'

'If you sang me a song, I'd rather jump,' Indu said, and Rana laughed all the way as they walked out of the theatre. She knew, she saw it in his eyes. She saw something that she was sure she wasn't wrong about. She wanted to hold his arm and stop him for a moment. She wanted to ask him what he felt for Runjhun, why he did not insist on her affection, why he gave up so easily. But she didn't say anything and just watched as he sat outside the theatre on the boundary wall. Indu sat beside him and they watched the people go by, smiling at each other. Some people looked towards them curiously, and some simply smiled.

'All these women get to spend stormy nights with Rajesh Khanna and then he sings poems to them,' Indu said to Rana. 'I don't know why I can't have that luck.'

Rana looked at her indignantly. 'Are you joking? You've got all these chances with me and you complain about your luck?'

She looked at him with her eyebrows raised high.

'What? I'm as close to Rajesh Khanna as you'll ever get—in looks and in poetry,' he said. Indu chuckled and got up.

'I didn't think Asha Parekh suited the role, though,' she said to him as he followed her. 'I think Waheeda Rehman would have been much better.'

'No way. She was so beautiful. You just want Rajesh Khanna for yourself, that's why you didn't like her.'

Indu called out to the *chaiwallah* who had set up his stall right at the crossing. '*Kyun bhai*, have you watched *Kati Patang?*'

Thrilled to be asked for his opinion, he spluttered an excited yes as Rana approached them.

'And don't you think Waheeda Rehman would have been better for the role than Asha Parekh?' she asked him meaningfully as Rana stared at them, sceptical.

'She would have, madameji,' the *chaiwallah* said. 'In fact, I say you would have been better. You are like Waheeda Rehman, but even better.'

Indu looked at Rana triumphantly as he spluttered exaggeratedly.

'Ha! Who looks like the star now, hun?' she asked, sitting down near the tea stall and ordering two teas for them.

'Very creative strategy to sell your tea,' Rana told the *chaiwallah*.

To the *chaiwallah*, Indu said, 'Actually, many other people have also told me I look like Waheeda Rehman.'

Rana shook his head in disbelief as he sat down next to her, folding his hands in prayer and looking up at the sky.

'And to think it could have been me that Rajesh Khanna saved from that rogue taxi driver, and who was offered a place in his house. Yet, here I am with this one, having chai on a street corner.'

The *chaiwallah* laughed and Rana pulled a pained expression.

'I can't imagine anyone brave enough to want to kidnap you,' Rana said. 'One look at you and they'd know you're trouble.'

They walked back to the library laughing and chatting. Indu told him she would talk to Esha's mother about her being tutored, and how she could manage it. Rana nodded and smiled.

'However,' she said, 'we should conclude the day by agreeing that yes, I do look like Waheeda Rehman.'

Rana let her pass through the door first. Then he leant toward her, his eyes deep and earnest, looking at her solemnly.

'You look like Waheeda Rehman,' he said, but added before walking off, 'if the lights are off.'

* * *

Sunita did not understand why her daughter had to be tutored. 'She is already good,' she had said, confused. Indu explained to Sunita that tutoring Esha would mean getting her ready for grade exams, so that she could finish school. Sangeeta would tutor her not only in maths, but also in other subjects in which Esha was far behind. And once she passed her grade exams, she could be made to do a specialized course in maths. Sunita was aghast at these plans and refused right away, saying that her husband would never allow Esha to sit for exams.

After the first rebuff, Indu and Rana spoke to Esha. Surprisingly, she said no to studying as well, saying that she did not want to get into all that, and that she did not want to study other subjects anyway. Crushed, Rana looked at Indu.

Later, she assured him that this wasn't it, that she would talk to Esha's mother again. But Sunita refused to relent until Indu finally went up to her own mother and asked for her help, and she decided to sit them all down together to discuss it.

Esha sat quietly in a corner while Sunita insisted there was absolutely no point in tutoring Esha, and it was about time she be married. Indu looked towards her mother, who patiently listened to it all, and then proceeded to explain in a firm manner that educating Esha would not only be important but highly beneficial, and that one day she could get a job and even earn money for herself, in case her husband wasn't able to. 'But she already has a job,' Sunita said. 'She works for Indu, and when Indu gets married, she can work at her new house as well, I don't mind.'

Indu looked at her mother in distress, and her mother continued explaining to Sunita why an education was important. By the end, Sunita agreed halfheartedly, but insisted that her husband could not know about this. 'He won't approve,' she said quietly, 'but maybe you are right, madame.' Indu told Sunita not to blame Esha for any of this, and that, in fact, Esha didn't want to study. She knew Sunita would take it better if she knew that this was being forced upon Esha.

'But this wasn't agreed on,' Indu told her mother later, as they prepared to sleep. 'You said Esha's agreement must be taken into account. This wasn't an agreement. You made Sunita say yes. It was a settlement.'

Her mother pretended that she could not understand what Indu was saying, and then shrugged and walked away.

Sangeeta seemed a lot more amenable to the plan and said that she would be happy to teach Esha—on the days that she herself came in, of course. 'But when will she do it?' Sangeeta asked them, 'if she's working?'

Rana had already suggested they do Esha's work in the time that Esha studied. Esha herself had been quiet throughout. Indu wished it were different, but knew it would benefit her in the long run. They couldn't ignore her aptitude for studies.

'What are you working on these days, by the way?' Indu asked Rana.

'Same old,' he said. 'Copy-checking some articles for the magazine, getting my own ready.'

'Do they criticize the government?'

'It's not fun if they don't.'

Runjhun had seemed smug about the whole Esha situation throughout, and Indu wondered whether it was her, not Rana's, idea in the first place. But it didn't really matter since it was because of the library that such an opportunity could be created in the first place.

They had also begun planning for the Partition-themed discussion Runjhun had proposed. They had called it 'Invitation to Dialogue: Discussions on Partition'. A problem arose when Indu saw the addresses the invitation letters were being sent to, and she questioned Runjhun about it.

'Why are you sending invitations to all these colleges?' she asked her.

'So people can participate.'

'I know, but these are mostly boys' colleges.'

'How does that matter?'

Indu gave her a long, hard look. 'It matters because this is a library for girls *only*.'

'Yes, but, of course, men can also participate in discussions. It's an intellectual event; you can't really keep half of the population out of it.'

Indu didn't reply for the moment, but later told Rana and Runjhun that only women would be invited to participate.

'That's madness!' Runjhun said, looking from Rana to Indu. 'The Partition didn't affect only women, they are not the only ones who can have a discussion about it.'

'It doesn't make sense, Indu,' Rana said to her.

Indu shook her head without looking at him. 'Of course it didn't affect only women, but the whole point of this place is to empower women so they can find a voice that they commonly lose in the presence of men! They won't be able to do that if there are men here.'

'Says who?' Runjhun said angrily. 'Women won't be able to speak in front of men, so let's give them a separate room? What kind of logic is that? It's a mixed world out there, and nobody gives you space if you don't demand it.'

'I don't agree with you,' Indu told her. 'It is because women traditionally have been denied such opportunities that I want to offer it only to them! The atmosphere will change completely if there are twenty men here, offering their opinions as if they were fact. I don't want that.'

Runjhun looked at Rana, aghast. Indu didn't have the energy to argue anymore, so she walked away.

On the way back home in the evening, she couldn't help the tears rolling down her cheeks as Natty tonelessly hummed his songs. He noticed she didn't rebuke his singing today and went quiet after a while.

'You're definitely more beautiful, madame,' Natty said when he heard her sniff, at which Indu laughed hysterically, but she was grateful for it.

The following day, Runjhun was absent and Indu found Rana quieter than usual. She sat next to him, and although unresponsive at first, he soon gave in to Indu's prodding.

'What will you do after the summer?' she asked him.

'I'll go home for some time, and then hopefully get a job.'

'You can talk to my father.'

'I will, definitely.'

His books lay open on the table, but he leant back in his chair, whistling a tune. Indu looked at him, her own face expressionless. He was unshaven and his hair was as messy as ever, but he didn't seem bothered by it. He stared back at her for some time, and then looked away.

'What about you?' he asked her, staring ahead.

'What about me?'

'In the summer . . . or after.'

Indu went quiet for a moment.

'I'll keep this running for as long as I can.'

'Will you be married?'

She didn't reply, and went over the logbook that she had in front of her.

'I suppose. I mean, whenever Rajat returns.'

It was a few minutes before he spoke up again.

'Will you still be living here after that?'

'I don't know,' she answered. And then added, almost as a respite from the situation, 'I didn't like what Runjhun said yesterday.'

'I think it made sense,' he said.

'I'm not opening this platform up to men, Rana!'

'Why not? It's just for a day, not every day, and the nature of the subject invites—'

'That's not the point! The very presence of men who think themselves as superior, of their opinions as more valid, is what holds women back from speaking. They feel that what they have to say is automatically less important in front of a man.'

'It's not about equal opportunity. Those riots affected everyone, and men should learn from them too. The world out there does not safeguard a spot for certain opinions or protect you from them.'

'In an ideal world, yes, this is not equality,' Indu said. 'But this is not the ideal world. How will those women narrate the torture they went through in front of men? Some people require extra encouragement and the right atmosphere to open up. Like Esha.'

He fell quiet after that and finally nodded.

'She means well, though,' he said to Indu, and she knew he was referring to Runjhun. Indu didn't reply.

11

Rana cleared his throat before reading the first part again, and his voice reverberated on the mic. Indu smiled, both nervous and proud.

> *'Ye daaġh daaġh ujālā ye shab-gazīda sahar*
> *vo intizār thā jis kā ye vo sahar to nahīñ*
> *ye vo sahar to nahīñ jis kī aarzū le kar*
> *chale the yaar ki mil jā.egī kahīñ na kahīñ*
> *falak ke dasht meñ tāroñ kī āķhirī manzil*
> *kahīñ to hogā shab-e-sust-mauj kā sāhil*
> *kahīñ to jā ke rukegā safīna-e-ġham'*

Indu heard the sound of every movement from the audience as he paused; nobody spoke.

'This stained, pitted first light,' he finished in English, 'this daybreak, battered by night; this dawn that we all ached for, this is not that one. This is not that dawn, this is not that dawn.'

Applause broke out along with a jingle of bangles. There were rows of chairs from the front, where Rana stood in front of the screen and the mic, to the back, all occupied by women dressed up in saris on this pleasant March morning. It had been cold and damp inside Number 7 when they opened it that morning, but now, with so many people inside, it was warm and there was barely any space to move. The clapping went on and Rana bowed, looking slightly embarrassed, for it was only a recitation. Indu went up to where he was.

They nodded at each other, smiling, and Indu took the mic. Her mother sat at the very back with her sister, and she nodded at them with confidence. Apart from Rana, there was no other male in the room, not even Fawad.

'I would like to thank you all for being here this morning,' she said, looking around the room. She had invited Mrs Bala and a few other teachers. Indu recognized some of her classmates too. Mrs Leela, her daughter, Sangeeta, Rosie, and all the others who came to the library every day were also in the crowd, some of them with their mothers and sisters.

'This year, we at the Number 7 Library would like to take this day as an opportunity to remember a ghastly past, the horrors and savagery of which must be remembered as well as it is possible to. We must be reminded that freedom came at a terrible cost, and India's heart today beats for the graves of those who were massacred in mindless violence organized in the guise of religion.'

She adjusted the notes from which she spoke and looked up to see Rana staring at her with bated breath.

'The partition of India in 1947 is the biggest mass migration of people in the history of the world, till date, and may remain so for a long, long time. A look at the statistics to understand the sheer scale of what actually transpired within those few days: estimates suggest that one crore, forty-five lakh people crossed the borders, that is, from India to Pakistan, and from Pakistan to India, both in the west and the east. While some figures claim the deaths of thousands of people, the actual number easily goes up to *hundreds* of thousands. Some reports suggest that anywhere between ten to twenty lakh people died, more than twenty lakh people went missing, and thousands and thousands of women were abducted and raped.'

There was absolute silence in the room, and Indu heard her own gulp sound much louder than it would otherwise have. Yet, the more chilling her content, the harder her voice became.

'Most people who had to cross over left within a few hours, lest the violence get to them. They left all they had ever known, the lives that they had built for themselves, departing for a new land where they didn't know what they would find, leaving by any means that they could. Some thought that one day, they would be able to return; most knew that was it and tried to carry as much with them as they could.

'As if the trauma of leaving their homes, the arduous journey, and the uncertainty of what lay in the future wasn't enough, on the way, they were subjected to every kind of misery and violence. There was carnage and looting, families were separated, women were kidnapped, raped and left to die, children murdered, and men killed, unable to help as their families disintegrated before them. Yet, the biggest trauma of all was that these atrocities weren't committed by a foreign, strange hand; it was brother against brother, wielding swords at each other after years of breaking bread together, simply because they belonged to different faiths.'

The silence was almost palpable, and Indu couldn't stop now.

'Centuries of peace and love broke down within a few nights, into hatred and slaughter. Swept up in the frenzy of the mob, humanity was forgotten. What occurred would be the biggest number of civilian deaths *by* civilians in this short a duration of time, as the world watched the annihilation unfold. Governments and officials might want you to forget what happened and start anew, but it is essential that what happened must not be forgotten, that the past is ever present in memory to remind and shame us, so that we may never repeat such sins, and construct a better future.'

'This event has been curated with the special assistance of Miss Runjhun Verma, and we hope to preserve the stories that we reveal today. I would like to invite on stage a few women who will share their experiences of their journey from what is now Pakistan to India.'

From the audience rose Kaur aunty, who came to the library every now and then. She was the first one who had agreed to tell her story in front of other people, eager that people should know her struggles, sure that what she had seen wasn't the worst of it. She was a heavyset woman and walked up to the mic slowly, holding her sari gingerly. Rana began clapping, the others joined him and she seemed slightly more confident when the applause died down.

'Thank you for having me here,' she began, slightly hesitant. She looked towards the audience, but her mind seemed to be somewhere else. Indu knew she was looking for a place to start. 'I was born in Lahore, nineteen years before the partition. My father was a trader and a strict, principled man. We were two sisters and one younger brother. I was the only one of the children to survive.'

Her words evoked an even deeper silence, and the room seemed colder than before.

'We grew up on the streets of Lahore, and I knew those inside out. I knew every shop at the bazaar, where the British made their offices. I knew them better than the back of my hand. In the summer of '47, I knew there would be danger soon. You could smell it in the air, as much as you could smell the summer air leaving. Gazes had turned hostile, and there was talk of arming yourself. "Do it for the peace of your own mind," they would tell us, but we had seen it coming long ago. My father took the decision too late, and it cost him everything.'

Indu held her breath and she saw everyone in the room doing the same; some held the sides of their chairs. Not a single eye left Kaur aunty.

'By the time we decided to leave, it had already spread on the streets. The violence, it was a disease, and it spread like wildfire. My father and brother had three women to take care of, and I had never seen them so scared. Yet, with courage, we packed up and left for the station.

'We heard screams from far away. They were much closer than we realized. We got on the bus safely, but it was one of the first buses to be attacked. When the bus halted, they hit the sides of the bus with sticks. We were terrified and clung to our seats. They entered and killed the driver and the men who sat in the front almost immediately. They hit a few others and ordered us all out, separating the men and the women. Some women were taken away; my sister and mother were among them. I never saw them again.'

Indu thought she heard a sob from the back of the room and forced herself to swallow the lump that rose in her own throat.

'They killed randomly, not caring who it was or what was their name was. But with each death, their confidence grew. They fed on our helplessness. Once all the men were dead, they began to march us women back, crossing towns where all we could hear were people screaming and begging for mercy. When I remember walking in the company of those women, being herded by those men who had killed all those people, I wondered where the God was I had prayed to all my life. I still do sometimes.'

'Yet, fate had something else in store for us, for soon, the police found us—the boundary force. Seeing them, these murderers fled. We cried when we saw them, and that dawn, each of those faces, the ones in uniforms, they far surpassed any Bollywood hero you see today. More than Dev Anand, more than Rajesh Khanna . . . they were the most beautiful men I had seen in my life.'

Indu's mouth was dry.

'My father survived too, and after a few months, I met him again in Amritsar, where I was staying with some relatives. We came to Delhi and built a new life here, but there is not a day when I don't think of that time.'

Her head was bent and she finally broke, her voice booming on the speakers. Indu clutched her arm and walked her back to her seat. She looked at Rana, and he took over.

'Mrs Kaur,' he said softly into the mic, looking directly at her as she settled down, 'we thank you for your courage and for sharing your words.'

There was another round of applause that refused to die down for some time, and when it finally stopped, he spoke again. 'We would now like to invite on stage Mrs Monga. She moved to Delhi from Faisalabad with her family when the riots were at their height. She has displayed immense strength in agreeing to talk here in front of us all. Mrs Monga . . .'

A lady sat in the front row, looking, to Indu, only slightly younger than her own mother. Rana had found her and invited her to talk. Before beginning, she cried for five minutes, by the end of which there was hardly anyone in the room who did not share her tears.

She narrated a harrowing tale, which began with doors being broken down in maddening rage, burning streets and demolished shops and houses. 'Men ran rampant, flinging swords they didn't know how to use, shoving them into bodies without a second thought,' she said, gazing blankly in front of her. She had left on foot with her family, but was soon separated from them. Yet, she said, she managed to stay with caravans that had police protection, and for days they walked the country, with no knowledge of where the rest of her family was.

'I had not the slightest clue whether they were dead or alive,' she said, 'but we had to keep moving no matter what, no matter who got left behind—husbands, children or parents. We had to trust fate to reunite us some day. If we paused, we would be dead too.'

She narrated how every day, in the camp, she cooked for hundreds of people, eager to use every last bit of her energy to make the situation better. She described how some people stood guard for hours, taking turns with the police, and how instructions would be given on the mic—more reassurances than instructions. One night, some crooks came into the camp and bribed the police, who let them take her away. They held her for a week.

Mrs Monga's face hardened at this point.

'Some yelled *Jai Shri Ram,* some yelled *Allah-hu-Akbar* . . . but they all did the same thing,' she said. 'I was lucky. I ran off to another camp and made my way to India. I was even more lucky that my family made it back alive and took me back willingly. A lot of the others weren't so lucky.'

The sounds of others crying were louder now and a couple of women got up and walked out, while the rest sat in silence.

A few minutes passed and a woman from the audience spoke, raising her hand.

'I would also like to say something,' she said, and Indu recognized her as the mother of the little Sardar boy who was always peeking inside. She was dressed in a plain *kurta*. She had put up her hand hesitatingly. Indu looked at Rana and nodded at the woman, indicating she should come up.

'My name is Parminder Chadda and I live on this floor, in the next flat,' she said. 'And I would also like to share my story.'

A silence followed her announcement and Indu nodded at her.

'It was a horrible time, enough to make me lose my faith. For a long time, I couldn't say the name of *waheguru*. It was hard for me. How can you, when it seems like everyone around you has forgotten all logic, all compassion, all humanity?

'In the town where I lived, Dera Ghazi Khan, men travelled together, telling each other to be ready, collecting weapons, and we could hear it. There was fire in their eyes. People sat on buses, took their cycles, walked, but it was hard to get out unscathed. They poured kerosene over things that were too big, vehicles and buses, and burnt them to ashes. The canals ran with blood and it was, truly, brother against brother. We left our house at half an hour's notice. A minute later and we would have been dead. But even the streets were burning. We could be noticed by the mob any second.

'Men on horseback, men in jeeps, men running, they all had the same, sole purpose—to destroy. The police force would attempt to save people, but the mobs shot in a frenzy, not knowing who they were killing. For days, we slept on wooden racks atop buses. I came from Multan and most of our family made it to this side too. But even if we got here, what then? Our life was over there.

'For weeks, we were in the camps. After some time, they allotted us some land near Panipat. Just some barren land, and said go, build your life here. What would we build it out of? We had nothing. Yet, we managed. My husband worked hard, so we sold it off and managed to shift here, to this sprawling city of Delhi, where there are so many like us rendered homeless by the actions of those who thought they know what was best for us. Today, life is better. We can give our children a good life, but we have to remember that at that time, nobody was spared the monstrosity. Not little girls, not infant boys, not the old, the elderly, the pregnant women—everyone met the same fate if they found themselves in the wrong place. Loot, rape, murder.'

Once she spoke up, more women began to raise their hands, offering to narrate how they had been affected, in whatever small or big way. After some time, Indu began writing what they were saying as Rana and Runjhun took over to mediate and moderate. Today, Indu could not bring herself to feel unfriendly towards Runjhun.

Minutes went by relating the horrors of Partition and finally, it was time to end the discussion. Indu thanked profusely everyone who had made the effort to go back to those haunting memories and find the courage to relate them. Formally, the discussion ended, but many women stayed back and Rana immediately got to work; noting down the new registrations. Many others walked up to Indu to say that they would be joining the library, and would be telling others about it too. Mrs Bala also came to congratulate her, telling her they would feature it in the college magazine, and that they would interview her. Indu almost laughed at the idea, but agreed.

Many of them sat about chatting, relating stories from their time. Indu's parents got nostalgic as well. The little Sardar boy's mother, the woman who identified herself as Parminder Chadda, found Indu and put her hands on her shoulders, thanking her for organizing the event.

'No, of course . . .' Indu said, putting the lady's hand on her hand, and then couldn't help adding, 'We see your son quite often.'

Parminder Chadda laughed, looking slightly embarrassed. 'Yes, I sometimes tell him to have a peek and see who all are there. You see, I have learnt some baking recently, and I was thinking, so many people come here every day, I could invite some of them to see if they would like to buy it.'

Indu stared at her, suddenly feeling embarrassed.

'If you want,' Indu began, 'you could bring the cakes here. I mean, we can think of some arrangement, to make it more regular, if you're willing . . .'

She looked at Indu in delight and thanked her profusely, promising to discuss it in more detail.

'Of course, Mrs . . .'

'You can call me Pammi,' she told Indu with a delighted smile, and was still smiling when she walked out.

Indu wanted to go up to Rana and tell him about Pammi, but noticed that he was standing with Runjhun and another woman who had just appeared. So she walked away to her own parents.

'Where is Rana? We want to congratulate him too,' her mother said, and then Indu had to bring him over. He greeted them cordially, striking up an easy conversation. He complimented both their daughters, causing Indu to remark that he was nice only in front of the parents.

Most people had left by the time Indu's mother decided to leave too. She wanted to pack everything up and then return with Natty; Amita had already left to see Govind. Rana told Indu that Fawad would come over in a bit, so they decided to bring lunch from outside and have it together in the library. Esha and Sunita put everything back in its place, with Indu instructing them. Fawad came in after some time with another man, whom Runjhun seemed to know. Indu wanted to ask who in the world these people were, but refrained from saying anything.

'It was horrible, of course,' Indu heard Runjhun say. 'We heard it today, the stories are horrifying. Yet, I mean, I can understand why Partition was necessary.'

They were sitting on the sofas—Rana, Indu, the other man that Indu didn't recognize, and another girl, one of Runjhun's friends who had come for the talk.

'What do you mean?' Rana asked.

'I'm not sure a "united India" would have even been possible, you know. So many people of such different faiths living together.'

'Lakhs of people died during Partition,' Rana said quietly. 'No speculation or possibility can justify that. And those people had already been living together!'

'I'm not justifying it, of course,' Runjhun said quickly. 'What happened was inexcusable. But suppose there hadn't been a partition; wouldn't there be frequent communal outbursts? Tension? More than even now? How would that have been handled?'

Indu sat down with them, breaking up her rhetoric. 'What's the point of thinking about what would have been? The fact is it happened. What we must think about is the action and consequences it invited.'

Runjhun nodded at her. 'I agree with that. I just can't help thinking whatever happened was for the best, even though it wasn't done in the best way.'

'How can you say that?' Rana asked. 'After hearing all this, what went on . . .'

'But I'm not saying what happened was right, Rana,' she protested. 'I'm saying it should have been done better. Tell me, would our democratic institutions have survived with that constant fighting? Would the Muslims have jobs in the government, the equal opportunities they demanded—'

'Of course they would have!' Indu said. 'We are a secular country.'

'In name only,' Runjhun responded darkly. 'In practice, we can't say for sure what would have happened if such a large section of the population, with adequate political representation and groups, wanted to separate—and couldn't.'

'So you are saying we couldn't have lived together if the separation hadn't happened?'

'The way the situation was, there were already two disparate nations, and to try and bring them together would have been foolhardiness. I just wish it had been done better. And we would have avoided the whole trouble over Kashmir as well if it were.'

'Walked in at the right time, haven't I?' Fawad asked, appearing at the door. Rana got up to greet him. Indu found this to be the right opportunity to avoid an argument with Runjhun.

Fawad folded his hands at Indu and she grinned at him, raising her eyebrows. 'Where have you been, mister? Why haven't I seen you in so long?'

'Because I'm always stuck on the road,' he said. 'I spend more time in the bus than at my own home.'

'That bad?'

'Campaigning is on in full force. On one side of the road they say *garibi hatao*, on the other side they say *Indira hatao* . . . then people start yelling *inhe road se hatao*.'

They couldn't help laughing as Rana chimed in, 'I heard another one a few days ago . . . what was it? Yes, *Jan Sangh ka saath do, beedi peena chhod do; beedi mein tambaku hai, Congress waala daku hai.*'

Indu raised her eyebrows but laughed anyway. 'What are they against, tobacco or the Congress?'

'I'd say both are equally fatal,' Runjhun said.

'Speaking of tobacco,' Fawad said, looking at Indu, 'I'd like to smoke some. May I?'

Indu nodded, and when Fawad went out to the balcony, she accompanied him there instead of sitting down with the others.

Fawad lit the cigarette and held it out to her. She was about to refuse when she glanced at Rana and Runjhun deep in conversation at the other end of the room and accepted it. He raised his eyebrows in surprise and gave it to her with a smile. She held it in her hand awkwardly.

'What do I . . .'

'Take a deep pull, as if you're drinking from a straw . . . yes, well done.'

Indu inhaled the smoke and coughed slightly. She took a couple of drags more and though she did not cough this time, she felt her head spin. As she handed it back to Fawad, he said, 'Don't do it too often though. It's a terrible habit.'

Indu nodded at him, looking around. She didn't want Sunita or Esha to see her, but obviously, she did want Rana to notice.

'What are you working on these days? Rana acts like it's some top-secret story that he's not allowed to talk about,' she said.

'It is,' he answered, grinning.

'Tell me what it's about!'

'Well, pretty much about how the party is a hotbed of corruption currently, and how we discovered official documents incriminating some officials. I've also allowed advertisements for the *morchas.* We are planning one of our own.'

'Are you even allowed to print all that?' Indu asked him.

'Of course I am—the free press of a free country.'

Indu stared at him, shaking her head, telling him he wasn't going to be let off easy if important people started having major problems with it.

'And who's important?' he asked. 'Your father?'

Indu gave him a hard look. 'He is. He is the Chief Advocate, and if there is trouble coming, he smells it from a mile away.'

Fawad laughed.

Indu wasn't sure how to react, and was saved the trouble of answering when Rana walked up to them. Runjhun and the other man seemed to have left.

'Since when do you smoke?' he asked Indu, raising his eyebrows sceptically.

She shrugged. 'Since when do you care?'

He looked even more surprised at her answer, but then shook his head and turned to Fawad, asking him when he wanted to go back home. She was annoyed there hadn't been more of a reaction.

'Where's Runjhun?' Fawad asked her. 'I'd like to talk to her about India and Pakistan separating, and the disaster that it was.'

'Ah, she's insistent that it was for the better.'

Fawad shook his head. 'Earlier, you had a commie for a girlfriend. Then you introduce me to Indu, and now this one. What's wrong with you, man? Why can't you choose girlfriends from one ideology?'

Rana contorted his lips, trying not to laugh at himself.

'He's a typical man, you see,' Indu said to Fawad, dropping the cigarette on the ground and stubbing it with her foot, giving Rana a derisive glance. 'Looks over books.'

* * *

Dear Indu,

It seems as if spring has finally sprung up here. There are roses everywhere, along with magnolias and dahlias. I wonder which ones you'd like. When you come here, I'd like to buy you these flowers sometimes.

When I have to spend hours in the library here, I think of you and your little library there. I wonder how it is faring. You haven't told me in the longest time. Unfortunately, I have some distressing news.

My brother Roshan—I don't think you've ever been formally introduced—got into a spot of trouble recently a few days ago with his friends but thankfully a family friend was able to sort it all out for us. I don't know all the details yet and will tell you more when I know.

There are some quaint little locales here that I've been looking at, with gardens in the front of houses, and it will be great to live here. I hope you wouldn't mind travelling by train sometimes, within the city—it's called the tube and it's always efficient and on time. And they never have strikes!

Pass my greetings on to everyone,

Love,
Rajat

She kept forgetting to reply to Rajat the next couple of days. Her conversation with Fawad continued to trouble her, both what he had said about his magazine as well as how easily he had referred to Runjhun as Rana's girlfriend. But even if there were no Runjhun , Indu still had another life waiting for her.

It was hard for her to imagine that life, especially if she would have to live elsewhere. She couldn't bear the thought of abandoning her library, especially to settle in a cold place where she would be nothing more than the wife of a man who was 'someone' there. She wondered what she would do all day. Would she have a job, and would Rajat even agree to letting her get one? She realized she had never asked his opinion, for their life together seemed so far away, and she still couldn't imagine the day when it would be a reality.

She thought of talking to her sister about this, but what would she say? *Didi, I promised to marry a man who is courteous, well-settled and approved of by everyone in our family. But I'd rather cry about another man who already has a girlfriend, partakes in seditious writing, and whose best friend might lead a march against the Prime Minister* . . .

In any case, Amita had enough troubles of her own. Her exams were drawing nearer every day and she had much at stake. Every day that she had spent living with Indu and their parents, the expectations increased. She had left her husband's home to study. Now she'd better do well, otherwise she would not be forgiven.

One look at Esha was enough to convince Indu that they had done well starting the library, and she was sure that she would want to find out how it all turned out. If Esha was thriving, one could imagine that others were also deriving some benefit from the library, even if it couldn't be assessed quantitatively. She thought of Sangeeta studying every day, passing her exams, which might have been, Indu dared to think, harder if she didn't have the library space. She thought of Mrs Leela finding an avenue to display her skill, which otherwise might have been lost in the monotony of household chores. Hadn't all the women who had spoken about their troubles during Partition found a place to make their voices heard?

She found Esha sitting in a corner of the kitchen floor, bent over the work Sangeeta had given her.

'What did I tell you about tying your hair when you work, hun?' she asked. 'If I see your hair spread about your face another time, I swear on your Sai Baba I will cut it off myself.'

'Sorry, *didi*,' Esha replied hastily, tying her hair into a braid.

Indu walked up to Sangeeta and whispered to her, 'Don't you think it's better to make her sit beside you?'

Sangeeta looked uneasily over her shoulder at the other women working. 'I mean, we could, but I am not sure everyone will be fine with that.'

Indu looked around the room and had to agree that someone might object to Esha sitting beside them. She looked at Sangeeta. 'Well, as long as she is studying, I guess it doesn't matter where.'

In the evening, in the car, Indu impulsively asked Natty what he thought of Rana.

'I don't think of him as much, madame,' he said, keeping his eyes on the road.

When Indu stared at him sharply, he nodded before answering, 'He's a good man, madame. I like him very much.'

She didn't reply immediately and heard him humming a song, but didn't know which one it was, and so was forced to ask him.

'"*Yeh shaam mastani*", madame. Rajesh Khanna.'

'That was really toneless,' she told him. 'I couldn't even recognize it. And I heard it in the theatre when I watched the movie.'

'We all have our talents, madame.'

She and Rana had sung '*Yeh shaam mastani*' under their breaths while watching *Kati Patang*. She remembered the obnoxious way he had laughed and said, 'I'm as close to Rajesh Khanna as you'll ever get.'

'So what do you think should be done, Natty?' she asked him plainly.

She knew he wouldn't ask her what about.

'I couldn't say, madame,' he said.

'But *what if* you had to.'

'I couldn't say,' he repeated, 'but you could.'

12

It was late April and already the weather was too hot for a walk, but Indu and Rana went for one anyway when they found themselves alone and free one evening.

At one point, Indu went on ahead and he caught up with her a minute later. He held out his palm, which had a jasmine in it. She looked at him, touched.

'It's just flowers, not my love,' he said, looking embarrassed, and ran his hand through his hair.

She stared at him for a couple of seconds and then shook her head, letting out a tired sigh. 'Why do you have to be like this? Why can't you be more like Rajesh Khanna, hun?'

'Are you joking?' he replied, pointing at himself. 'Have you seen this? If I were also romantic like him, uff, that would be very unfair.'

She shook her head again. 'I want to see some *amaltas* trees now.'

'You deserve it. You've been a good girl today,' he said, smiling cheekily.

They walked in the outer lanes and the trees seemed to pop out in a burst of yellow among the green, as if planted there deliberately by someone to break the monotony. They stood beneath a big one and found a few of its flowers on the ground, brightening up the concrete. They gazed at it for some time and then walked slightly farther away as Indu wanted to look at it from afar, when its yellowness wasn't that pronounced.

'Next year, though,' he said, looking at Indu, 'I don't know if I'll be here to see them.'

'Why, where will you go?'

'I don't know where a job might take me.'

'But most likely Delhi, right?'

'Could be Bombay. In fact, it's more likely it will be Bombay, that's where all the jobs for me are.'

'Really? And you don't mind?'

'I don't know. It would be even more crowded, I'm sure, but I think I would like how fast-paced it is, with so much happening all the time. I'd like to live in that pace for some time.'

They walked back slowly towards the library, and she tried to imagine him in Bombay. She had never been there, but she could imagine him fitting in, making a life for himself, walking by the beach. She wondered if she herself would be here to see the *simal* and *amaltas* bloom next year, and knew at least where her life was headed. She'd definitely be married. She couldn't imagine herself in this new life, especially when she thought of Rana living in Bombay, making new friends, meeting girls. She had heard everything was more relaxed in Bombay, that all the girls had boyfriends, and that they went to discos together.

She looked at him now as he walked next to her, his hands in his pockets, looking ahead but clearly lost in thought, probably musing about next year. She saw the uncertainty, but also the excitement on his face. She tried to think of herself in Bombay, pursuing some kind of career with Rana by her side. It seemed impossible.

Entering the library, they looked at each other and smiled, and he seemed warmer than ever, his eyes the lightest shade of brown, looking into hers. Indu felt like grabbing him by the shoulders and asking him why he wouldn't ask her how she felt.

But the next morning, he smiled just as easily when he saw Runjhun arrive. His words repeated themselves in her head. 'It's only flowers, not my love.' He had his life and she had hers.

She watched him through the day and when she couldn't bear it anymore, she went out again, wandering the street alone this time, coming across Natty, who had parked the Ambassador a little way off. She sat on the bonnet of the car, and neither of them said anything to each other when she put her head in her arms and hated herself for crying again.

'I am sorry for you, madame,' Natty said to her quietly. When Indu didn't reply, he added, 'You should eat a banana. Bananas cheer you up.'

She smiled at his kindness and then asked him if he knew a place where she could sit in silence for some time. He suggested that she could spend some time at the *gurudwara* down the road, and offered to drive her there.

The hum of the *bhajan* was background noise for Indu, and she smiled back at the *karsevaks* who smiled at her. She took off her heels outside and covered her head with her *dupatta*. The marble floor felt cool at this time of the day, so she sat on the rugs at the back, leaning against the wall, and stared ahead at the canopy where they sat fanning the *granth sahib*.

Her mind was a whirl and she thought of Amita to distract herself. She wondered if Amita and Govind would ever properly reconcile. Why was any marriage set up at all if it did not guarantee at least some possibility of happiness? Practically, it should be possible to make any marriage work as long as both were willing to adjust to their circumstances.

But she couldn't help but think that there had to be something more to a marriage, some love and understanding deep enough to have brought them together, to make them want to spend a life together, more than being told that this was the way of the world.

Her thoughts went back again to Rajat and Rana. She did not know Rajat and who he was as a person. There was absolutely no guarantee their life would be a happy one; she wondered what the preconditions for happiness were. Surely, some common passions, the affinity that your body has some with people which it simply doesn't with others, a genetic inclination that you can't control. A particular kind of humour that one might specifically prefer, more so than that of other people.

And so what about Rana, then? No fool would deny that they worked well together, that they clicked, but the fact remained that they did not have space for each other in their lives. Thinking of Rana tired her, so she shut her eyes, leaning her head against the wall.

Some time went by before she woke up, but she couldn't say how much. They were still singing a *bhajan*, and on the other side, there was a short queue of those who waited for their blessing. She got up and walked out the other way, taking the *halwa* they gave her in her palms.

When she reached the flat, she let Rana take the keys and rode home with Natty, and by the time they reached home, resolved not to let herself think of things that would remain just flights of fancy. She promised herself she wouldn't be carried away by despair and let herself feel wretched. She told Amita this too, finally finding courage to talk about what was on her mind. Her sister said she was proud of her. When she asked her why, Amita shook her head at her and smiled. 'You found it in yourself to listen to your heart and acknowledge your feelings. I was never able to do that.'

As the days stretched longer and May came upon them, a mania gripped the country—a mania that said that the tide of politics had turned the other way, that what had been around for years was now slated for a downfall. Young men roamed the roads shrieking slogans like, '*Indira hatao, garibi hatao, JP ji ko aagey laao*'. Her father remained busy with the party, often away with Shashi uncle and Govind *bhai*, sometimes sucking in even her mother into the vortex, as Amita spent more time at home and at the library with Indu. The opinion became increasingly divided as there was counter-sloganeering—'*Hawa nahi yeh aandhi hai, desh ki Indira Gandhi hai.*'

Indu could see that it took its toll on her father. He ate little, grunted in response to questions, and refused to read the newspapers. Indu knew she must talk to him about it, but he wasn't exactly at his friendly best.

'But what is going on? Why this hue and cry suddenly?' she asked her mother.

'It's because of a case that was filed some time ago, for not following some silly rule or something, and it's starting to get serious.'

'What do you mean?'

'Her candidature might be revoked; she might have to step down.'

'What?' Indu asked. 'But then what will happen?'

'It doesn't matter, madame,' Natty replied, yawning, having just walked in. 'This one on top or that one, life will remain exactly the same for us. I will still be driving this Ambassador while you make me sing Rajesh Khanna songs.'

'You mean you will still be driving this Ambassador while you make me listen to you sing Rajesh Khanna songs?'

* * *

The upcoming court case became a sore topic at the library soon as opinion became increasingly polarized there as well. Runjhun led what Indu called a crusade against Indira Gandhi, constantly counting the injustices that her government had meted out to the citizens of India, insisting that if the Prime Minister wasn't asked to step down, it would spell doom for the country.

It became even more contentious when Rana told her that Fawad had a run-in with some Congress workers and got hurt. He had apparently asked them some offensive questions at a press conference, and didn't back off when some party people threatened to roughen him up.

'But what happened?' she asked him.

'They apparently targeted him and some of the people with him. I don't know much yet, he is resting at home. I'll ask him more when I go back.'

'I want to see him too,' Indu told him. 'If you want, we can go to your house in the evening with Natty.'

She was glad to see that Fawad was smiling as usual when he saw her, but she could tell he had been badly injured. His forehead bore an ugly bump and so did his chin, with a gash along his cheek. He wore a cast on his shoulder, leaning against the back of the bed. His hair was a mess, but he smiled widely when he saw Rana, Indu and Runjhun. Indu told Rana she would help him cook dinner. Fawad joked that he should get hurt more often so they could get the girls to cook for them.

'The good life, eh?' he said, winking to Rana before Runjhun admonished him.

'Where are the vegetables?' Indu asked Rana, looking for the refrigerator.

'We don't have a fridge,' Rana said, handing her the bag on the table. 'We buy fresh vegetables every morning.'

She began chopping onions, hearing the faint murmurs between Runjhun and Fawad, and put the rice to boil as Rana cooked vegetables in the pan.

When they sat down to eat, Fawad told them he had gone to a press conference on the Prime Minister's electoral malpractice case.

'Was she there?' Indu asked.

Fawad snorted. 'Of course not. Her lawyers were there.'

From the corner of her eyes, Indu saw Rana give her quick glance.

'Well, what did you ask that ticked them off so much?'

'Same old,' he said grinning, which made him wince, but he continued anyway. 'What was the government's explanation for the considerable downward plunge of the growth rate. If the injustices committed during last year's railway strikes were going to be answered for. Why they were unable to regulate the rising prices of essential commodities and rate of unemployment. Oh, and also if the Prime Minister already had an alternative profession in mind once her Lok Sabha seat was revoked.'

'God, Fawad,' Rana said, shaking his head, 'do you not fear for your life even a little? What will happen to your future wife and three kids—two boys and one girl?'

Fawad began laughing and, though Indu found nothing amusing about it, she refrained from commenting.

He went on, telling them how a bunch of Congress workers had cornered him on the street afterwards, telling him to mind his tongue. 'When I refused, well, things got a little heated. I kind of challenged them, said that they couldn't do anything because they'd be going out of power soon, hurled a few swear words, and here we are.'

'Well, have you learnt your lesson, then?' Indu asked.

'And which lesson would that be?' Runjhun asked hotly.

'To keep his mouth shut when needed.'

'I'd rather teach that lesson than learn it, to be honest,' he said.

Nobody said anything, but she could feel the weight of the blame being directed towards her, at least from Runjhun. Indu wasn't responsible for all the actions of this party, which had hundreds of thousands of workers under its umbrella, just like the Prime Minister wasn't responsible for all the injustices that took place in the country. She felt outraged on Fawad's behalf as well, but could do little about it.

She had seen the irritation on Rana's face every time she vocalized her support for Indira Gandhi, and so she made it a point to tell him that she felt sorry for Fawad and that what had happened was wrong.

* * *

A few days later, when Rana noticed Esha studying on the floor, he told her to go and sit with everyone else. Esha refused and started crying when Rana insisted, which left him completely confused.

'She feels embarrassed about sitting with everyone at the table,' Indu said to him softly.

'So you're going to just let her do her work on the floor?' he asked her, his face indignant.

'It's not about the floor, it's about where she is comfortable. It will be too much for her to sit at the table.'

'It will be too much if we make it seem too much. If we treat it normally, as it should be, then everyone will get used to it.'

She tried to tell him to be patient, but he didn't relent. 'A girl told me once that the first dissent to oppression always arises from a place of privilege. Well, let this be the place of privilege that gives birth to dissent, then.'

And so Indu explained to Esha that it would be better for her posture and concentration to study at the table. Scared at first, she agreed after some coaxing. Indu set her seat at the corner of the long table, but everybody stared at her all the same when she sat down.

Two women at the table, who had recently signed up, asked Indu pointedly if anybody could be a part of this library. Indu forced a smile and told them it was free and open to all women. Yet, that wasn't what was assumed, for anybody who could afford to spend their time in the library, or could afford to dedicate herself to study, was already coming from a place where money wasn't the biggest problem.

Esha's hunched figure, poring over the books in her chair, with her darkened, rough feet folded under her, struggling to write out letters that she had only recently learnt, did not invite their sympathy. They had come to treat the place as, Indu realized with dismay, an elite club of sorts to discuss intellectual ideas. When Esha sat on the chair, she would make herself look as little as possible, and rarely looked up. Sangeeta too did not know how to deal with the situation, but gradually, they all got used to it. One day, Mrs Leela said to Rana before leaving, 'It's good you treat your servants with such respect, even at the cost of your *own* respect.'

Rana made a brutally unkind face at her, but she had turned her back on him by then and had left. 'Can you believe her?' he had asked Indu, and she wanted to tell him that she could, because everyone typically had the same reaction, but didn't say anything.

The other problem was that Esha didn't seem to be making much progress, which greatly worried Indu, but didn't seem to bother Rana that much. 'What, you thought she'd study for two months and emerge a genius? She needs training, practice, focus—things she hasn't had all her life.'

'I know,' she told Rana, 'but girls always face a deadline. If she doesn't perform soon enough or well enough, her mother will go back on her decision and assume she doesn't need education, that she'd be better cleaning a house or married.' Rana told her to take it easy and wait, that it would all work out and pay off. Already, her mother was giving Indu reports of trouble between Sunita and Esha at home, and Indu made up her mind to talk to Sunita about it.

Outside, a wave of agitation rippled through the city as the date of the verdict of Indira Gandhi's case drew nearer. Every day, they read reports of how crowds flocked to greet her, 'infants suckling at their mother's breasts, the elderly stumbling through rocky paths, and men finishing their work early' to stand in the sun that shone more harshly every day. But the streets told a different story, where popular opinion seemed to be turning against the government. Wild stories began cropping up of how Indira Gandhi had black magicians advising her, that she had learnt some occult art that enabled her to be at multiple places at the same time, that she had signed pacts with the United States of America, selling a part of India to them so they could use it against the Soviets, in exchange for winning the case.

Her father spoke little, not allowed to discuss anything besides what was necessary, but dropped ominous hints that things were going to change soon, and Indu wondered what that meant. But she noticed he no longer spoke of Shashi uncle with the same camaraderie, that there were now differences in the management, and that they all waited for the judgment. Everything depended on June 12.

When it arrived, nothing seemed real. Her father had sent word that they should not expect him home anytime soon, and they had just been able to catch a glimpse of him on the television, a part of the Prime Minister's motorcade. The Prime Minister had lost the case and would be stripped of her membership to the general assembly, and would subsequently have to step down. Indu could not accept that a woman she had been named after and looked up to all her life had been publicly declared a defaulter. It seemed as if the chants against her grew louder each day.

It was as if winds of change blew in Indu's life as well. Indu noticed Runjhun's absence after a few days, especially when she would have had the chance to gloat about the results of the court case against Indira Gandhi. Despite herself, Indu asked Rana about it.

'Oh,' he said. 'Well, she moved away.'

'What?!' Indu sputtered, her heart bubbling with hope, although she tried not to show it. 'Why?'

'Well, she kind of got this opportunity in Bombay, at the Blitz—'

'What's the Blitz?'

'It's a kind of, well, magazine, and they were opening up a film offshoot of it, Cine Blitz or something.'

'What? She'll get to meet Rajesh Khanna?' Indu asked, a streak of jealousy rising in her again.

'Sooner or later, I'd say,' he replied.

'And you think you won't go there?'

'Not for some time, no.'

'But sooner or later?'

'I don't know,' he replied, 'so we decided it best to end it. But there was also but there was also another problem.'

'And what's that?'

'You. You're in the way.'

Indu's heart skipped a beat, but she finally managed to sputter, 'Me? I'm in the way? You're in the way! Ever since I've met you, you've always been in my way!'

He didn't speak for some time, just shook his head, sighing as if he shouldered all the problems in the world. Indu asked him after a while, 'Did you love her?'

He paused before answering, 'I think I could have. If it weren't for certain things, mainly you, I could have loved her. But every time I saw you acting stupid whenever she was with me, it felt like I wasn't being true to her, because I could see that you do have feelings for me, and it reminded me that I do as well.'

'I wasn't acting stupid,' Indu said lamely, and Rana laughed.

'When will it be, then? Your wedding?' he asked her.

She looked at him silently before answering, 'I don't know. Sometime next year, I suppose.'

'Am I invited?'

She saw that he was grinning. 'I'll have to think about it. You'll anyway be in Bombay, living your fancy life . . .'

He laughed, looking towards the sky. 'I can't wait. I want to live in one of those high-rises or at least by the sea. One day, eh?'

She stared at him for a while longer. 'I envy you a bit, you know.'

'I mean, obviously. But why exactly are you saying that?'

'Because you can live freely.'

'So can you.'

Indu shook her head, and he glared at her, saying, 'Yes, you can. You have everything you could possibly need in life, and you're smart.'

'Yet, my circumstances don't permit it as yours do,' she said.

'I always thought of you as someone who was more than what her circumstances might make her.'

There was that warmth in his eyes that Indu had grown accustomed to, and which Indu believed, despite everything, was reserved just for her. It made her sad that she couldn't have it.

'I agreed to marry Rajat quite willingly, without any qualms, even looked forward to it. It made sense to me; I mean, I had to be married anyway, and he is someone I had met a few times, heard that he was doing well. But then . . . I met you.'

She couldn't look at him for a while and felt his stare upon her. When she finally saw his face, his expression was inscrutable. They stood like that for a while. He was about to say something when Kittu interrupted, asking Indu if she looked good in pink, that her mother had suggested it for her engagement.

13

Indu lay on her bed watching the fan rotate on the ceiling. Two of her *kurtas* hung on hooks by the side of her cupboard, the curtains were drawn across the window, and a bunch of fresh flowers sat in a vase next to her dresser. The card on the flowers read 'Love, Rajat', and she knew he had asked his parents to send them to her in his stead, probably to fill the gap that had appeared as their conversation had waned.

The house had been absolutely still for some minutes, since she had heard her mother's footsteps going to the kitchen. She lay in the silence, her sister sleeping next to her. Before Amita went off to sleep, Indu had told her, 'I am proud of you,' in a rush of affection and honest love. She wished that her sister had never married Govind *bhai* and instead found someone she genuinely cared for.

Amita was talking about moving back in with Govind. Indu had known it would happen. There was no way out except to try and make it work. Just a few days ago, Amita had completely broken down in front of her, and Indu had attributed it to her exam results, which would come out any day now. But it was so much more than just the results. A bad relationship, her sister had said, is something that you always carry with yourself. 'You go to bed thinking about it, you wake up with it—it's always on your mind.'

Perhaps it's only in retrospect that you wonder how life could have gone so wrong, but when it's happening, you don't really realize what's wrong. Every blow to Amita's crumbling relationship Indu felt in her own self, forcing her to re-examine her own life.

The Queen of Practicality, her sister used to call her, and Indu was quite proud of the title. She felt weak each time she caught herself thinking of Rana, of letting her head go up in the clouds like that, no better than the silly girls who used to giggle while boys would line up outside their college. But life gave her no answers.

She couldn't help thinking of her sister and rued not having a solution, not being able to do anything about it, and wished someone would show her the way. She remembered Govind *bhai's* thunderous face when he had come in yesterday, demanding to know who Fawad was, and Indu, scared for a moment, had looked at her sister in panic. She must have mentioned his name when they went to his birthday party. Indu had tried to pacify him by asking him what the problem was, and Govind *bhai* had just stopped himself from lashing out at her. He had asked Indu again who the boy was, and she, hesitant at first, had said loudly and clearly that he was her friend.

'Look what he writes!' Govind *bhai* had said in contempt, shoving a magazine at her, in which there was a whole feature titled 'The Numbered Days of Congress', with subheadings like 'Five People Taking it to its Downfall'. Indu saw that one of them was Shashi uncle, charged with promoting corruption and hooliganism in the party. 'What kind of company is this RSS maniac for a young girl?' he had said to her. She had coldly told him she could watch out for her own company very well.

The next day, on the way in the car, she thought back to Rana's expression when she had said to him 'until I met you'. She had been unable to judge what he thought of it. She couldn't decide whether what she had seen in his eyes was warmth or surprise and pity.

They didn't speak for the first hour in each other's company at the library, until he finally came and stood in front of her with a meaningful look. She walked outside into the corridor, where he followed her. She faced him, reminded of the last time and what she had said. He hadn't said anything about it to her yet and the hurt of it rushed to her cheeks.

'What is the meaning of that?' she asked him quietly. 'What is the meaning of naming, *incriminating*, my—'

She needed a moment to articulate, in which time he looked confused: '—my sister's husband's uncle like that in your magazine!'

His face screwed up in confusion, trying to understand who she was talking about, before realization finally dawned upon him. 'Pardon me that we don't check your extended family tree before writing a story.'

'Don't joke about it! Did you know?'

'That he was writing it? Yes, of course!'

'So why didn't you say anything?'

'I didn't even remember that he was, well, *related* to you, and even if I had, I still wouldn't—this is different. What would you do? Erase his past?'

'There is no proof he did anything.'

'Don't be a fool. It's probably his people who got into a scuffle with Fawad the other day,' Rana said, staring coldly at her till she looked away. She walked back inside, deciding to ask her sister about it later in the afternoon when she arrived. He avoided speaking to her after that and they each went about their work. Indu looked at Esha sitting next to Sangeeta, hoping that they were making progress. When it was time for lunch, Esha got up to make tea for those who would have it, later going around to serve it, and Indu noticed that most women now treated Esha even more dismissively, evidently annoyed at her intention to improve herself. Indu wondered if she should have her stop doing the work, but knew that it was also the reason she was allowed to come to the library—she earned money, which was why her mother was still okay with her not being married yet.

She and Rana didn't talk much the rest of the day, and she tried to guess what he was thinking, but his expression was inscrutable. She wondered if she should write him a letter, but felt she had already said too much. She considered the possibility that he was using Fawad's situation as an excuse not to address the conversation they had had before.

In the evening, Indu and Amita sat at the back as Natty drove, and Indu asked him to stop at an old park nearby. Now that the sun had almost set, it wasn't that hot anymore. They walked around for some time, talking. When there was a lag in the conversation, Indu looked at Amita and couldn't help asking, 'Are you unhappy?'

Amita didn't reply, but Indu saw the tears in her eyes and felt helpless against them. 'I don't know,' Amita finally said. 'I don't know how I am. All I know is that there isn't much I can do to change the situation. I always thought life would begin once I got married, had my own family, people to be responsible for. Sometimes it feels like there's nothing left, that the best has gone by, and it wasn't even that good.'

Indu held her sister's wrist, putting her shoulder against Amita's as they went on walking. 'I don't think that I felt in love with him for even a moment,' she said, looking at Indu now. 'In the beginning, it was exciting because there was attention, the promise of something new . . . but after a while, I realized that I just didn't admire him as a person.'

'Is there nothing else you can do?' Indu asked her.

Amita shook her head before answering, 'I just don't have it in me to be able to break it off. These exams, this study time felt like an escape, but I have to go back to him now. I know it's not very strong of me, but it's hard to go against the tide of the world. Nobody would approve of it, and there is no "problem" as it is. In fact, people might go so far as to say that Govind should be the one to break it off, you know . . .'

'But you can,' Indu said fiercely. 'If you choose to do it, I swear I will support you till my last breath.'

Amita squeezed her hand tightly. 'Thank you, but I am pretty sure I can't do it. I can tell you this much, though: if you are not convinced about Rajat, don't be afraid to take the decision. It's not too late.'

Indu walked on, looking ahead, then looked away. 'Rajat is not Govind *bhai*. He's different.'

Her sister patted her on the back. 'That sounds like a plea. I hope he is different, but you have to consider if you can fit your life around his. If something goes wrong, I know you won't take it quietly. I know you will raise hell. But it's better to avoid it altogether . . .'

'It doesn't matter, it doesn't matter if there is Rana,' Amita continued. 'Think about yourself. If you can live the life Rajat desires, well and good. If not, there will be better things in the future. I know you feel it's too late for that. It will be hard, but better now than later.'

Indu walked on troubled by these thoughts, looking unseeingly at an old man ambling along the bushes.

* * *

When they met Fawad next, Indu saw that his gash had almost healed and his cast was off. She saw him a dart a quick look at Rana, who nodded discreetly. Fawad pursed his lips in acknowledgement and pulled out two chairs politely, asking Indu and Amita to sit down.

Fawad explained to them that he didn't really have any intention to hurt anyone. To Indu's surprise, Amita seemed to understand him completely, nodding the whole while, and even seemed sympathetic. That led Indu to think that maybe she knew some things about Shashi uncle that she didn't.

Amita said, 'Fawad, I would say that you love this country a lot more than those who claim to serve it. But I would ask you to take care of yourself. I don't know why, but I feel something major is brewing, and this piece has really angered them. Something is not right.'

'But what—how do you mean?'

'I am not sure, but there are many meetings being held about what to do, because it is certain that she will not take it lying down.'

'So she won't step down?'

'She doesn't want to.'

'I appreciate your concern,' Fawad said, looking respectfully at Amita, 'but I have to write what I see. We have a series of, one could say, *explosive* pieces coming out, and it might be taken up by the BBC. I—I won't stop it.'

Neither of them knew what to say to that. Fawad added that he was grateful she had thought of him and was sorry if she had felt offended. Rana smiled at them from the other side of the room. He had set up his transistor, and "*Yeh Shaam Mastani*" had begun playing on it softly. Indu squealed excitedly when she heard the opening strain.

'Oh God, no, please,' Amita said, putting her head in her hands. 'I've heard this one too many times now. She and Natty have gone crazy. They sing it all the time.'

Rana threw his head back and laughed, increasing the volume as Indu began singing.

Amita walked over to Rana and said, 'Do you know, she even mumbles Rajesh Khanna dialogues in her sleep?'

'No,' Rana said, laughing even harder. 'Tell me that isn't true.'

'It's quite true. A few days ago, I was sleeping next to her and she woke up in the middle of the night, said something like "*zindagi badi honi chahiye, lambi nahi*", and went back to sleep.'

Rana laughed so hard that he had to sit.

'That's not true!' Indu yelled in the interlude of the song. 'She's completely making it up!'

'I'm sure she dreams of him all the time,' he said. 'Oh *babumoshai*, I love you so much, *babumoshai*. Do you know how much she cried when she watched *Anand*?'

'I cried at just the last bit!' Indu answered indignantly.

'Yeah, she cried only for the last two hours.'

Indu threw a cushion from the sofa at them, which would have hit the transistor if Rana had not caught it in time. He glared at her as she muttered an 'oops'.

* * *

Indu did not get a chance to speak to Rana alone for a week as his exams had begun. The weather turned hotter, but the streets became livelier. Promises from political parties hung in the air, thick and strong, but the people wondered what would actually come of them.

In such an atmosphere, Indu always wondered how she would live in another country. She had no intention of leaving. She had a reputation here, people knew her, and she had achieved something for herself. If things went on as they were going now, she could really make a name for herself, a name that was unattached to any man's.

Yet, she did not know how to navigate such a future for herself and constantly put off dealing with the thought. She wondered if she would be attracted to Rajat if she got to know him better. She sometimes wondered what his life was like, and if he would appreciate what she was doing.

A few days ago, Esha had passed her school exams with a better-than-ever grade. They had enrolled her in a correspondence course that would allow her to graduate. All Indu had to do was imagine how her future might be changed to remain convinced that this must go on. She was sure Esha's future would look very different if she continued to study like this.

Sangeeta, however, brought up several problems. She told Indu that it was not as if Esha could not study—she simply did not want to. This was because the people of her community had begun isolating them, especially since they had refused to marry Esha to another boy in the community. Esha's stepfather had lost his temper and kicked Sunita and Esha out of the house, so they were renting another room. Nobody in their community supported them, because they didn't understand the reason for allowing Esha this freedom. Indu told Esha and Sunita that the only way out of this was for the young girl to study hard and earn money, which would bring them the respect they weren't getting now.

The other members of the library were proving difficult too. They were beginning to mutter that their families didn't send them here to mix with this kind of crowd. When Indu insisted that they must rise above such pettiness, Mrs Leela and Bharti aunty told her unapologetically, 'Listen, Indu dear, though it may be 1975, it's still naïve to think that we can sit and study with our servants. Today there is one, tomorrow there will be many more. We'll say it to you now: you need to have some kind of entry and admission standards for the library. You can't let just anyone come in.' Indu ignored what they said, but it seemed to be an increasingly popular opinion.

Rana walked in one afternoon as June entered its last week, announcing to everybody that he had given his last exam and that he might be called to the bar. Everyone clapped for him, Indu the loudest of all.

She was sitting at the desk when he came up to her. 'I fell asleep for a few minutes before you came in,' she told him.

'Were you talking to yourself again?' He looked at her and she narrowed her eyes at him.

He held up a jasmine. She got up, taking it cautiously, making sure not to bend any of its petals, and smelt it. 'Thanks,' she told him quietly, and he smiled at her, looking down as she bowed her head to smell it again.

'Do you want to go out with me this evening?' he asked her. 'We can leave a bit early.'

She knew he wanted to talk, and felt nervous. She thought about pretending that it was long over for her, but by the skittish way she said yes, she doubted whether he would believe it. He nodded and went back to look at what Esha was doing.

When the evening rolled around, he suggested they take a walk through a *mela* nearby and then sit in the park. It had gotten very hot by now, so Indu was grateful for the light breeze that kicked up in the evening, even though it meant that the dust from the parched *mela* ground often blew into their faces. At the far edge of the ground, there was a giant wheel, which would be lit up after dark, and a few more rides around it. Hawkers and stalls surrounded these, selling knick-knacks. They sat by a bench where it was slightly quieter, having *chana* from a paper cone.

'I'm done studying,' he mused.

Indu looked at him curiously. 'Do you look forward to it?'

'To what?'

'Life.'

'I guess so.'

'Do you think it has good things in store for you?'

He looked into the distance for some time before answering, 'I think so, yes. I mean, I don't know where I will go. But I know I want to enjoy it, every bit of time we have.'

She nodded at him, and he turned to face her, 'What about you?'

She answered, distracted by the lines on his face, 'I think it does for me too. But the onus of it feels too much, you know. I feel I have taken a decision. I'm scared that if I mess it up, I'll end up somewhere not good. Like my sister.'

They fell quiet again for some time before he turned to Indu once more. This time, his face was different, his eyes earnest. 'I didn't know what to say to you.'

Indu realized what he was referring to and looked away, concentrating her gaze on a balloon seller a little way off.

Round, colourful balloons floated in the air, tied by strings to a long wooden stick. Soon, it would be too dark to make out the different colours, and they would be silhouettes against the sky.

He knew she was listening. 'I still don't. I don't know what you want. Actually, maybe I know what you want but I'm not sure you know if you want it.'

She didn't reply and they sat in silence for a while till she turned to him and said, 'I don't know why I met you. I was alright. I never thought of another possibility. It was all chalked out for me until you came waltzing in, calling yourself Salim, telling me with your stupid, moony eyes, oh, I want to make a library with you. Tell me honestly, did you actually come to me for that?'

He laughed at that, leaning back against the bench, putting his arm around its back. 'Of course not. I just wanted to get to know you, and I found a good opportunity to do that.'

She shook her head at him. 'It's completely your fault.'

He bent again, putting his head in his hands. 'I know, and I was so confused, I didn't know what to feel about it. And then I thought, if I were with someone else, it would be better. For both of us.'

She looked at the balloon seller again, and the balloons bobbing on the stick.

'I have to say,' she told him, 'that made it much worse.'

He sighed, his palms on his face. Indu was glad that it affected him. She watched as a mother bought two balloons for her child. The child held one in its hand and set the other free, which floated upwards slowly; it would soon be invisible against the sunset.

Neither said anything for a while and Indu stared ahead. Would she have met someone else, if not Rana? Did the problem lie in her not knowing Rajat?

'Since you won't stop staring at them, I'll buy you a balloon, unless you want to retain some respect and decline the offer,' he said.

She laughed, looking at him, and so they bought a big orange balloon. Indu set it free even though it was dark and they couldn't keep it in sight for very long. They walked through the park and headed towards Number 7.

When they were nearly there, both stopped. He looked at her for a couple of seconds and stepped closer. She knew what was about to happen. He tilted her chin up and brushed his lips lightly against hers. A few seconds passed. She squeezed his shoulder and he looked at her with a question on his face, but his grin remained.

'You have to ask, mister,' she told him.

She knew he wanted to laugh, but instead, he made his expression very serious, folding his hands. 'May I?'

She flung her arms around his neck and kissed him back.

14

Early the next morning, they were woken by the loud ring of the telephone. Indu was still groggy, but her mother was already up and rushed to the phone to answer it, knowing it would be her husband. It was a ten-second conversation, and her mother put the phone down without saying anything.

'What happened?' Indu asked while her sister emerged from the room, rubbing her eyes.

Her mother walked over to the radio, telling them that their father had asked her to turn it on. 'Isn't father at home?' Amita asked blankly, but nobody replied. They all gathered in the drawing room, around the radio.

The broadcast ran loud and clear for a few minutes, and they took in every word. The Prime Minister's dainty voice formed every word with precision, enunciating clearly. She spoke about internal disturbances, external threats and the price of maintaining security. While Indu understood every word, she was unable to understand the overall message, and looked quizzically at her mother and sister. When the broadcast ended, she asked, 'What does it mean?'

'What it said,' her mother replied. 'A state of emergency has been declared.'

'Yes, but what does that mean?' Indu asked impatiently, and her mother and sister looked as clueless as she did.

Her mother shook her head and went to phone her husband again, and this time, the conversation lasted a minute. Indu and Amita looked at her impatiently, waiting for her to explain.

'You will read all about it,' her mother started, 'but mostly, it means that civil rights have been taken away. There can no longer be any protests or any kind of bandhs or strikes. Certain schemes and rules will be enforced. Many opposition and other vocal leaders have already been arrested. Most importantly, there will be press censorship.'

'Press censorship?' Indu asked. 'Like, how?'

'All publications will have to get approval for whatever they publish, and the same goes for television and other media.'

'Where is the newspaper this morning?' Indu asked.

'No newspaper today. Electricity to all presses was cut off last night. Nothing will come out until all publications start to follow the rules.'

'But why is all this happening?'

'It had to happen,' she said. 'She didn't want to be unseated.'

'What now? And when will father come home?'

Her mother shrugged, unable to answer either question.

* * *

The streets seemed unchanged, although there was less traffic. She asked Natty if he had noticed anything different.

'*Kis baat ki emergency?* Everyone here anyway walks around as if they are in an emergency, never giving way to the other person! The only emergency we need is the emergency of common sense!'

She decided she would discuss it with Rana and Fawad. She was really looking forward to seeing Rana, now that what was between them had been acknowledged. The trouble was that she had to make a decision about Rajat now, and knew that breaking it off would mean a long and rocky path ahead. Her parents would try everything in their power to make her change her mind; Rajat's family and hers went back a long way and they would not want relationships to be ruined over the whims and fancies of a twenty-three-year-old.

They would convince her that it was just a phase and that any boy could be forgotten. Her father certainly would think so. What would she say about Rana as an actual possibility in their lives?

Moreover, could she count on Rana? It was one thing to exchange banter, all fun and games, but he still hadn't discussed how they should take it from there, and Indu was too proud to ask. She guessed he too was making up his mind, but that reeked of uncertainty. Also, neither had mentioned Runjhun. If he could end things with her so suddenly, didn't that just reinforce that he was not dependable? And could she rely on him to give up his cavalier lifestyle? What of the next time he saw someone he found attractive and found an opportunity to get to know them, just as he had done with Indu?

And what of Rajat? He certainly seemed more accommodating and didn't provoke her with banter, although for all she knew, his politeness was a garb.

When Rana came in to Number 7 the next time, he shared with her a smile that contained the knowledge of their last kiss, but he didn't address it, so Indu went about her work, not giving him undue importance. When he sat next to her with his hands folded in a steeple, she gave him a questioning look.

'I'm going to go home in two weeks,' he told her. 'For the summer.'

They sat in silence for a couple of minutes when he turned and began staring at her.

'What?' she asked, refusing to look at him.

'I have something for you,' he said, and got up from his chair. Indu sighed, making a show of getting up and shaking her head at him, following him outside into the corridor. A large, flat package was resting against the wall. Indu looked at him questioningly and he nodded at her to open it. As soon as she touched it, she knew it was a canvas and could not stop grinning. He had made a painting for her. She delicately tore off the outer packing, holding the canvas tenderly. She wanted to see all of it in one go, so she opened it from the back, finally turning it around and gazing at herself on paper.

She was painted with her head tilted to the right, the neck of her beige *kurta* ending at her collarbones, her hair long and open, parted in the middle. Her eyes twinkled with laughter, eyebrows were raised, lips turned down as if mock-marvelling at something, and she knew he had captured her looking at him, for there was amusement on her face. She definitely thought he had depicted her chin raised to support his theory that she always looked snobby, but it was a beautiful painting nevertheless, white jasmine tucked behind her ear, its petals fresh and white.

Indu's painted face glowed against a mustard background, making the whiteness of the jasmine stand out. She ran her thumb across the canvas, its roughness smoothened by patches of the oil paint, its strokes following masterful patterns. 'It's beautiful,' she said, looking up at Rana. 'Not just because of me, I mean,' she added, and he laughed.

'Fawad helped me with it,' he said. 'I knew—I had an idea what I wanted to depict, but he helped me execute it.'

She wanted to say so much to him, but the words got caught in her throat. She wanted to tell him that she had never felt this way about anyone, that the days she didn't speak to him felt sad and incomplete, that nothing would thrill her more than planning a life with him, but she couldn't, and instead held the canvas tightly, her eyes sparkling with tears.

'I hope you like it,' he said, suddenly unsure, and she nodded. He looked at her closely for a few seconds before going on. 'Ever since you told me that you—well, I couldn't put it out of my head. I think I love you.'

How she had waited for him to utter these words! But now that he did, she found it hard to trust them. Despite herself, she couldn't say anything in reply. She stared at him without blinking.

'That doesn't mean anything,' he went on. 'I don't expect anything from you. I don't know what you're looking for in your future, but whatever it is, I would like you to lead your life as you will, you know? How you want it to.'

She nodded at him, clutching the canvas tightly. 'Should we go in?' she asked, and he paused before nodding. But she did not move. Instead, she put the canvas down, resting it against the wall, and impulsively put her arms around him, holding him close for a few seconds. Then just as suddenly, she let him go before turning to pick the painting up.

'I should thank Fawad too,' Indu said, touched. 'Where is he? And oh, did you hear it this morning?'

Rana shrugged. 'Hear what?'

'The broadcast!'

'What broadcast?'

'The emergency one! What kind of magazine writer are you? Where is Fawad? He would know!'

'I haven't seen him since yesterday, he didn't come home. I think he might be staying with someone else.'

'Don't you know? An emergency has been declared. I thought I'd ask you what it means.'

'What do you mean an "emergency"?' he asked, stopping in his tracks.

'I don't know, something like an emergency situation, I didn't get it, my mother was telling me but I don't know. You noticed there was no newspaper this morning? Some kind of press censorship.'

Indu turned around to see that Rana had stopped dead in his tracks. 'What?' she asked him.

'I need to go,' he said, rushing inside to pick up his stuff.

'Where?'

'I'm sure there will be some team meeting or something. How do I not know this? The streets did look a bit empty this morning. Where is Fawad?' Rana darted out in an uncharacteristic hurry, and Indu shrugged it off.

When Indu took the painting home that evening, Natty decided to narrate a story from his youth.

'I fell in love once, you know, madame,' he said.

Indu looked at him in the rear-view mirror, surprised. 'Really?'

'What, you think this Natwarlal doesn't have a heart, madame?'

'No, but, I mean, you have a wife.'

He pffed. 'I mean before her, I fell in love once. She had the biggest brown eyes, you know, madame. And she wore *payals* so big, I could hear them from a kilometre away. Her father was also very liberal, you know, for that time. Many days, we passed each other and made eye contact, she always smiled at me. Rajni was her name.'

'*Arre waah,* Natty.'

'Wait, it has a tragic end, madame. Before I could muster the courage to talk to her father for her hand in marriage, my best friend did it!'

'No!' Indu said, outraged.

'Bastard. He did, and now they are happily married with five fat children.' He shook his head in disappointment, hitting the steering wheel lightly in dismay. Indu didn't know whether to believe him or not, but he certainly seemed regretful enough.

'It was a difficult time, madame. A different time. We didn't have the opportunities you have now, to be able to talk so freely. One must always talk freely, you know?'

She didn't reply. Natty had an ability to say one thing and mean another, and she understood what he was implying.

Putting up the painting in the house led to considerable grumbling and suspicion, although they thought it was beautiful. Her father, in particular, glared at it every time he passed it, but his eyes softened whenever he stopped to admire his younger daughter's expression captured on canvas.

* * *

Rana didn't turn up the next day, and so Indu busied herself deciding what else could be done at the library. She could barely imagine a life without it now, but all thoughts about it were inexorably linked with Rana. She was already imagining a life with him. He would need a proper job, though, she decided.

Her mind wandered back to the Emergency. The newspapers had all carried it today, how the government had declared a state of emergency, and how it would affect people. From the outset, Indu couldn't help but think that it didn't seem to make much of a difference. It wasn't possible to protest now, and so those students might actually attend some classes, she couldn't help but think to herself wryly. If the decision had been taken, maybe it wasn't such a bad one.

What shook her more was when she got home that day and asked her mother casually where Esha was. She was informed that Sunita had taken Esha away to their village to get her married off.

'What?' Indu asked, shocked. 'But what—why?'

'Sunita said that everyone around them had started to taunt her that her daughter would never get married. I can't say I blame her, it really created a mess for her.'

'How can you say that? She was doing so well!'

'You're doing well too,' her mother answered, walking away. 'But will you give up a set future for it?'

Indu stayed silent, not wanting to reveal the extent of what was going on in her mind. She feared never seeing Esha again, and wanted to tell Rana, but he didn't come the next day either. She raged and seethed to her sister, telling her how he was completely undependable, master of his own will, doing as he wished without any care or consideration for others. Once she got tired of it, she decided not to think about him at all and instead, pondered what to do about Rajat. The answer had been obvious to her the whole time, but she didn't want to acknowledge it.

It would be one of the biggest decisions of her life, for marriage was what she had imagined. It was an eventuality, a natural progression in the events of her life, something so obvious that she never sought to question it. She had known of Rajat for some time, and so when their match was discussed, she thought about it and said yes quite agreeably, for the logic of it was obvious to her. She would have to marry somebody, and he seemed like a decent enough man, liked by everyone she knew. There hadn't been a reason to turn it down, and so she had consented quite readily. When she learnt that he would study for two years first, it seemed an even better decision, since she wouldn't be rushed into it.

But the past year had changed everything. Now that she had a room of her own, a job to call her own, a purpose in life, and they eclipsed everything else. And then she had met Rana. After meeting him, after knowing what life could be, everything had seemed different. The conversation and attraction that constantly drew her to him—she didn't want to settle for less. She couldn't take that chance. But it would be the most difficult thing she would ever do.

She was ready to face the fire from her parents. She decided she would first write to Rajat and try to explain the reasons for her choice as well as possible. She also told Amita her final decision while her sister was packing to move back in with Govind *bhai*. She would have to talk to Rana before talking to her parents.

But he didn't turn up at Number 7 for a few days after he had given her the painting. As she wondered why for the umpteenth time, the little Sardar peeked into Number 7. '*Haanji paaji, kya hua?*' Indu asked him and he quietly handed her a note. She stared at him quizzically. 'Who gave you this?' 'Bhaiya' the boy said and scampered away.

She opened it to discover a hurried scrawl from Rana, asking her to meet him at Bheem House at 5 p.m. that day. She didn't understand any of it but was curious to hear what he had to say.

When she reached Bheem House, someone suddenly pulled her into a corner.

'Shhh!' Rana said as soon as she opened her mouth, indicating that they should quietly sit on the corner seat. There was less hustle-bustle here than in the rest of the place.

'Where have you been?' she hissed at him.

Instead of answering, he looked around them, as if expecting someone. Indu noticed that the usual sparkle was gone from his face, and he constantly fidgeted.

'Hello, mister?' she asked him, 'what's wrong?'

'You came here alone, right?' he asked her.

'Yeah, with Natty. What's wrong?'

He shook his head and ordered two coffees.

She asked him a few more times what was wrong and he finally began after he had finished his coffee. He smoked as he told her.

'Fawad's gone,' he said.

'Gone? What do you mean?'

'He's gone under the radar, with a bunch of other magazine workers.'

'But whom are they hiding from?'

'The government, of course! They are arresting people left, right and centre.'

'You too?'

'No, not me. I wasn't as involved.'

'We'll look for him,' she said confidently.

'At first I thought he was being paranoid, but the mood everywhere is strange.'

'Alright, let's do one thing—let's talk to my father about it and he can—'

'No! Of course not! We are not going anywhere *near* your family.'

'What do you mean?' she asked him, hurt.

'Your father helped set this up, this emergency, I'm sure, and even if he didn't, he has to defend it. He can't hear about it.'

Indu laughed in confusion. 'I'm sure he didn't set it up or whatever, but you don't have to hide from him. I mean, how can you, you're with me.'

'I'll have to go,' he said.

'Go where?'

'I have to find out where Fawad is, figure out our next move. I can't stick around.'

She looked at him incredulously. 'I don't get it. Because of what, an "emergency"? Where do you want to go, and what are you even saying—what about us?'

'What about us?'

She hoped that the hurt didn't show on her face. 'What do you mean "what about us"? Are we not—what is wrong with you?'

He shut his eyes before answering and extended his hand, which she didn't take. 'Indu, I . . . I can't say anything right now. You don't understand. But right now, I can't promise you anything. I have nothing to promise.'

She slid her chair away from him, wondering if she was seeing him for the first time. She hoped she had heard him wrong, but she knew she hadn't. She stared at him for a long time as the din around her seemed to fade. Or maybe it was her own thundering heartbeat that quieted. She realized that all the fears she had with regard to Rana suddenly rang louder in her ears and seemed more valid than ever. *Unreliable*—the word went around in her head. Life had to be more than just fun and games. She got up from her chair, finally.

'Then you better never see me again,' she said, and almost ran to the Ambassador. She thought she heard him call out her name, but even of that, she could not be sure.

END OF PART 2

15

1 year later

Clouds changed shape in the lull before the predicted storm, gliding slyly across the smoky, grey sky, filtering the rays of the sun as a light breeze skipped across the city. The air was heavy with the promise of thunder, and Indu hoped to make it back home before it broke, but the pace at which Natty was driving, her expectations weren't very high. She sighed as he continued his rendering of '*Yeh Dosti Hum Nahi Todenge*'.

'Oh, do continue the song,' Indu said, feigning sweetness. 'It's not like we are in a hurry.'

Natty laughed. 'Coming and going is a matter of fate, madame. How can a simple song halt its course, of what's been written for us lifetimes ago?'

Indu pouted at him for a few seconds before turning her head to look at the road. 'Why don't you start writing dialogues for movies? You can put your talent to good use, and maybe I'll finally get my debut alongside Rajesh Khanna.'

'You flatter me, madame. You must be very troubled.'

Indu *was* troubled. The day had begun ordinarily enough and she had left for the library after the usual breakfast, wearing a beige and light green *chanderi* sari with a light blue paisley print on the border. The switch from *kurtas* to saris had not been without reason. The season seemed to demand it. She felt different, more grown-up, and it seemed to reflect in her dressing.

Indu had pinned the sari tightly to her shoulder, stepping into her heels, standing by the garden gate as Natty had brought the car to her. While the rickshaws and bicycles still zigzagged with disdain across the roads, which always sent up dust, they flouted traffic signals less often. The Ambassador in which Natty drove Indu had the Congress symbol displayed front and back. Everywhere they rode, people hurriedly backed off and stared curiously inside, and Indu never went out without her sunglasses.

The morning had started out sunny and Indu was glad for the new curtains they'd had tailored for Number 7. For the past few months, every time Indu walked inside, she couldn't help but look around and smile—Number 7 looked more and more like a proper library every day. Bookshelves lined all the walls now, colourful book spines slanted against each other. They had added tables, which looked big and inviting in the morning, and slowly got occupied through the day. Now Kittu helped Indu during the day. Indu had agreed to give her a small sum of money, which she proudly took home to her parents. Kittu wasn't the smartest chip on the block, and there was only so much that Indu could tolerate of her negligence, but she realized that there was nobody else who lived close enough and was available to stay there throughout the day.

The first of the girls began arriving around 11 a.m. Indu made entries of the books that had been returned and the ones that were pending, handing them to Kittu, who would run and put them on the correct shelves. She thought of Rajat, who would arrive in three weeks. She wanted to make sure that it looked busy and vibrant when Rajat saw it, and was hoping to have an event on the day she would bring him here. She finished filing the last of the returns and looked up at the doorway.

Rana stood there, one hand in his pocket, the other touching the door. The shirt was untucked, and his hair messier than before. He stared at her long and continuously, pouting, his face in a frown uncharacteristic of him. She half expected him to walk in with a cheeky grin, ready to say to her, 'Could you stop staring at me? I'm starting to get uncomfortable.' But he didn't. He didn't move from the doorway. He looked thinner and had shadows beneath his eyes, but suddenly he smiled and the twinkle in his eyes seemed to come back.

Indu didn't smile back, just looked at him instead. She couldn't tolerate his audacity. She finally walked towards him, her sari trailing behind her. She wondered if he would notice the change in attire.

She came to a stop close to him, looking at him with indignant, raised eyebrows. In a firm voice, she asked, 'What the hell are you doing here?' and saw that he heard the anger in her voice. She hoped it would hurt him.

It was as if he had forgotten how to speak, for he kept staring at her. She looked at him in exasperation and then glanced around to see if the others had noticed him. Kittu and two of the older girls were grinning widely and the rest of them stared curiously till Indu shot them a sharp glance. They hurriedly turned back to their books. When she turned around, Rana was still staring at her.

'Why are you here?' she asked him again.

He didn't reply for the longest time, and she didn't know what to do with him as he stood in the doorway of her library, leaning against the wall, staring at her without a care in the world.

Just as she was about to open her mouth again, he asked her, 'How are you?'

She mustered all the contempt that she could and brought it to her face, telling him coldly, 'Better without you. I don't want to talk to you.'

His expression did not change, and she was going to re-emphasize her point when he finally said it. 'I need to talk to you.'

'I don't want to talk to you,' she hissed at him, and she meant it. 'How can you show up—after months—at my door like this—how can you even *think*—'

'Indu, please—'

'Don't you dare take my name!' It came out louder than she had expected, and suddenly her eyes threatened to spill tears. She took a deep breath. 'Please, go.' But she knew he would not.

'I'm not leaving without talking to you.'

'I'll call the police,' she said.

'You're worse than the police,' he replied.

She knew he thought she would laugh, so she didn't. 'Get out,' she told him.

'Indu, I need to speak to you.'

'I don't have time.'

'I'll wait.'

'I'm not interested.'

'It's a matter of life and death, Indu.'

She stared at him, refusing to soften her expression. If he thought he could turn up after a year and use big words like 'it's a matter of life and death' and expect her to relent, he was wrong.

'What is it?' she asked.

'Come with me.'

'No.'

He looked at her for a few seconds. 'At 5.30?'

She paused before asking, 'Where?'

'You know where.'

She raised her eyebrows and he gave her a knowing look. She turned around to go back to her desk, and by the time she sat down, he was already gone.

* * *

The day Rana and Indu had met at Bheem House Diner, one year ago, was the last time she had spoken of him, when she had told her sister what had transpired. She didn't mention him to anyone after that, but spent months dwelling on the memory of his face, his voice. She hadn't expected to see him again for many years. One day, she thought, they might randomly spot each other walking down Marine Drive, where Indu would be taking a walk along the city of dreams and Rana would pass her, wearing a suit. They would look at each other with the same warmth. She would smile at him, give him a courteous nod, ask about his welfare and walk off. She wouldn't tell him that she thought of him every day, and that he came to her mind every time she laughed, and watched Rajesh Khanna on screen.

When Rana had left, Indu had been convinced, knew *for sure*, that he would return soon, apologizing for his brash words, sorry for his hurried decision, and then Indu would take her own sweet time to let it go. But she knew in her heart that she would definitely let it go, enamoured by the sweet things he would do to make up, and they would again discuss being together. Every day she sat down with the draft of the letter she would send to Rajat, gently apologetic, saying that she had met someone else.

But with every passing day that Rana did not return, she felt increasingly the fool, felt that he had played her. She berated herself for being stupid enough to fall for his wobbly promises and casual claims, yet could not believe that all that he had said and done had been empty. It might have been sincere at some point, but just like with Runjhun, just like with everything else in his life, his attention had wavered, the shine had waned and he had left as quickly as he had come. When she realized he wouldn't come back, she channelled all her pain into ignoring his existence, refusing to talk about him to anyone who asked, erasing all traces of the time he had been a part of her life.

Now she entered Indian Coffee House and looked around. She found him waiting for her at their old table. He got up when he saw her. Taking a deep breath, she walked towards him and took the seat opposite, crossing her arms across her chest.

For a few minutes, neither said anything. Indu didn't want to be the first one. Rana finally asked her if she wanted coffee.

She shook her head and gave him a look of loathing.

'It's a valid question—we *are* in a coffee house!'

She hoped he could see the disgust in her eyes. 'I'm not here to have coffee with you. I'm here because you said something's a matter of life and death. Not that I believe you, but I have to give you the benefit of doubt before I ask you never to show me your face again.'

She thought she saw a twinge of pain on his face, but he turned and asked the waiter for a coffee.

'I'm going to have one, though, if you don't mind. Couldn't sleep all night,' he said.

'Listen, mister—'

'I know you're angry, okay, but give me a chance! I know you've decided to give me a chance because you are here.'

She still refused to look at him.

'How are you?'

She didn't reply.

'You look beautiful. As always.'

She yawned pointedly, still looking away.

'Yet, there's something missing.'

She shot him a contemptuous look. He extended his hand and opened his fist to reveal a fresh, white jasmine. She looked at the little flower on his palm, and then at his face. She picked it up and crushed it with her thumb and forefinger, letting the ruined petals fall to the table as he watched her, wide-eyed.

It took him a few seconds, after which he said, 'Ouch.'

'Anything else?' Indu asked in mock curiosity, raising her eyebrows.

Rana stuck out his lower lip, leaning towards Indu across the table; his eyes were wide and he extended his arm again, while Indu still kept hers folded across her chest. He propped his elbows on the table, away from his coffee, and stared at her sadly. 'I miss you,' he said.

She felt herself melt for a moment, but didn't let it show, and instead, composed herself to ask him coldly, 'What do you want?'

His eyes looked sadder and browner than ever, and Indu was tempted to sound less harsh.

'Don't you want to know where I've been?' he asked.

'Not really,' Indu said.

'I'm going to tell you anyway.'

Indu sighed, turning to the waiter, and requested a coffee as well.

'When we met at Bheem House that day—'

'You left, Rana!' Indu suddenly said, banging her hands on the table. She noticed people turning to stare at them, and so she lowered her voice. 'I don't care where you've been, what you've been through, or whatever cock and bull story you plan to feed me—the fact of the matter is, you left.'

'You told me never to see you again!'

'Then why are you here?'

'I know you didn't mean it! I wanted to come earlier, but I couldn't!'

'That's convenient,' she said, turning away from him again.

He put his head in his hands, massaging it as if this conversation had given him a headache. He then sighed loudly and shut his eyes.

'When I met you that time,' he began, 'I told you things were going to go wrong, but I didn't know how true that would turn out to be. I told you Fawad had already gone into hiding. We had heard that some opposition leaders had been arrested, but we didn't know anything for sure. Our printers had also been sealed.'

'Your printers got sealed?' Indu asked him.

'Of course! Did you not know that already?'

'How would I?!'

'Well, anyway, that evening, Fawad came home and told us we must leave. He looked deranged, throwing clothes into his suitcase, moving around distractedly, telling me we must pack up and leave. I told him no, of course, that he needed to calm down. I told him the prime minister would never be allowed to keep this up. It seemed such an impossible situation then, all those measures. But he left anyway, saying he couldn't stay, and moved to a friend's house in Uday Park. I thought he was being paranoid, but I humoured him.'

Indu waited for him to go on.

'Two days later, they knocked on my door. It was in the middle of the night and I woke up groggy, hoping that it was Fawad. But my worst fears were confirmed. There were three people, one in a police uniform. They pushed me aside and entered, heading straight for the rooms. Fawad was not there and they started going through our things. I told them that Fawad had gone home to visit his family. It was a good move as they seemed to believe me. Yet, they took me along with them.'

Indu stared at him in shock. 'Took you where?'

'I don't know what it was, but someone's office, I suppose.'

'What did they want?'

'To convince me that Fawad was a Kashmiri nationalist, that he wanted to blow up the government, and that I should tell them whatever I knew about him.'

'Oh my God,' Indu covered her mouth with her hand. 'I can't believe it.'

'They kept me for a few hours, trying to drill it into my head and convince me that I must report him as soon as he returned, that I must give up his addresses, his friends, his family. They even asked if I had any of his documents,' Rana said. 'I obviously told them I didn't know anything, that he didn't share very much with me. Then they questioned me about what I had written for the magazine. I said it was mainly sports and poetry.'

'Oh God.'

'They let me go after a few hours, but I knew it wasn't over. They kept an eye on me. I did not dare call anyone, but I had to somehow get to Fawad and warn him. One day, I made sure I wasn't being followed, went to the place where he was staying, and managed to tell him they had come to get him.'

'But—why did they want to arrest him?'

'You read the stuff he wrote. Article after article against the government, attacking everything they had ever stood for. The question is, why didn't they arrest him the same night they declared Emergency? The day it all changed, he was already at the forefront of one of the few big marches against her. He was a marked man. Of course, I didn't know the extent of all this. I knew he was involved in activities other than the magazine, but I never bothered much. The people who tried to get him took too long, and it bought him his freedom. He stayed low. I knew I was being watched all the time. I did not dare speak on the phone, I didn't know whom I could ask for help—it was very confusing. I also had no news from the others because nothing was allowed to be reported. We obviously expected that this wouldn't last. It was impossible to think that it could go on so long this way, and that no one would do anything.'

'But why didn't you go back home to Lucknow?'

He shook his head. 'Whatever it was, I didn't want to voluntarily lead them to my family, just in case something went wrong. I didn't want them to be used as bait. The farther away I was from them, the safer they were.

'After a few weeks passed, we realized the situation would continue that way. I didn't know what to do, the magazine had been shut down. I couldn't come to the library—'

'That's the part I don't get,' Indu interrupted. 'I mean, not that I care, and whatever, you are free to make your choices—but how does that stop you from . . . from . . . one whole year!'

His elbows were on the table again and he held his head in his hands, unable to look at her. Indu watched the others around them, the waiters bustling about. A signboard above them said 'Political discussions are banned.' Suddenly, Indu couldn't look at Rana anymore. She pushed the chair back and got up, shouldering her bag in haste. 'I'm sorry, I have to go now,' she told him.

'Indu, wait!' He held her arm and Indu shook him off. 'Indu—I didn't know if I could trust you!'

She looked at him scathingly. 'What do you mean?'

'Will you please sit down? I don't want to call attention to ourselves.'

She stared at him for a few more seconds, and sat down again.

'What do you mean you didn't know if you could trust me?'

'I came to Number 7 a few times, never went inside, of course, but I did try and look for you. I saw you thrice, but each time it was with some officials or the police, and I didn't know what to make of it.'

'What to make of it?! I was trying to make sure the library remained open. They put a ban on all public meetings. I had to answer the questions of twenty different people before they gave me permission.'

'That's exactly why I didn't meet you! It was too dangerous to take the risk. Everyone knew we were close, that I worked with you at Number 7. What if they used you to get to me? I was dodging them all the time. To come to you wouldn't be wise.'

'And also because I had told you to never see me again,' she said.

He hung his head. 'It's true. I was mad at you for not understanding what all this meant, but that anger evaporated, believe me. I thought about you every day, all the time. And anyway, I didn't have many chances to get to you before I had to move again.'

'What do you mean?'

'Fawad and I moved to Gujarat. We paid off our landlord and in the dead of night, moved everything down to Ahmedabad.'

'Why, what was in Ahmedabad?'

'It's a different government, so it was much safer. Moreover, there was nothing left for us here. The magazine had been shut down, Fawad had a warrant out for his arrest, and they were looking for the slightest reason to arrest me as well. There was a movement growing in Ahmedabad, with lots of discussions about the Emergency. We knew some people there and stayed there a few months, doing odd jobs, while Fawad got right back into the resistance, organizing protests. I was more cautious at first.

'I thought about you all the time. What you were doing, and if you were wondering where I was, and what you made of all this.'

At this point, a little tear rolled down Indu's cheek and she wiped it away hastily, but when she spoke, her voice was muffled and teary.

'I even went to your house once,' she said.

'You did?'

'On the pretext of returning some things you left at the library, but I did.'

He put his head against the palm of his hand and stared at Indu with sad, wide eyes. She looked away.

'What happened then? After you went to Ahmedabad?'

He paused before answering, asking Indu if he could eat something first. She watched him scan the menu, his eyes squinting at certain items, asking her what she wanted to eat. She refused and he finally ordered a masala dosa.

'Nothing really happened immediately. I had kind of gotten carried along, I didn't really know what I was doing there. I needed money so I got work doing odd jobs for a lawyer. I was careful to change my name, though. I was paranoid. I had a forged ID.'

She looked at him doubtfully. 'What did you pick?'

He laughed to himself before meeting her dubious gaze. 'Rajesh, ha.'

Indu couldn't help the smile on her face.

'Soon, we began hearing pretty disturbing stuff. So many people that we knew had been arrested without warrants or explanations, picked up in the middle of the night, tricked into coming to the police station or blackmailed. Little did we know that was just the tip of the iceberg. We joined a kind of underground resistance, where we constantly tried to pass around information about what was actually happening instead of all the doctored news.'

'Like what?'

'Well, at first it was just the whereabouts of important leaders, meetings to discuss what was going to happen, the future, et cetera, but then we realized that it was important to print and circulate material about secret arrests, torture and blackmail. Soon, it grew into a full-scale operation, and we, of course, started *Goonj* again. But it was very dangerous work.'

She stared at him. 'Why did you keep doing it, then?'

He shook his head. 'You would have too. Anyone would have—once you see the injustice happening in front of your eyes, you cannot un-see it. It's impossible.'

'You did all this on your own? Joining this "resistance movement", publishing material for it?'

'No, of course not. This movement—' he paused. He scanned Indian Coffee House once again, looking carefully at each person dining there. Indu's stomach twisted in a knot as she remembered the sign above their table. 'This movement has its own political affiliations, of course, and lots of people come into play here, but we, Fawad and I, came under the charge of this one Leader. We discussed all our plans with him and did as we were told.'

'Who is this guy?'

Rana shook his head.

Indu felt hurt. 'Do you still not trust me?'

'No,' he said quickly, reaching out for her hand, which lay on the table, but she pulled it away. 'No! It's for your own good. You don't want this kind of information. It immediately puts you in danger.'

Indu looked away. 'Are you staying with him now?'

He gave a small nod. 'It's a kind of a safehouse. It's not just me, there are probably a couple more people there as well, they come and they go. Anyone who needs to stay safely in Delhi for some time can stay there.'

'Do they know that you're meeting me?'

He shook his head. 'I can't tell them. I've done enough for them. I want to do what I came here for.'

'What do you mean?'

'Well, once we started doing this kind of work, and some months went by, I came up with the idea of making fake identities.'

'What?!'

'These were dangerous times, and it seemed to me the best way to save people. Of course, we couldn't do it for people who were already known, but we could for small-timers, the "collateral damage", as they were called—the fake identities could save them. These people were either able to buy enough time to hide or convince the authorities they were someone else.

And it was quite a success, this scheme of ours. Soon, we had to expand.'

'Expand?'

'You know about all the forced sterilizations?'

Indu shook her head. 'I mean, I heard some vague rumours, but I was not sure it had actually been done.'

'I wouldn't know where to begin. There were stories everywhere, of people, old or young, married or unmarried, being forced into sterilization. Incentives, schemes, they were all coercions to fill sterilization quotas. We decided to forge sterilization certificates.'

Indu nodded as he continued, 'Men couldn't claim benefits, receive their pensions or even their salaries if they weren't sterilized. Everything depended on meeting the quotas, and even the officials appointed to implement the scheme couldn't help it. So we started making the certificates, identical to the ones given out by the government, so that people could carry them around to show that they had already been sterilized. They were an insane hit; I mean, we started making more than fifty a day.'

'Oh God, but how?'

'We had printers—unlicensed, of course. I collected data and put them in identical cards that we got printed. Fawad got them laminated, and there was a Kishore *bhai* who distributed them. It might have been the most dangerous thing to do in the country then.'

'And you still continued?'

He looked at her, shrugging. 'There was nothing more satisfying. To feel that you've been able to save someone's life, their family, in this regime, there was nothing else like it.'

She didn't reply and looked away. It was hard to believe he had done these things, none of which she had been privy to.

'It was then that everything started going wrong.'

She looked at him.

'We were still printing stuff in *Goonj,* but then there were reports of problems in Lucknow. The camps there were pathetic, apparently, and truckloads of people were being taken there every day. The authorities did not care who they were, if they wanted to go or not. The government apparently wanted to achieve that one million mark. One million sterilized. We thought we would get pictures of it. It was also a chance for me to go home. I was sure that by now, I had dodged the people who were watching me, otherwise the two of us would already have been arrested.

'But it was a mess in Lucknow. Some people attacked the officers and doctors in a sterilization camp near the city, and in retaliation, the police, of course, opened fire. Hundreds of people died, none of which was reported. It was very volatile for some time.'

Indu put a hand on her mouth, unable to believe what she heard.

'But we got pictures of it all. It was incredible. The lathi charge, the tear gas, the injured people, we got it all. It was like sitting on a gold mine, and we would publish it in *Goonj*, of course, but we knew we needed to take it to a wider publication. The only way those people would get justice was if the world got to know about it, if those who did it were held accountable.'

'And you tried to get it published?'

He nodded, somewhat dejectedly. 'We got in touch with some BBC journalists and had to carry these pictures with us to Delhi to give to them. For safety, Fawad and I travelled separately. We said goodbye when we left, but I haven't seen him since. All I know is he made it to Delhi.'

Indu didn't know what to say. 'But where do you think—'

'I am pretty sure they've found him somehow, and if I was with him, they would have taken me as well. They already had a warrant out on him, they didn't need any other reason.'

'And the pictures?' Indu asked quietly.

'I have them—I think.'

'Hun?'

'I mean, I have reason to believe Fawad hid them before being arrested. I just have to figure out where he would have hidden them.'

'Oh dear God.'

'It's been a few days, I have no idea where he is. I've nobody here who I can approach or trust. I dare not write to or call anyone. It's with great difficulty that I even got to you.'

Indu noticed again how careworn he looked. His eyes seemed like dark hollows. His smile still had the same crinkle, but his skin seemed creased, older and more fragile. The jasmine lay broken and crushed on their table. Someone had picked up their coffee cups and the plate of masala dosa, and Indu hadn't even noticed. She checked the time and realized they had been sitting there for almost three hours, while outside, the sun threatened to turn fiery and red before setting.

Rana again leaned towards her and extended his hands, touching Indu's, and she didn't pull away this time.

'Please help me find him,' he said, his eyes pleading.

She stared at him and wanted to cry, but she pulled away.

'How can I help you? I didn't even know these things were happening.'

'If there is someone who can help, it's you.'

She shook her head and really began crying this time. 'You didn't bother to contact me for a year. How do you think you can walk into my life like this and demand miracles from me?'

He hung his head again, unable to offer any comfort as she continued crying.

'I'm going to go now,' she said, suddenly getting up, picking up her bag. He didn't reply, and sat back, staring at her. 'Rajat is coming back to India in a few days, and so it would be better if you didn't see me again,' she said, walking out of Indian Coffee House.

16

Summer had arrived, bringing a crippling heat that was interrupted by the occasional thunderstorm. The sun was enveloped by the foggy air that sat heavily over the city, refracted through the clouds, and cast a reddish-pink glow ever so slowly. A part of the sky was midnight blue while the other part was still on fire.

Indu sat on a steel bench at the edge of the walking path that encircled the park, looking at the flocks of birds that twittered and circled endlessly. Only a few people were still walking. The sky got darker with every passing minute. She knew it would soon be time for the park gates to be locked, but she didn't have it in herself to get up and move, and so she kept sitting and staring ahead, focusing on the dome that lay quiet and ominous in the gardens. She had once told Rana that it was the tomb of Mohammed Shah, and he had nodded, impressed that she knew.

When all movement ceased around her and she was sure that they would lock the gates if she didn't leave, she got up and walked towards the exit where the *chowkidaar* had begun blowing his whistle. As she walked out, the waft of sweet potatoes being roasted hit her. She looked around for the white Ambassador and walked towards it. Natty leaned against the front door, munching on a *bhutta*.

'*Chalein*, madame? Had a good walk?' he asked her.

'Won't you ask me if I want *bhutta*?'

'The world is yours, madame, *bhutta kya cheez hai*! But you never eat it because it gets stuck in your teeth.'

'Today I want one,' she said, folding her arms across her chest. An old woman was fanning the corn on a tray of coal, which lay on a jute mat. The *pallu* of her sari was wrapped around her head and her face was dark and scrunched, her smile revealing crooked yellow teeth. The corn crackled as the woman fanned it, and Indu looked at Natty, who stared ahead in contentment.

'Are you worried, madame?' Natty asked her.

'About what?'

'Amitabh Bachchan.'

She looked at him with her eyebrows raised.

'That he is taking the place of Rajesh Khanna, especially after *Sholay.*'

'What have I told you about Rajesh Khanna, Natty?'

'That there never was anybody like him, and there never will be.'

'So why are you asking me this silly question?'

'Amitabh Bachchan is also tall, madame.'

She snorted. 'He may have done well with his couple of hits, but Rajesh Khanna is the ultimate superstar. Didn't I tell you? Form is temporary, class is permanent.'

Natty nodded wisely as Indu tried to remember where she had heard this.

'Still, madame, I think this Bachchan hero will go somewhere. *Kuch baat hai isme!*'

The woman handed Indu her *bhutta*, wrapped in its own green leaves. Indu carefully kept one hand beneath it and took a bite, crunching on it slowly, staring blankly into space.

'What do you think I should do?' she asked him quietly.

Natty had finished eating, so they both got into the car.

'Do you remember, in *Kati Patang*, madame, when Rajesh Khanna finds out Poonam is actually Madhuri and she was lying all along?'

She gave him an incredulous look; had he not realized that she had changed the topic?

'Do you remember, madame?' he asked her again.

'Of course I remember, Natty.'

'Rajesh Khanna finds out that Poonam is actually Madhuri, that Poonam had died some time ago, and that Madhuri had been lying to him all along. It was quite a big lie, madame.'

'What's your point, Natty?'

He laughed. 'There are many points, madame, but the most important one is that Rajesh Khanna forgave Madhuri because it was something she had done under difficult circumstances. Her choices were not easy, and in that moment, she did it believing it was the best course of action. Rajesh Khanna understood that, and that's why he still went back to help Madhuri.'

Indu now looked out the window, and Natty said no more. She knew she shouldn't have turned her back on Rana, and therefore on Fawad, like this, but couldn't bring herself to accept that he had just walked back into her life like this after a year and demanded help from her. And it was help that she couldn't even provide. How was she supposed to find a missing person at a time like this? How was that a realistic expectation from someone who didn't even want to talk to you?

She knew that talking to Amita would provide a better perspective. When she reached home, she told her mother that she would visit her sister at the hospital the next evening and that Kittu would lock up the library.

Amita had started working at the City Hospital after she finished her studies; when she had picked up studying again, the last and final part of her MBBS had been pending, which she had left before getting married. That out of the way, she was allowed to practice, and so she moved back to Govind *bhai*'s house. The same people who had sniped at her sister when she was studying were now quick to comment on her success and tell Amita they were proud of her.

* * *

The walls of City Hospital were as sombre as ever as Indu walked toward her sister's office. Nurses bustled about as people sat worried in the waiting area. Entire families were squatting and camping in the corners. '*Ae mere watan ke logon*' played faintly on the speakers, dispersing its sad, melodious tune throughout the hallway. Her sister, though, smiled widely upon seeing Indu, and the off-white colour tones suddenly seemed less sombre. The peon brought them tea and her sister proceeded to narrate the ordeals of the day.

'Ten times as many patients as we are equipped to handle, of course. Everyone beats their chest and cries that their turn hasn't come even after months. Our hands are tied, we tell them. Hospitals are far and few in between, and everyone anyway wants to come to the City Hospitals. They are willing to wait for months for the best treatment at a low cost. Bihar, UP, Punjab, Haryana— every family living north of Madhya Pradesh wants to be treated here, for everything from muscle sprains to tuberculosis.'

'How are you managing?' Indu asked her.

'Don't ask. These days, especially, when strict timings are followed, I'm afraid to leave even a minute early. And if it's one of the "VIPs", everyone else is pushed back down the line, of course.'

'Tell me something,' Indu asked, stepping closer and staring at her sister. 'I heard some disturbing stuff. Is it true that there have been . . . forced sterilizations?'

Her sister narrowed her eyes at her. 'Where did you read that?'

'Is it true?'

Amita glanced at the door and asked Indu to shut it, which she did promptly.

Amita took a sip of water before answering, 'Not only is it true, nobody knows the extent of it. Some people say thousands are being forced into this every day, while others say that these are false and baseless rumours spread to malign the government. It's definitely happening. There are now campaigns urging only two children in a family, some incentives for people who have had the operation and what not. But it's affecting a lot of people, definitely.'

'Then why don't we hear more about it?' Indu asked her.

'Who is allowed to report all this? The press cannot, and it's something that is only affecting the lower-income groups as of now. Yet, every week, I get at least one case of an operation gone wrong. Last month was horrible. A man was brought in with infectious boils all over.'

Indu winced. 'Don't tell me!'

'Exactly. Nobody wants to acknowledge it, but it's happening all the same.'

Indu remained quiet. She was happy to see that in a short time, her sister had done well enough to have been given this office. Of course, some of it might have to do with Govind *bhai* being her husband, but it was a connection that her sister never advertised.

Indu swilled the milky tea around in the plain, white cup. Finally, she broached the topic of Rana. Her sister's expression went from surprised to sceptical to concerned, but she mostly nodded and said little.

'Don't tell Govind *bhai*,' Indu said immediately.

'Of course not,' her sister responded. They sat together quietly for some more time, until her sister announced that they must meet Rana again and see how they could help. 'I will meet him with you,' she said.

It was a hard time for Indu to deal with her feelings for Rana now, considering that at home, preparations for her and Rajat's wedding were beginning. Her mother had already decided that they would all go pick him up when he arrived in another three days, and she constantly wanted to discuss clothes with Indu. She insisted that Indu ditch the saris and wear a suit. Together, they had chosen a beige silk one with hand-embroidered black tree motifs all over and a thin orange and green border. 'To go with the spirit of the nation?' she asked. Her mother laughed. She wondered whether to tell her mother about Rana and what he was asking of her, but decided not to. It could be dangerous.

It was with a feeling of awkwardness that Indu left with her parents for the Palam Airport, wondering how she would find this man after two years of correspondence. Why couldn't Rajat return after a few more days, once she was done with this Rana drama? Or why couldn't Rana have come earlier? But she reminded herself that her mind was already made up. It had been made up the day Rana went away.

He might have been in a difficult situation, but was she expected to wait for him to finish his adventures and then make up his mind? She had considered breaking off her engagement to someone else and going against her family, all because she loved him and had told him as much. And what had he done? Maybe he had wanted to leave her out of it, but if he really wanted to let her know how he felt, he could have sent her a message. If he could do all that he did, transfer banned material from one place to another, go to violence-ridden states, maintain a network of people communicating secretly, then he could have somehow sent word to her.

Indu greeted Supriya aunty and Balwant uncle as well as a host of their relatives, who were all excited to meet Indu. Her parents got involved in the animated chatter that surrounded the gates of the international terminal, everyone waiting to welcome Rajat. Supriya aunty had readied a *pooja ki thali* full of flowers and a garland, ready to welcome her son after two long years. They waited for another half an hour till Rajat walked out of the gates. The driver ran ahead to help Rajat with his luggage, and when Rajat reached them, he was smothered by the hugs and tears of a family he had not met for two years. His hair was short and cut neatly, and he wore matching trousers and a blazer, with a scarf tied around his neck. He looked much the same as Indu remembered him. He had small dark eyes, dark eyebrows and a very fair complexion. He seemed slightly shorter than Rana, but wider.

Supriya aunty put a tilak on his forehead with two grains of rice, while he kept a hand on his hair, which wasn't even long enough to need being held back. People took turns to kiss him on the cheek, a few more tears were shed, and then they started looking expectantly in Indu's direction. Rajat eventually reached Indu's parents and touched their feet. He turned at Indu. She looked at his small nose, groomed beard and polite smile. He bowed when he saw her, and Indu folded her hands into a namaste. He courteously kept a hand on her shoulder and asked her how she was doing, while everyone around them smiled.

Everyone got into the waiting cars and the party went to Bukhara for lunch. Indu and Rajat were made to sit together. She wasn't amused by all the giggling and excitement, but she put on a smile nonetheless. Dishes upon dishes were ordered and questions were thrown at Rajat as he struggled to answer them all, but Indu was glad for it as that meant she didn't have to keep up the conversation. He seemed kind and sensible, and she made more of an effort to be interested.

Her parents were seated at the far end of the table along with Supriya aunty and Balwant uncle. Seated close to Rajat was his brother, and Indu noticed that he kept a sharp eye on her, watching constantly how she reacted to whatever Rajat said. Indu didn't say anything to him, but when she met his gaze once, he didn't even bother to look away.

'How was your flight?' she asked Rajat courteously, conscious of his brother's gaze on her.

He leant towards her and answered politely, his eyes happy and smiling, 'My flight was quite comfortable, thank you. I thought I would be tired upon landing but I feel fine now. Must be the excitement of getting to meet you.'

Indu smiled at him but didn't reply and instead, poked her fork at her *haryali kebab* moodily, suddenly wondering how he managed his food in London if he didn't eat meat. She was about to ask him that but his parents had engaged him in conversation. On reaching home, Indu's mother told her she'd be able to talk more to Rajat when he came to lunch at their home in two days, which he had promised.

But now she was completely preoccupied with meeting Rana again. As instructed, she had left word with one of the waiters at Indian Coffee House that she would like to meet him again, and received a handwritten note the next day at the library. A little girl arrived on the pretext of returning a book. Just as Indu was about to tell her that the book didn't belong to them, the girl opened the book and put a note into Indu's hand.

Dear,
It is not safe for us to meet there. Meet me where I first gave you the jasmines, today at five.

R.

Indu crumpled the paper immediately, stuffing it inside her bag, and phoned her sister, arranging for Natty to pick her up from the hospital and bring her here. Amita was not happy about having to leave the hospital early, but told her sister she would manage somehow.

Only the uppermost leaves of the trees were getting any sunshine by the time Indu and Amita reached the park and took the path towards the jasmine bushes. The sun was a harmless, deep orange that had started dipping lower on the horizon, and the birds were chirping louder in the last of the daylight before settling into slumber. Feeling nervous, Indu held her sister's hand as they walked towards the bushes. Indu had decided that she could trust Natty, and had told them they were going to meet Rana, but nothing more. He had nodded understandingly.

She was looking around for Rana when he suddenly appeared from behind a tree, his face and head covered with a scarf, sunglasses on his eyes, and his hands in his trouser pockets.

'Amita,' he said in surprise, completely forgetting Indu for a moment, and Indu saw him smile under his scarf. Her sister folded her hands in a namaste and gave him a wide grin, which quickly changed to a stern expression as she remembered what they had come for.

'Is it time for disguises already?' she asked him and he nodded, looking around suspiciously.

'It's better like this, *didi,* don't you think, when we cannot see his face?' Indu said, and Rana raised his eyebrows at her.

'Are you sure you weren't followed?' he asked, his voice muffled.

'We don't think so,' Amita replied, looking at Indu, taken aback by his suspicious manner.

'Let's walk,' he said urgently, 'but only on this path.'

They made for a strange group—Amita in her neat sari, looking very much like a doctor, Indu in her ironed sari and shawl that lay gracefully across her shoulder, the library ID around her neck, and Rana, wearing trousers and a jacket that he seemed to have put on hastily, with a scarf and sunglasses on his face.

'Have you decided to believe me?' he asked.

'I believed you,' Indu replied coolly. 'I just don't like you.'

Rana shook his head. 'Amita, what about . . .' he looked at Indu uncertainly.

Indu didn't answer and looked away, while Amita shook her head. 'Don't worry, I won't tell Govind.'

Rana nodded. 'You've met Fawad, you know what a truly sincere, good man he is, but he has ended up on the wrong side of these people now, and he's been arrested. I am under threat, anyone in contact with me is under threat. I hope that you understand the situation and can help me.'

Amita's face was more forgiving than Indu's.

'Of course we want to help you any way we can,' Amita said, putting a hand on his arm, 'we just don't understand how.'

The sky was a darker blue now and a group of birds flew in formation, making trails across the sky. Rana's scarf had slipped slightly downwards and Indu could see him biting his lip, staring ahead at the path in trepidation, as her sister looked at them uncertainly.

'Where do you think he could be?' Indu asked.

He looked at her for a few seconds, and then back at the path.

'I can't say for sure,' Rana said, 'but all political prisoners, everyone detained in relation to the Emergency, is known to be in Rohtak Jail.'

'Rohtak Jail?'

'The chief minister there apparently had to build this new, big jail for all the thousands of people arrested. I've heard it's a huge cantonment, acres and acres of jail blocks, but it is still overflowing as they keep arresting more people every day.'

'Really?' Amita asked in amazement.

'You'd be surprised what all actually goes on in there. If something is not in the newspaper, we think it can't exist.'

'But do you think Fawad is there?'

'It's quite likely that Fawad is there.'

Indu looked at her sister, who seemed as disturbed as she looked surprised.

'If this Rohtak Jail exists—'

'It does exist.'

'Well, if it definitely exists, then Govind would know about it.'

'So would father,' Indu said, and both her sister and Rana looked at her.

'But you know he is not allowed to speak about all this,' her sister said.

She remembered a conversation they had had when she had peppered him with questions, and he had refused to answer, flatly denying some facts that Indu had heard were true. After a couple of days, her father had taken a walk with her and told her that he couldn't speak about these matters as he was fighting the case for the Government of India, and the stakes were very high, and that he would be very surprised if he wasn't on record all the time. Indu had asked him if he meant that he was being monitored, and he had told her that he was sure he was being monitored.

In the past year, her father had turned into a very cautious man. 'Not only our reputation,' he had said, 'our places in society, our very lives are at stake.' He said little or nothing about his job and stayed away from the public eye, hardly meeting anyone outside of work.

'Say he is in Rohtak Jail,' Amita said. 'Even then, what do you plan to do? I mean, it's still a jail, not a visiting centre.'

Rana said, 'I don't know. I thought you would already be in the know of someone who's aware of all that is going on, and could help us. In secrecy.'

'Everything you told us, we've heard it for the first time.'

He sighed loudly and went back to staring at the path ahead of him.

'What about Shashi uncle?' Indu asked her sister.

'Yes, he would know for sure. But Indu, there is no way he would help us.'

Indu was quiet for a moment, before looking up at the two of them. 'Should we ask Rajat if he can help us?'

Amita glanced at Rana before answering, 'Come on, that's impossible. Why, I mean, how would he help us?'

'I don't know how. We can't ask father because it threatens his position, we can't ask Govind *bhai* because he might turn on us—the only other person I can think of is Rajat. Balwant uncle and Shashi uncle are close as well, and Rajat, well—he won't tell on us. And also, I don't know if it makes sense, but I remember Rajat writing to me once that his brother got into a bit of trouble once and a friend of theirs had to sort it out. If it can be done for Roshan, well, maybe it can also be done for Fawad.'

'Really?' Amita asked, her curiosity piqued. 'What trouble?'

'I never asked,' Indu said. 'But his brother does have this mean look about him so I don't find it hard to believe.'

'But still, I mean, why . . .' Amita trailed off, and Rana looked away.

'I'll ask him,' Indu said, her voice firmer. 'There's no harm asking.'

Rana looked from Indu to her sister, opened his mouth to say something, and then shut it again. They walked to the road in silence.

Natty was standing coolly outside the Ambassador, and on seeing Rana walk up with Amita and Indu, he straightened and couldn't help smiling. Rana was amused at his reaction, but suddenly realized they were back on the road and pulled his scarf tightly around his face and neck, putting on the sunglasses, even though it was completely dark now.

Natty raised his eyebrows at Rana's get-up. Rana smiled back at him.

'*Kaise hain Natwarlal ji?*' he asked him, teasing.

'I'm not Natwarlal, Rana sir, I am Natty,' he replied, 'or have you forgotten?'

Rana threw back his head and laughed. 'How could I forget?'

'You seem to have forgotten a lot lately.'

Rana hung his head, 'So I did. But just because one is not around doesn't mean one has forgotten, Natty. Wasn't that one of your favourite lines from the movies?'

Natty seemed satisfied by this and bowed. 'Anyway, we cannot be forgotten easily. What makes you cross our path?'

'To find someone who is lost—but don't worry, Natty, I'm not only crossing paths, this is where our paths merge!'

Natty glanced at Amita, not knowing what to say. Indu sensed this and stepped forward, opening the car door for herself.

'Once the time has gone, the paths become two. And what's gone may not come back, it's time people knew.'

Rana looked at Amita and Natty in shock. 'Who taught her how to rhyme?'

Indu slammed the car door shut, and Amita walked to the other door resignedly. 'See you tomorrow!' she called out to Rana, and Natty drove the two sisters home, sniggering at the wheel.

* * *

As the days passed, the fact of Fawad's incarceration bore heavy on everyone's mind. For Indu, life hadn't changed significantly after emergency was declared, but now that Rana was back in her life, she understood the threat involved. And if she felt it so keenly merely by extension, it was hard to imagine how they had been living this past year. But at the same time, she also had to think about Rajat and getting to know him, now that he was here.

He was polite, well-mannered and liked by everyone around him. He constantly looked to her to make sure that whatever was happening had her approval, but he still felt like a stranger to her. They hadn't yet had much time to spend together. And Rana was here now, bringing a new set of problems.

And now the only way to resolve these troubles seemed to be through Rajat—she had to talk to him.

17

Indu went about it systematically. She began asking Rajat questions about their future house, flattering him and telling him constantly that he had made a great decision to study in London. Over the next few days, she told him again and again how much she appreciated his calm nature and polite speech, so he would be amenable when she told him about Rana and Fawad and how she expected his help. She also made it clear that she was passionate about politics, but he appeared to know very little about the topic.

She asked her mother if she might go out to dinner with Rajat one night, and her mother readily agreed, seeing it as a sign that Indu was finally making an effort. She wanted to broach the topic of Fawad's release during the dinner. With that in mind, she dressed in one of her good saris and wore a large, red rose in her bun. Rajat picked her up, looking dapper in a grey suit, and as they stepped out, Indu felt a thrill, but soon realized it was to be short-lived. He often interrupted Indu as she told him about her life over the past two years, or else stared at her unblinkingly, wearing a smile on his face. When Indu asked for his opinion on something, he proudly told her he hadn't heard her as he was too busy admiring her.

'How is Roshan now?' she asked him, taking a little bite of the *gulab jamun* sitting in a brass bowl.

'What do you mean?'

'Well, I remember you once wrote to me that he got in a spot of trouble with some friends of his, and it had to be handled.'

Rajat's face fell, and Indu felt bad to having to bring it up with an agenda in mind.

'He's just . . .' Rajat said, agonized, 'he doesn't use his mind sometimes. Gets influenced by friends easily. He and his friends were in private club, and well, one of them fought with some other guy over something frivolous, and guns were raised. I think there was a shoot-out.'

'What?!'

'Yes, but . . . Roshan was definitely not involved too much. That's why Dhar uncle could get him out, he's a coordinator in the party. Also, I don't know too much—I don't partake in such behaviour.'

His dismissive and condescending tone discouraged her from asking for his help, so she remained quiet and decided that she needed Amita when she spoke to Rajat about it.

The following day, it was with a certain reluctance that Amita and Indu arranged a meeting with Rajat. Indu stared at him as Amita talked and realized that though he looked kind and concerned, with his glasses, he constantly looked at Indu with a panicked face. She would nod reassuringly, holding up her hands as if everything was under control. Yet, she could see Rajat getting really uncomfortable, opening the top button of his shirt in response, wiping his forehead.

'I need some water,' Rajat said when they finished, and Indu quickly got him a glass of water, wondering if he was about to start hyperventilating.

'Let me get this straight,' Rajat said, gripping the edge of the table as Indu put a hand on his arm to make sure he wouldn't slip. 'You want to, together with me, help your business partner—'

'Former business partner,' Indu said. Rajat paused for a few seconds and nodded. 'Former business partner. So you want to help, I mean, his former roommate, a *fugitive*, escape from prison.'

Indu looked at Amita with a shrug; the plan definitely sounded crazier than it actually was.

'Release,' Indu said, 'is actually what we're hoping for. I know it seems difficult and problematic, but we have to do something.'

'Indu, this man was arrested for a reason, do you even—'

'And what reason,' Indu asked immediately, trying to keep the anger out of her voice, 'allows the government to randomly pick up innocent men in the middle of the night, keep them in prisons without a fair trial, without charges, without the benefit—'

'How do you know he is innocent?'

'Because I know!' Indu replied, looking from him to her sister. 'I know because I've been here for the past two years, I know what's been going on. Rajat, this is all a sham. So many people are suffering, nothing's been reported in the papers. People are disappearing and dying and the news is censored, just so they don't lose power.'

Rajat gaped at her as she said all this, glancing occasionally at Amita. 'Why do you care?' he finally asked. 'It's no danger to you.'

Indu's mouth fell open, and before she could say anything, Amita intercepted her. 'Rajat, you said it yourself. Why do you care? Laws are being broken to make this happen, right, so what's one more? What's one more law broken if we can take care of someone known to us, and get him out of prison?'

He scratched his head in distress. Amita shook her head at Indu; she must not lose her temper.

'Look, I asked you only because you told me about Roshan, and how he could be helped out, and well, I thought you would help me. I trust you.'

'Don't get me wrong, I do feel sorry for this chap,' Rajat said. 'But . . .' his words trailed away. Indu thought that perhaps he was starting to consider how it might affect his relationship if he refused outright the first real help his future wife asked of him.

'I just want to be able to do all that is in my power to help someone I value,' Indu said, and he looked at her strangely.

'Even if I wanted to do it,' he went on, 'I've no idea what's going on, I just returned from a different continent!'

'We can try the same person who helped Roshan,' Indu said.

By the end of the evening, Rajat had promised to help Indu, but not without asking her to forget about all this madness afterwards, saying that they must get away as far from all of this as quickly as possible.

'We'll move to London permanently, Indu, and I swear you will love it,' he said, his eyes earnest. 'There are so many bookshops there, and libraries! You like libraries, right? The national library is so huge, you can spend your days there, especially the rainy days, which is every day, really, and read as much as you want, and–'

'Have you seen Number 7 yet?' she asked him, and he shook his head.

'But this library would still be very limited, right?' he went on. 'You can find all the books of the world in the national library there—'

'Yes, but,' Indu said, cutting him off, 'Do you want to see it? I can show you.'

He nodded and Indu smiled. 'Don't worry, once we get him out, Fawad, that will be the last of it. We can then focus on the wedding.'

Rajat beamed.

* * *

'Ah, I had forgotten your braids in the picture,' Rana said, chortling shamelessly as he gazed at Indu's campaign picture on yet another hoarding they could see from where they were standing. 'How many marriage proposals did you get because of this picture, again?'

In a swift movement, Indu threw the water bottle she had brought along straight at Rana's head. He dodged and caught it, used to the assault.

'How many times have I told you not to aim for my face? It could take out my eye, you know.'

'I only aim for your face so you can see it clearly and dodge it,' Indu said, suddenly unsure.

'Yeah, but you're getting better at it.'

'How many times have I told you not to comment on this picture?'

'But you look so *cute* in the mini braids and the red ribbons,' he said, laughing.

She was about to retort but held back, refusing to give in to his flattery. Indu knew he had been trying to pay court to her for the past few days, hoping that she wouldn't see through it. But only an *idiot* wouldn't see through it. She tried to keep the joking to a minimum. It was hard, though, because he found something to joke about even when his best friend's life was under threat.

They were waiting outside the address Rajat had given Indu, waiting to see this mysterious Dhar uncle. She knew that Rana was indulging in more nonsense than usual because he was even more nervous than her.

Rajat had told her that Dhar uncle was known to 'make trouble disappear'. But what made Indu really uncomfortable was that Rajat's brother would also be coming along, and she had told Rana as much. She remembered how he kept checking Indu's reactions to what Rajat said when they had dinner the first time together.

'What's his brother's name?' Rana had asked her.

'Roshan.'

'Don't worry,' Rana said, 'I mean, what, he's only going to be your brother-in-law, right? You only have to see him at the most important moments of your life.'

She threw him a dirty look, and he muttered an apology. A few minutes later, a Fiat arrived and Indu straightened up, sending silent encouragement to Rana. She clutched the end of her sari and looked over to find that Rana had his hands in his pockets.

Rajat was dressed in his usual shirt and trousers, while Roshan had his shirt untucked and wore sunglasses. From afar, he looked less menacing, but when they came closer, Indu's heart beat faster. She stepped forward to give Rajat a hug and nodded at Roshan, giving him a little smile. He smiled back widely in return. Both brothers gazed at Rana without any sign of greeting and Indu cleared her throat loudly, introducing them.

They stared at each other without saying anything. 'Uh, shall we go in then?'

Rajat nodded and Roshan led the way. Indu walked in step with Rana.

In the garden, they saw that Dhar uncle was already seated in the shade. When they walked in, he got up and folded his hands in a namaste, ordering tea for them. He was a towering personality, taller than most men, dressed sharply in trousers and a blazer. He had a full head of white hair and sharp eyes. He bowed to Indu and shook hands with the men.

It was an odd scene. Rana was seated on one side of her and on the other, Rajat. Roshan sat next to Dhar uncle, his legs stretched out in front of him and his arms folded, staring at her unblinkingly. Indu decided to begin the conversation.

She introduced herself, and when Dhar uncle gave her a smile, she felt encouraged to continue. She introduced Rana, telling Dhar uncle about his excellent work in the magazine, his work as a lawyer and how he helped her build up Number 7. Rana did nothing but nod, and she wanted to nudge him into making one of his stupid jokes to lighten the mood, but he did nothing of the sort. She told them about Fawad, feeling nervous. As she recounted what had happened, the one thought that had plagued her—that Dhar uncle, or Rajat and Roshan, for that matter, had no reason to get Fawad released—made her voice shaky.

Dhar uncle gave a heavy sigh when Indu finished and stared towards the sky, apparently deep in thought. Thanks to Roshan, he was saved the trouble of replying.

'This man, Fawad, he's in jail?' Roshan asked.

Indu nodded.

'There are so many in jail.'

Indu's heart sank. She knew it would come to this. She looked at Rana and saw the veins on his arm move as he clenched his hands.

'And we are sorry for them all,' Indu said, 'but he is the one we want out. If there was a way, I would gladly help all those who have been imprisoned incorrectly. But I don't, which is why I've come to you.'

'Why do you care about him so much?' Roshan asked, adding, 'Indu *bhabhi*.'

Indu narrowed her eyes at him. 'He's my friend.'

'You have interesting friends,' he said, gazing at Rana.

'Roshan . . .' Rajat said, a hint of warning in his voice.

Indu shot Rajat a look of anger; she hadn't walked in here to be insulted, and blamed Rajat for involving his brother. If he couldn't help her, he should have just said so instead of making his jerk of a brother question her intentions.

'What I mean is,' Roshan said, putting his hands up, 'how can rules be bent for one person?'

'Listen, mister,' Indu replied, 'the rules have already been bent, and they have been bent especially for you. Everything that has happened during the Emergency, the arrests, the family planning programmes, all of that is illegal. If one man's life can be saved by an extra effort, it's important to us that we do all that is in our power.'

Roshan smiled widely. 'Does your father believe all this is illegal as well?'

'We'll keep fathers out of this,' Rajat said, looking from Indu to Dhar uncle. Indu was fuming.

'I think what Roshan means is,' Dhar uncle said, 'in this time, arrests have been made for a reason. To get someone released will involve bribing all sorts of bureaucrats, threats, warnings, jeopardizing the reputation and position of everyone involved, right from the person who unlocks this man's door, to me, Rajat, and even you. I see no reason why such a risk must be taken.'

Indu stared at blankly at them. Wasn't it obvious? Because she was asking them to. She couldn't believe that he was actually asking her what they were to gain by helping them let Fawad off. Perhaps her father was right; perhaps there was no point in getting yourself involved. Maybe she should just move to London with Rajat, taking him as far away as she could from his monster of a brother.

'What will be gained?' she asked him. 'If even one innocent person's life can be saved in all this, wouldn't you consider that a gain?'

Roshan shrugged, and then yawned pointedly.

Indu looked at Rana, who was now bent forward, propping his elbows on the table in front of him.

'Well, what if you had no choice?'

Dhar uncle looked quizzically at him and asked, 'What do you mean?'

'What if you didn't have a choice about whether to help him get out or not?'

Roshan bent forward as well. 'And why wouldn't he have a choice? You would threaten him in his own house?'

Rana shrugged and Indu tried not to look completely clueless; she had no idea what he was talking about.

Rana sat back again, now in the same posture as Roshan. 'Fawad wrote anti-government rhetoric that was declared illegal, took part in protest marches, and joined a resistance movement seeking to destabilize this Emergency.'

'I wonder why he got arrested,' Roshan said sarcastically.

'You really think he didn't document all that he was doing? Or that he embarked on all this without having conclusive proof of what he found?'

'What do you mean?' Rajat asked.

'Fawad had a stack of photographs that documented the government's mishandling of things. Deaths of people. He planned to release the photographs to the BBC, that's why he came to Delhi, and was arrested before that could happen. The photographs, however, are still with us.'

Indu thought that Dhar uncle was either a very good actor, or was genuinely unfazed by what Rana said. Indu heard Rajat's breath catch, while Roshan just raised his eyebrow.

'Sounds like an empty threat,' Roshan said.

Rana shrugged. 'As you wish. Maybe you've not realized this, but I'm in no position to make empty threats. All I'm doing is playing the last hand left to me. I have no other resort left except to barter these photographs for my friend's life.'

'It's still empty, as I see it,' Dhar uncle said. 'First of all, we cannot be sure that these photographs even exist. If they do, what do they show? And whatever it is that they reveal, how does that affect us? If some photographs do come out in the BBC at some point, I hardly feel responsible for them.'

Indu couldn't help but think he was right.

Rana bent forward again and looked straight into his eyes. 'Are you sure about that? How will the other members feel about the fact that you could have prevented this leak, that you had the golden chance of these photographs never seeing the light of the day, but you . . . just didn't?'

'I'm not liking your tone in this conversation,' Roshan said.

'Or maybe,' Rana went on, ignoring Roshan, 'these photographs come out, are widely condemned, and the Congress is suddenly under the scrutiny of the world media, its top members under investigation for their involvement in what could potentially be crimes against humanity itself . . . then what? Will you still be minding my tone?'

Indu caught on.

'Dhar uncle, you asked me why you must put yourself at risk to get someone out of prison,' she said. 'Well, this is what's at stake. This is what you would be averting.'

She could see from the corner of her eyes that Rajat was staring at her, maybe in disbelief, but she ignored it, and instead kept looking directly at Dhar uncle, with occasional glances at Roshan. At long last, Dhar uncle spoke, and he looked only at Rana when he did.

'You threatened me,' he said finally. 'You came to my house under the pretence of seeking help, but it was actually with the intention of blackmail.'

'You said you'd help us and now that we are here, you've started evaluating profit!'

'Why would he not?' Roshan spoke up. 'Who are you to him? Who is *she* to us?' Indu glanced sideways at Rajat when Roshan said that. His expression remained unchanged.

'I'm sorry, but it's my last hand,' Rana said. 'If Fawad is let out, we will turn the photographs over to you. If he is not . . . well, I can't promise anything.'

A long silence followed, punctuated only by the dirty looks Roshan threw at Indu.

'Very well,' Dhar uncle said. 'We will need to see the photographs first. I'll need time to get things arranged. Once it's done, I will give Indu a call. Then we make the barter.'

Rana clapped his hands, getting up from his chair. 'Then there's nothing more to bicker about. Roshan, shall we have another cup of tea?'

Roshan gave Rana a dirty look and walked away, followed by Rajat, who left without saying goodbye.

'What?' Rana asked Indu, turning to her, 'What did I say?'

* * *

On the way back, Indu and Rana talked about all that had happened as Indu replayed their meeting over and over in her head, thinking about the wounded look Rajat gave Indu, Roshan's insinuating questions full of suspicion, and his remark, 'who is she to us?' She knew that it wasn't correct that they coerced Dhar uncle.

'Why didn't you tell me you wanted to use the photographs?' she asked him.

'I'm sorry! I just felt like I had to, there was no other option—'

'No, it was brilliant! But why didn't you tell me beforehand?'

'I thought of it on the spot,' he said.

'Well, where are the photographs, then?'

His face fell. 'That's the problem. That's the reason I couldn't offer them right away. I don't know where they are. I know Fawad must have hidden them, but I have no idea where . . .'

Natty stopped the Ambassador at a petrol pump and got out. Indu gave Rana a sideways glance, but turned away when he saw her. 'Did you,' she began, wondering whether she should go on, but then went for it anyway, 'Did you think about me, at all, while you were away?'

Rana tilted his head before giving a rueful, lopsided smile. 'I did. Every day.'

Indu raised her eyebrows at him.

'Did you think about me?' he asked her.

She shook her head in a clear no, and he laughed. 'You don't have to lie, you know.'

When Natty got back in the car, he began in his baritone, '*Yeh dosti, hum nahi todenge . . .*'

'How dare you sing this Bachchan song? In my presence!' Indu hissed at Natty.

'What can I do, madame?' Natty asked. 'There isn't any recent movie of Rajesh Khanna to sing from.'

'Hello? Which world, hun? What about *Prem Kahaani?*' Indu replied.

'But I was singing it all of last week, madame, and you didn't like it.'

'Well, I don't like this either, and I'm going to turn off this non-stop Natty radio if you don't stop promoting your Bachchan hero.'

Natty chuckled, looking at Rana resignedly, who was laughing as well. 'Madame has started feeling insecure about Rajesh Khanna. Everyone has, ever since Bachchan has come up.'

'Oh but Rajesh Khanna is the *original* superstar,' Rana replied in a high-pitched sing-song voice, in what Indu presumed was an imitation of her.

18

Indu's most vivid memories as a young girl were of the times when people would crowd around her and ask her what she would like to be once she grew up. The aunties would pull at her cheeks, making pouty faces, yelling their favourite suggestions at her, 'Indu, say princess! Say you will be a princess when you grow up!'

Indu usually ignored them. Instead, she would flip her hair, which was generally tied up in a ponytail by her mother, and say, 'I'm going to be a Bollywood superstar,' while everyone would laugh and compliment her mother. 'Look at the next Madhubala!' they would say to her mother and pat her on the back. But for a brief period before Indu decided she would become a Bollywood superstar, she not just wanted to be, but *was sure* that she *would* be, the prime minister of the country. She knew it in her heart that if there ever was a post for her, it was to be that of the prime minister of India.

When her namesake was appointed the prime minister, Indu, who had just become a teenager, decided that while that Indu would rule the country, she would rule people's hearts: she would be the superstar of Bollywood. Age had brought its own lessons—Indu had learnt that Bollywood was not for her, and that she was content with *an* Indu being the prime minister. The prime ministership meant just one thing to her—the post held by Indira Gandhi. Nobody else, not even herself, Indu had decided, could take that place.

With every passing day, however, Indu felt her faith and reverence dying in the face of all that she saw and understood. It didn't matter, whatever the reasons behind the Emergency and whatever else they said. Someone Indu knew and valued was suffering unjustly, and there was nobody they could go to. She certainly couldn't broach any of this with her father, as he would immediately seek to put an end to it, questioning why she felt the need to take such measures for Rana. She couldn't appeal to the police because they were most likely mixed up with everything going on. She couldn't reach out to the newspapers because they weren't allowed to report these things. She couldn't even ask for the support of people, because how could people protest something they didn't even know was going on?

Indu thought she felt a similar helplessness in her father, but even of that she couldn't be sure.

When she tried to speak to him, all she had received in response was grunts and hmms, with a complete refusal to divulge any information about the Emergency. 'It is not to your interest, any of this,' he had said to her. 'Just concentrate on enjoying your library. Anyway, you will leave soon.'

'But what if I want to stay?' Indu had asked fiercely. 'What if I want to stay here and fight?'

'Fight what?' he had asked, exasperated. 'This is not your fight.'

'So you admit that it is yours!'

Her father bowed his head. 'I cannot do anything to stop what is happening. All I can do is make sure that I keep my family out of trouble.'

* * *

Rajat visited Indu's house and insisted on taking her for a drive. Indu sat in the car with one leg crossed over the other, looking outside at the road going by. She could feel Rajat's sideways gaze boring into her. She finally gave in and looked at him, asking if he wanted to say something to her.

'Say *something* to you?' Rajat asked incredulously. 'Saying *something* would be a bit of an understatement, don't you think?'

Indu had to agree with that one. 'Look, I know I've gotten you in a bit of an adventure, I'm sorry, but I think things will work out.'

He shook his head at her, astonishment on his face. 'Things will work out?! I came here to marry you, and you're basically taking me on a *chor-police* chase, with criminals! I don't even get what's going on!'

'They are not as criminal as you are making them sound; this is the Emergency, and they have been wrongfully arrested—'

'I don't know if they have been wrongfully arrested, and I don't care! There is a man in jail, he must have done something!'

'Can you relax? It's not like that. Rana is willing to give up the photographs, and then you can see for yourself in these photographs what has been happening all around us in this country! Tell me if clicking that makes them criminals.'

She stopped talking as they stopped on the side of a road and he put his head in his hands, finally speaking after a couple of minutes of silence. 'Listen Indu,' Rajat began again, 'if you want me to help you, you have to promise me: as soon as this is over, you will end all this madness and focus on the wedding. Can you give me your word?'

She imagined how Rajat must be feeling. To return after two years, looking forward to meeting the woman whom he was going to marry, and instead, getting dragged into having a fugitive released. In the face of all that, his demand did not seem very unreasonable.

She nodded.

In the middle of all this, it seemed like the stupidest question in the world when Indu's mother asked her when she planned to have the final fitting for her wedding sari. Indu had completely forgotten about it, but said they could do it after the weekend. Her mother was already suspicious, as it was not like Indu to take her clothes lightly. What made her even more curious was when she and Amita spent hours whispering together, discussing the plan.

Meanwhile, Rana was trying his best to lay his hands on those photographs. He got in touch with everyone they were associated with, which was a task on its own as the people in the movement were, obviously, hard to trace. He disappeared for days at a time, and Indu would then curse herself again for getting into this mess with him. It was a couple of weeks later when Indu met him at Indian Coffee House, where he arrived panting with the promise of some news.

'What?' she asked, getting up from her chair, 'Did you get them? The pictures?'

'No,' he said, still out of breath, 'but I might just know where he hid them. I got to know that Fawad had visited the safehouse when he reached Delhi—before I arrived!'

Indu looked at him, confused. 'The safehouse?'

'The place where I am staying!' he whispered impatiently. 'I told you, where people can stay if they wish to remain in the city . . .'

'Oh! Yes. So? What if he went there?'

'I have a hunch he hid the photographs there, right inside the house! I can't believe I've been there all these days and never thought about this!'

'Is it a strong hunch?' she asked him. Rana nodded.

'Let's go then,' she said, getting up immediately.

'Go where?'

'To the safehouse, where else?'

'But . . . Indu, you can't go there.'

'What do you mean?'

'It's a protected house, nobody apart from the people in the resistance can know about it . . .'

'Listen, mister, haven't I proven myself loyal enough to know your secrets? You came to me after a year asking for help and I put everything I have in jeopardy to do that. Now you better not tell me where I am and am not allowed.'

When Rana didn't reply, Indu got up and told him she would look for Natty.

'No!' he exclaimed. 'We definitely can't take Natty. We can't have anyone else knowing the location. No, if we have to go, we must do it ourselves . . .'

* * *

It was a single-storeyed, yellowing building a little way from a parched, fraying park somewhere in Mehrauli. A board outside it read 'Shreemati Kamala Devi Organization for Women'.

'That's it?' she asked him.

He nodded.

She thought she might be missing something. 'You're blocking my view with your big head,' Indu said to Rana as she looked towards the building.

'Well, it's time your head got used to seeing something other than its own reflection.'

'*What* did you say?'

'I mean, your head should get used to seeing my head, as it's going to be a-round. Do you get it, ha ha ha?'

'What now?' she asked him, ignoring his frivolousness.

Rana suddenly looked very nervous and Indu patted him on the back as he gulped, and finally nodded.

As they walked towards the building, Rana's pace quickened, became more purposeful. He held Indu's hand tightly and glanced around furtively, but the thought of Fawad must have prevailed, for he kept going.

'How many people live inside this safehouse?' Indu muttered to him.

'Maybe three or four, nobody really knows,' he said. 'The thing is, people come and go, and nobody talks to each other. Most of the times I've come back, there's hardly anyone, save for footsteps I hear on the staircase. You aren't introduced to anyone unnecessarily for the sake of your own safety. You are allowed to stay here only if someone on the inside vouches for you.'

The sky was a light blue, and the sun shone steadily on the park in front of the building. When they were close to the building's gate, Rana suddenly stopped and looked at Indu, unsure. 'Maybe you should stay outside,' he muttered to her. 'I'll try to figure out where Fawad could have hidden the pictures.'

'Don't be silly,' Indu hissed. 'Why do you think I have come all this way? Two eyes are better than one.'

'I have two eyes.'

'I mean two pairs of eyes are better, Rana, don't—'

They heard the gate creak as it swung lightly in the wind.

The iron gate was unlatched and Rana walked in, Indu trailing him. A dusty corridor led them to what seemed like a government office. He pushed open a rickety wooden door to reveal a sad, old room that looked like it hadn't been inhabited for ages. Cobwebs covered the grimy walls, while old, bent steel almirahs stood against the walls. Files upon files lay on shelves across the walls, gathering dust. Some rocky wooden tables took centre stage, looking surprisingly clean.

Before Indu could ask anything, Rana was rummaging through his pockets, taking out a set of keys. 'Come,' he said to Indu, moving farther into the office, heading towards one of the bookshelves. She followed him, lifting her *dupatta* so it wouldn't do the much-needed sweeping that the place required.

'Uh, what are you doing?' she asked him as he began removing the books from the shelf one by one, and putting them on the table. He didn't reply and continued removing books, maintaining the order, and finally Indu saw why: behind the books was another door. Rana inserted the key into it, rotating it with a click.

'That's the safe—' Indu began, but Rana shushed her. He began putting the books back in the same order, and Indu helped him. He then stepped back and gave the bookshelf a little nudge, unveiling a dingy staircase that Rana immediately moved towards; when Indu didn't follow him, he looked back at her.

'What?' he asked her.

Indu didn't reply and simply gave him a dubious look.

'Now you take a moment to doubt my intentions?' he asked incredulously. 'Come on!'

The stairs were dark and unlit, leading down to some kind of basement, and Indu felt the wall beside her so as not to trip. When the stairs ended after turning a corner, Indu's mouth fell open.

The dust and dinginess of upstairs was suddenly gone. Although the area was dimly lit with lamps only in the corners, Indu saw that right in front of her hung a huge noticeboard. It had many scraps of paper, with messages to one side, and the centre had a layout of the Parliament. The entire surface of the noticeboard was covered with paper, some with slogans written in bold letters, some which seemed to be code words.

Indu tore her eyes away from the board to see lockers stashed untidily in a corner, stacks of newspapers, a desk on which lay multiple open files, some of which were full of charts and figures. A room from there led into what seemed to be the kitchen. The whole area seemed to be a bit haphazard. On the other side lay a couple of telephones on a desk, along with a typewriter, behind which, on a slab of a wall, lay a transistor. Indu wondered how they kept all this functioning, when Rana interrupted her train of thought.

'Okay, doesn't look like anyone's here,' Rana said in a low voice. 'All the better for us.'

'What about your Leader—'

'Shh,' he said, alarmed and looking around. 'Let's go to my room, come.' He grabbed Indu's hand and pulled her through a labyrinth of shabbily built rooms to step inside a tiny area, no bigger than a storage place or a prayer room, where his bag lay neatly in a corner, next to the mattress where he presumably slept.

'Let's just try and look for the photographs quickly, okay, without drawing too much attention to ourselves.'

'What about the lockers?' she asked him.

Rana shook his head. 'Somehow, I can't imagine him giving up these photographs— other people would have access to these lockers. It was our work, you see? No, if they are here, he would have hidden them somewhere hard to find . . .'

Indu was at a loss. How could they find the photographs in this clutter of a house? She felt a stab of annoyance at Rana. Why did he mention the photographs to Dhar uncle when he didn't know where they were?'

It's my last hand, she remembered him saying.

They came out of his room and walked further into the corridor, which was lined with paintings, and she wondered how someone had found the time to decorate this place.

Now that they were here, it seemed ridiculous to Indu that they had gotten themselves in this mess. She had forgotten how it was before Rana had come into her life, and she had thought about him every single day. It wasn't her fault, she decided. He was the one who had waltzed in uninvited with his poems and paintings, flowers and fancies . . .

'Let's just start looking around' he said, 'and I know we'll get it.'

She opened a couple of drawers, going through the sheaves of paper, frequently distracted by the writing on them. Rana too listlessly went through some stuff as the futility of the exercise hit him, and they caught each other's eye. Indu didn't want to give up so easily, so she tried hard to think where it was in this place that Fawad could have left the photographs.

'Fawad arrived here from Gujarat,' Rana was saying to himself, 'stayed here a couple of days, went outside and then got caught.'

Her gaze again fell on the paintings on the wall. Indu asked Rana who brought in the paintings and he shrugged, saying they must be possessions of the residents who had been driven away at some point. She stared at the one with the blue lake and white lilies and houseboats. It was beautiful, like the hands had magic: the artist's hands had magic. She heard a noise and looked immediately at Rana.

'Someone must be coming,' he said. 'Don't act alarmed. Just stay calm, and act like you belong. People come and go frequently.'

Sure enough, in a couple of minutes, a man dressed shabbily emerged from the corridor and looked at them curiously for a few seconds, then nodded, ducking inside a room and shutting the door behind him. A couple of minutes later, the same man came out again and went back, exiting by the stairs. Rana sighed.

'Look, maybe we should just . . . lie to Dhar uncle, meet Fawad and ask him where . . . I don't know . . .' he murmured, but Indu was again staring at the painting with the lake and the lilies, and turned to look at him. He stared quizzically at her for a second, and then lunged for it. She told him to be quieter as he removed it from the wall and turned it around.

There was nothing on the back of the painting. Indu whispered, 'How did you not recognize earlier that it was Fawad's?'

He shook his head, stunned, and suddenly felt at the back of the painting. He unhinged it, and out fell a package. Rana opened it with quivering hands, and took out a bunch of photographs.

'Oh my God,' Indu extended her hands towards them, and they quickly saw a couple of pictures. Rana held her by the shoulders.

'Let's go now, Indu,' he said, 'come.' He led her to his room and picked up his bag, stuffing the photographs inside.

He grabbed her hand, and they left the room to find another man examining the painting they had just ripped open.

'Hello,' he said, revealing a set of bad teeth.

19

The man had a thin stubble on his head and his face, and a dark complexion. He wore a shirt and a pair of trousers. He smiled at them graciously, leaning against the wall where the painting had hung. Indu thought he seemed like someone who meant business. He examined the dismantled painting and looked up at Rana for an explanation.

Rana had become very still and refused to look at Indu. 'Namaste, VP ji,' he said.

Indu wondered whether this was the leader; he certainly looked it, with the dark shadow over his face, but he seemed too ordinary, and had an open, welcoming smile.

'Why would you tear this up?' he asked Rana, glancing occasionally at Indu. 'And who is our lovely companion?'

Rana grinned broadly. 'VP ji, meet Indu . . . uh, my girlfriend.'

Indu gave Rana a sharp glance; had he forgotten the terms of their deal? VP ji looked pleased, however, and stepped forward to shake her hand.

'But that's wonderful,' he said. 'I'd love to get to know you. We must sit down for a chai!'

Indu smiled uncertainly and looked at Rana, who nodded and immediately put his bag down. As he put some water to boil on the stove, VP ji sat down opposite Indu on a chair, staring at her with interest.

'Indu,' VP ji said, his fingers drumming the table, 'short for . . . Indira?'

Indu said yes with a weak laugh, and VP ji seemed absolutely delighted, unable to stop smiling in amusement.

'The woman of the moment!' he exclaimed. 'It's perfect that we have you here. You know how much Indira*ji* would love this place, don't you?'

Indu simply laughed, not answering.

'So Rana is your boyfriend?' he asked her, and Indu looked up at 'her boyfriend'. He deliberately had his back to her.

'Yes,' she said, fiddling with her *dupatta*, and then added with an eyeroll, 'unfortunately.'

VP ji chuckled and looked fondly at Rana. 'And you will get married?'

'Of course,' Rana replied from over the brewing chai. 'Otherwise what kind of man would I be?'

VP ji twiddled his fingers and looked at Indu with twinkling eyes. 'So! Tell me about yourself! What do you do, how did you meet?'

Indu again looked at Rana with trepidation; she wasn't sure how much to tell VP ji, again wondering why he had said she was his girlfriend. Probably because they weren't allowed to bring anyone here unless they trusted them implicitly.

'Well, I met him through a teacher, he helped me set up a library of sorts, and then we got to know each other.'

'Amazing,' he said, clapping his hands together. 'He's very charming, isn't he?'

'Deceptively so,' she said.

Rana grinned from the kitchen, pouring the chai into cups and bringing one each for the three of them.

'So how did you get involved in the resistance?' VP ji asked, still smiling.

Indu took an extra large sip of her tea and burnt her tongue as she thought about what to say, and then cleared her throat.

'Well, I heard about Fawad, and have also been hearing about the government's . . . *injustices*. I am sympathetic to the cause, and eager to learn more about it.'

VP ji nodded, waiting for her to say more, and when she didn't, he looked at Rana.

'VP ji,' he said, leaning towards him over the table, and staring at him with intensity. 'We are going to get Fawad out.'

His mouth fell open and he held Rana by the shoulder. 'Make him escape? From prison?'

'No,' Rana said in a tone that Indu thought was almost rueful, 'no, we have something else in mind. We are getting him in a barter.'

'Barter for what?'

Rana glanced at Indu, and when she didn't react, went to his bag and retrieved the pictures.

'Here,' he said, laying the pictures on the table, one next to the other. There were several pictures of the streets: policemen holding up *lathis*, armed men in cars, a policeman with his gun up in the air, an advertisement that said, 'Sterilization is the best method of family planning. Incentives: Male—Rs 40, Female—Rs 20', a man bent over on the ground, people lining up outside a makeshift doctor's clinic with similar papers in their hands . . .

'Incredible,' VP ji said, going over them, passing a few to the other man. 'Yes, I remember Fawad mentioning these. A few other boys also took similar pictures; they are still in Ahmedabad, though.

Yours are definitely incredible.' He turned to Indu and said, 'This is the kind of work that will bring down the government, Indu. This is what a few of us must do, to undo this tyranny.'

Rana nodded, holding a picture. 'We need to let go of these, though, for Fawad.'

'And who is the source? Of the barter? Who is getting him out?'

Rana looked at Indu, and VP ji nodded. 'Her father has some connections,' he said. Indu nodded, knowing that he couldn't very well say 'her fiancé'.

'And who is your father?' VP ji asked mildly.

Neither Indu nor Rana answered for a few seconds. 'Ajit Narayan,' he finally said hesitantly, 'chief advocate.'

VP ji nodded, his fingers on the table. 'It will definitely work, VP ji,' Rana said again. 'I don't want him to suffer. I want to bring him out.'

'And what is your father's position on the issue?'

'He is sympathetic to the resistance,' Indu said.

'Oh. He is?'

'As far as he can be . . . in his position.'

Indu sensed a change in his manner and looked at Rana. Perhaps they should never have told him. She wondered if Rana had been foolish in trusting him.

'And does your father know that you are here?' VP ji asked her.

'No,' Rana said, 'of course not. No one knows she's here. She doesn't even know where the safehouse is located. We followed all the rules, she was blindfolded when I got her here.'

Indu nodded vigorously, but it seemed like the damage was done.

'And how does your father feel about your upcoming . . . alliance?'

'Well, that's our business,' Indu said briskly. 'Also, I think we should get going now, we don't want to miss our meeting.'

Rana nodded and Indu collected all the photographs again, putting them back in the package. VP ji nodded and got up swiftly, walking back into the corridor as Indu picked up her *dupatta* and Rana stuffed the package back into his bag. 'Uh, yes, I should blindfold you again when we go out,' Rana said. Indu widened her eyes at him but didn't say anything more, as Rana was obviously thinking of what he could use as a possible blindfold, and indicated her *dupatta*. She handed it to him with a glare.

He put it over her eyes, wrapping it around her head and tying it at the back. 'Okay, give me your hand,' he muttered to her.

'What do you mean "give"? Take it! I can't see where your hand is.'

He grabbed her hand and they had barely walked a few steps when she felt Rana stop dead in his tracks. 'What?' she asked but he didn't reply. A long silence followed, she felt another presence, and guessed that it was VP ji.

'Rana?' she asked again, but he didn't reply, and clutched her hand tighter instead. She had opened her mouth to say his name again when he pinched her thumb and she shut up.

They were suddenly moving backwards. Rana made her sit on the chair again. She prised off the knotted *dupatta* from her eyes and gasped. VP ji stood with a gun pointed at them, all smiles gone from his face, and she turned to Rana, who seemed as unnerved as she was. Beads of sweat formed on Indu's palm and she held Rana's hand tighter.

'Sit,' VP ji said, his voice crisp, and Rana sat next to Indu.

'What are you doing, VP ji . . .' Rana began in a small voice.

He looked sharply at Rana. 'How much does she know?' he asked.

'She's on our side, VP ji,' Rana said immediately. 'I can swear to you, I vouch for her completely. I vouch for her on my life. She's helping us get Fawad back, we swear to you it's true.'

Indu nodded vigorously, noticing how much Rana had paled, and how VP ji's hand remained steady, holding his gun. A silence followed, and Indu thought VP ji was trying to make up his mind about her. When Rana tried to get up from the chair, he jabbed the gun in Indu's direction.

'VP ji, why are you doing this?' Rana protested.

'Don't speak,' he retorted. Indu sat with her heart beating thunderously, waiting for the worst. They both sat staring at VP ji and Indu glanced frequently at Rana.

She tried to signal to Rana to say something. After what seemed like hours, VP ji slowly lowered the gun and Rana smiled, encouraged. 'That's right,' he said, pacifying him, 'she doesn't mean any harm, VP ji, you were being paranoid. You can see, I will blindfold her and lead her outside, right until we reach the city. She has no idea about the location of the safehouse.'

'Come here, I want to talk to you,' he said, now staring right at Rana.

Rana made as if to move towards him, and then stopped himself. 'Anything you want to say can be said here, VP ji. I'm telling you, you can trust her.'

VP ji stared daggers back at them, and then continued. 'I'm sorry to have pulled the gun out,' he replied shortly. 'I wasn't sure what to think about her.'

Indu tried not to look exasperated, for he still had the gun, after all. Rana nodded, holding up his hands. 'It's fine, we must be cautious, after all, these are dangerous times . . .'

But VP ji was staring at Indu. She looked at Rana, feeling conscious under his gaze.

'Your father is getting Fawad released,' he said—a statement, not a question.

Indu nodded after a pause.

'Why not more people?'

'What?'

'Why won't he get more people released?'

Indu gaped at him. 'Because he can't. Even getting one person out is very tough!'

'But he's doing it,' VP ji said.

'Yes, he's doing it because we asked him, and also . . . these photographs!'

'So he's not really on our side, is he, then, if he's asking for something in exchange?'

'You don't understand! You don't know the position we are in, how we are even managing this!'

'VP ji,' Rana began, 'it's not just her father, we are taking the help of other members of their family and Indu's . . . fiancé. Her father doesn't even know about any of this. We have to exchange the pictures for Fawad.'

VP ji got up from his chair, his hands folded behind his back, and began pacing up and down the corridor.

'What if we keep her here?' he asked, looking at Rana. 'Her family would exchange way more people for Indu, wouldn't they?'

Indu's heart turned to stone, and she could tell that Rana too was completely shocked. She heard forced patience in his tone when he spoke next. 'VP ji, think about what you are saying. Holding an innocent woman hostage? Using her as leverage, putting her life in danger? We don't do that, or we would be like them, ready to dispose as we will, use as per our interests and profits!'

But VP ji now paced faster than ever, shaking his head. 'Rana, you're not thinking about the big picture here. Forget about your relations with her for a moment, not that what you told me was honest anyway—as you said, she has a fiancé—but think about how valuable she could be. We could get several of our top people out if her father or fiancé or whoever valued her life. She'd be far greater political leverage.'

'Are you out of your mind, VP ji?' Rana yelled, getting up from his chair. 'Using an innocent woman in this. I thought this movement was greater than that!'

'Think coolly, use your head! It's not only Fawad's life that is important, there are so many of our valuable members inside—'

'Okay, I am not a part of this anymore,' Rana said slapping his hands on the table. 'Indu, come on, let's go.'

Indu got up from her chair, but found her path blocked by VP ji. Rana sighed in frustration.

'Look, we won't harm her, if that's what you are thinking,' VP ji said. 'It's not about her—it's about the bigger movement! She can stay comfortably in your room, and not a hair on her head will be touched! We are not mistreating her in any way, but we can't just let an opportunity like this get away.'

Rana now sat with his head in his hands, silent. He stayed that way for a long time and then looked up at him again. 'So you are saying she won't be harmed in any way?'

Indu couldn't believe her ears and stared at him incredulously.

'Not at all,' VP ji said soothingly, almost laughing at the suggestion. 'What will we achieve by harming her? We are not monsters. She can stay here. In return, we will ask that in addition to Fawad, a few more of our top men, who also have been unjustifiably imprisoned, be let off. Innocents released for an innocent released. Is it not our duty to do all we can for those whom we swear to protect? Is it not up to us to save as many human lives as we can? In fact, considering what's at stake, the price she can fetch us, if she's truly on our side, she should volunteer to be held hostage!'

Indu couldn't help it; she laughed at the preposterous suggestion, unable to control her guffaw, and to her astonishment, looked up to find Rana not laughing. She gaped at him, betrayed that he didn't find it ludicrous.

'This is how it feels when someone close to you is incarcerated for no apparent reason,' VP ji egged him on. 'It's the perfect plan, and the way I see it, we have nothing to lose. They let our people go at a certain location, pardoning all charges, we let Indu go from here, chastity, dignity everything intact, not even the ends of her *dupatta* crumpled. Everyone is happy.'

'You have got to be kidding me,' Indu said, now standing next to Rana, nudging him. 'Can you believe this guy? Has he gone nuts because he's been trapped here for so many days?'

But Rana didn't wear exasperation on his face, and looked, in fact, to Indu's chagrin, pretty convinced by what VP ji had said.

'He's not saying anything wrong, Indu,' he said in a low voice to her. 'Just think of what we can achieve. Using your name this way was what we should have done all along, instead of other petty things.'

'Have you lost your mind?' she shrieked. 'Do you know how much trouble we will be in, how much trouble my father will be in? Have you absolutely no sense?'

'Indu, dear,' VP ji said, now grinning broadly, 'just think! Your father will be so ecstatic just to have you back that nothing else will matter, absolutely nothing else! A few prisoners would be nothing.'

'Stop this madness now.' Indu got up from her seat and attempted to walk away, but found her path again blocked by VP ji.

'Rana!' she yelled, looking at him.

Rana walked towards her, looking apologetic. 'Indu, try and understand, nothing is going to happen to you. All VP ji is suggesting is that we fake this "kidnapping" and see what we can get out of it. You said that you wanted to help Fawad, didn't you?'

Indu couldn't believe what she was hearing. She felt her way to the table, picking up their chai cup, and threw it straight at Rana. It hit him on the forehead and fell to the floor, cracked. Rana winced in pain as VP ji came up behind her, holding her arms in a lock. Indu struggled against his hold and began screaming at the top of her voice as VP ji yelled at Rana to help him. Rana went to a drawer in which there were ropes.

They tied Indu's arms and legs, and put a gag over her mouth so she wouldn't scream; Indu shot Rana looks of pure venom as he massaged his forehead. She didn't want to believe what had just happened. Yet, as the minutes passed, he avoided looking at her.

'Do you want to know how I came into this movement, Indu?' VP ji asked her, and Indu raised her eyebrows sarcastically. VP ji gave a low chuckle. 'I was forced to join it. There I was, sitting peacefully in my home one day, not really bothered by any kind of emergency, when they arrived at my doorstep and declared my home was illegal. I was confused; how could homes be illegal? They said our entire colony was illegal, that it didn't exist on paper, and so we must leave. My wife asked me what to do, but I had no answer. The next day, when we sat outside our homes, refusing to move, they beat us and kicked us aside, knocking over all that we knew to be home.'

If he expected Indu to show sympathy, she displayed none. 'Did your father think about the legality of destroying 200 homes, chief advocate that he is?'

Indu wanted to tell him that it wasn't up to him, but was barely paying attention anymore. All she could think about was Rana's betrayal. Her mind turned to whether anyone at home had noticed her absence already. She was dimly aware of Rana hovering around her.

Rana and VP ji huddled together in front of her, murmuring in low whispers. The cloth was tight around her mouth. They sat that way for some time, discussing plans in low voices, and she even saw VP ji pat Rana on the back once. She wondered how she could have been *so* wrong, so many times, about a person. As she simmered in anger, she saw Rana say something in VP ji's ear and then pin him against the wall, swiftly grabbing the gun from him.

She stared at him as he pointed the gun straight at VP ji's face. 'Stand back,' he growled at VP ji, whose expression went from shock to anger.

'You will regret this, son—'

'Shut up!' Rana yelled at him, backing up to where Indu was, removing the cloth from her mouth.

'If I give you a knife, can you cut the ropes?' he asked urgently.

'So you're . . . you're not on his side?' Indu asked him.

He couldn't help looking at her in exasperation. 'Of course not! Did you actually buy that?'

Indu shrugged.

'I told you that if anybody could act like Rajesh Khanna, it's me. Anyway, wait,' he headed over to the kitchen counter slowly, still pointing the gun straight at VP ji, and brought back a knife. 'Do it,' he said to Indu, 'I need to keep this bastard in sight.'

VP ji shut his eyes and began singing *Aye mere watan ke logon*. Indu and Rana looked at each other, incredulous, but Rana shook his head and urged Indu to hurry up.

'Rana, this is not the way to *insaaf*,' VP ji said after a while.

'I know,' Rana said shortly, 'but yours isn't the way either, you freak, keeping her hostage. Now don't talk or I'll blast your head off.'

VP ji smiled. 'You're not a killer, Rana, I know that. Especially not one who kills their own leader.' He began to walk forward with his hands up in the air, and Rana warned him to stand back. When he continued walking, there was a deafening blast. Indu jumped, and the knife fell from her hands. As the smoke from the gun dispersed, she saw a bullet embedded in the wall. Rana's expression was fierce. 'I thought I told you to stand back.'

Indu saw VP ji gulp and take a step back, horrified that Rana had actually fired. Indu then continued cutting the ropes on her wrist, and finally freed herself.

'Go,' Rana said. She grabbed her *dupatta* and shot VP ji a look of the deepest loathing.

'If you dare come after us,' Rana said to VP ji, 'we will make sure the police comes knocking on this safehouse next.'

20

Their autorickshaw wobbled dangerously on the road, but neither Indu nor Rana cared, still reeling from the shock of what had just happened. They didn't say anything for about a minute, and then Indu let out a sound of relief and hugged him sideways, surprised to find that he too was shaking. The auto driver watched them in the mirror, but they ignored him. She wrapped her *dupatta* around herself.

'I thought you had really turned on me back there,' Indu said.

'Is that why you hit me so hard with that cup?' he asked.

'Of course!'

'Pity all the practice of dodging things before didn't work out . . . but only because you caught me unawares.'

'*What* in the world was that, though? Why did he suddenly flip like that?' Indu asked him.

Rana seemed to be having trouble processing what had just happened, so Indu gave him some time.

He finally looked at her, a vacant expression in his eyes, and said after a few seconds, his voice cracking, 'I'm sorry. I didn't know. I felt a bit nervous about taking you in there but I just never knew that he could . . . stoop to this level . . . got greedy… what's the difference . . . shattered my faith . . .'

He was now murmuring bits of phrases, and Indu patted him on the back. 'I always knew he was ruthless,' he went on, 'but to this extent—he could dare to even suggest that we kidnap you . . . after I said we will be married . . . what sort of madman . . .?'

Indu nodded sympathetically, lost in her own thoughts. She had thought she understood how things worked, how authority and dissent functioned. She thought that the lines between the good guys and the bad guys would be clearly demarcated. But this encounter had left her more confused than ever.

Rana bowed his head in shame. 'I don't know what to say. I wonder what the other people in the movement will think of it if they find out. Just goes to show that humans, even well-meaning ones, can go to any extent to get what they want.'

Indu reflected on this, finding herself agreeing, and yet it was hard to make peace with it. 'Nice game of bluff there, by the way,' she told Rana.

A grin spread across his face. 'Once I saw how seriously he believed in his plan, I knew there was no way to change his mind, so I had to act convinced. I was hoping he'd keep talking to me.'

'Why?'

'It's easier to fool talkative people,' he said, matter-of-factly. 'That's why I'm always able to pull a fast one over you.'

'Oh, please! When have you ever pulled one over me? And you're the talkative one . . .'

The conversation kept them going as they headed toward Ganpati Tower. It was quite late at night, and Indu knew she would have a lot to explain when she got home. But for now, they had a more pressing problem at hand: where in the world was Rana to stay?

'Just stay at Number 7 tonight. It's safe, nobody will expect you to be there, and tomorrow, in the morning, before the girls start to arrive, I'll come and let you out. I'll tell Dhar uncle we have the pictures, and are under a lot of pressure, so if he wants to make the exchange, it needs to happen . . . very soon. We'll make the exchange and get this over with once and for all,' Indu said.

He stared at her for a few seconds and then nodded. She got down at Ganpati Tower as well when the auto stopped.

'And Indu,' Rana called out as she walked away. She turned around and stopped right at the apartment gate.

'What?'

He was silent for a moment, but only a moment. 'I wanted to tell you that I love you,' he said suddenly in a rush.

'I mean it,' he went on, 'I really do. When I think about you, I know it immediately in the way my heart swells. If I could go back in time, I'd tell myself not to be an idiot and tell you the first time I met you that I loved you and wanted to marry you and would do anything in the world to give you a beautiful life.'

Tears now streamed down her cheeks, but she refused to look at him.

'But I see you struggling with it, bending to pressures, and I hate that I complicated it for you like this. More than that, I can't bear that every day, I put you in even more danger. I want to be able to end this for you. I'll go away and never contact you again after this.'

'But I love you too,' she said before she could stop herself.

She saw his jaw tighten with emotion. He extended his hand to her, and Indu saw that he was about to say something, when the little Sardarji popped up at the gate. She cursed him silently and was about to signal to Rana to hide, but realized it was too late when she saw the boy already waving enthusiastically at Rana.

Rana's eyes grew wide too, but he recovered quickly and smiled, while Indu tried to think of an excuse.

'Rana *bhaiya*!' the little boy said, jumping in excitement as Rana patted him awkwardly on the head. 'Where were you all these months?'

'I was away on some work,' Rana said lamely.

'I am so happy you are back!' Indu saw that he looked genuinely happy. 'It was always fun to have you here. Indu *didi* scolds everyone a lot.'

Rana chuckled quietly.

'He is not here to stay,' Indu said. 'In fact, he was just here for two minutes to pick up a book. He is now going—to Kerala—and he doesn't really want to stay to say hi to anyone, so don't tell anyone he was here, okay?'

'No,' he replied with a pout. 'You're going again? Stay here, you can stay with me!'

'I would love to, but I have some more work these days. When I am finished, I'll definitely come back to see you,' Rana replied.

'Don't tell anyone that he was here,' Indu said to him strictly again, 'or I will set the ghosts of Number 7 on you.'

'There are ghosts in Number 7?' he asked, his mouth slightly open.

'Of course!' Indu said with a cackle of a laughter. 'Who else do you think stays here at night? An empty house is very comfortable for ghosts. I lock them in the house, but if I let them loose, they like to go to the homes of little Sardars and cut off their *joodis* . . .'

At that, the little boy put his palms to his eyes, pretending he couldn't see Rana, and walked back to the building.

Realizing how late it was, Indu rushed away before Rana could say anything about their interrupted conversation.

She reached home to find her father at the door, and felt nervous again.

'Where have you been, Indu?' he asked her carefully, and she guessed some of the distress might be showing on her face. Indu took a deep, calming breath before answering.

'I was just out, you know, with some friends, watching a movie, that's why it took so long. *Hera Pheri*,' she said, naming the first movie that came to her mind.

'Really? I thought you didn't like Bachchan.'

'I don't, of course, but my friends dragged me.'

'Why didn't you ask Natty to take you?'

She suddenly fell quiet. 'Uh, just like that. I didn't want to bother . . . I just used the bus. I have to get used to it for London!'

Her father looked at her strangely and she wondered how high-pitched she sounded.

'Come, sit here,' he said, indicating the sofa. 'Tell me how your day was.'

She followed him to the sofa, taking a seat beside him. 'Good, regular. Kittu's getting better at handling everything, and I was—you know, I'm very glad about it. I really love being there.'

Indu hoped he understood the meaning of her words, and he took some time to answer.

He nodded. 'It's good you started this, right? I remember you were so excited.'

She laughed nervously. 'I still am.'

'You fought Govind so hard to get hold of Number 7.'

She didn't answer.

'Amita was also on your side. Perhaps that caused a rift . . .but never mind that now. And then you found that chap, what was his name again . . .'

'Rana,' she answered carefully, now looking around for her mother. She must be in bed already.

'Quite smart, that one, wasn't he?'

She didn't answer, again, and her heart began pounding; was it possible he knew? No, it couldn't be. Natty would never. Not in a million years.

'Smart fellow, he asked me for a job at some point. He will do well in life, I can tell. I know you two were friends . . . but alas, everything was already fixed.'

He was talking to himself now.

'What are your intentions, then?' he asked her.

'What . . . what do you mean?'

'Your intentions. To marry Rajat.'

The question left a bitter aftertaste in her mouth. 'I don't think my intent was considered very much,' she said.

Indu wondered why her father made a face, as if this piece of information was news to him. 'Indu,' he said, holding the side of the sofa, 'I never—we never . . . we are very liberal. We would never stop you from . . . that is not fair.'

Indu restrained from retorting. 'I know, but . . .'

'You knew all along you would marry Rajat. You've known it for two years, and you never said anything!'

'Yes, I never did say anything! And so this is the last thing you should ask someone when their marriage is already fixed.'

He stared at her before shutting his eyes and leaning against the sofa, and she walked out of the room, too scared to stay longer, unsure of where the conversation would lead.

* * *

'*Jai Ram ji ki*,' Natty said when he saw Rana early next morning, slouched comfortably on the couch, his arms behind his head.

Rana grinned at Natty's greeting and held up his own folded hands, bowing his head.

'So you are back in the library?' he asked him.

'I just couldn't live without it. The flip side is that to see Number 7, I have to bear her as well,' Rana said, pointing to Indu.

'You have to take care of this idiot, Natty,' she said. 'He has nowhere to go for the day. Take him around, feed him something, go sit in a park, chill out, I don't care. Bring him back in the evening and hopefully, we will get this situation sorted out soon.'

Half an hour later, girls started arriving and took their seats. Indu called Rajat and told him they had what was needed. She asked him if Dhar uncle might possibly be ready to make the exchange, as more complications had arisen.

'You should ask him,' he replied testily. She decided she didn't have time to analyse his mood.

'Please give me his number,' she said, and noted it down. 'I'll tell you what the plan is, okay?' she added, but he didn't answer and just said goodbye. She then called Dhar uncle and told him that they must make the barter as soon as possible, and after much cajoling, he said he would try his best for the next day.

The morning hustle had settled down, and Indu had been idle for just two minutes. Her thoughts constantly wandered to how her mother was already discussing their living arrangements in London with Supriya aunty. Indu marvelled how this part of her life was so distant from the rest of what was happening. She thought her day would pass uneventfully till Dhar uncle called her back and told her it could be done tonight. Finishing their talk, she immediately called Rajat back.

'Okay. We should make the exchange tonight here, then,' Indu said. 'At 11 p.m. okay? Most people should be in their homes already. I'll tell my parents I'm sleeping at *didi's* house.'

'Right.'

'Will you come?' she asked him.

'Uh, I'll see.'

Her day passed in anxiety, and she could hardly pay attention to anything, constantly flipping between what had happened last night and imagining how tonight would go. She informed Amita, who promised she would be there with Indu. Amita told Govind that she would be sleeping at her parents' house.

Indu's mind worked non-stop. She found her father's behaviour the previous night odd. Why had he asked her what her intentions were? Maybe Rajat had said something to him, or maybe her mother had commented on how her mind wasn't fully on the wedding preparations. Most importantly, she stopped herself the moment her mind strayed to what Rana had said when they had said goodbye. In the evening, she called Dhar uncle again to check that everything was on track, and was glad to know that it was.

Just tonight, Indu thought. After tonight, all this would be over and she would be free to think about other things—not to think about so much as get used to Rana leaving her life again, Indu thought. And to focus on her new life with Rajat.

It was late evening by the time the last of the girls left and Amita strolled in, greeting and smiling them on their way out. Sangeeta had just been telling Indu how she had been feeling quite low recently. Indu nodded sympathetically and casually asked her if she remembered Fawad. Indu noticed Sangeeta's eyes light up as she nodded keenly.

'Of course! He was so funny, just like Ranaji! I wonder where he went.'

Indu shrugged nonchalantly, trying to hide her delight that Sangeeta had gotten so excited at the mention of Fawad, and how happy that would make him.

'Yeah, I really wish I had the chance to speak to him more, you know,' Sangeeta said, as Indu marvelled at the ironies of life. 'I mean, I don't know, but I thought there was something about him. He was always so sweet to me too. I wanted to ask you where he was but then, you know how girls like to gossip here . . . oh well, what's gone is gone.'

She eventually left with a melancholic goodbye. It would be something nice to tell Fawad when Dhar uncle brought him there that night. Indu and Amita had been sitting and talking when Rana walked in with Natty. Indu instructed Natty to go back home and leave the Ambassador there, and tell her parents that Indu had been dropped off to Amita's. Indu asked Rana in a low voice if he still had the gun that he took from VP ji, while Amita unpacked some food she had brought along. He nodded slightly.

'Get rid of it as soon as possible,' she said.

Rana nodded. 'I can't wait to see Fawad, ask him how he is.'

The three of them played cards for some time, as evening turned to night.

'Oh,' Indu said, 'I forgot to tell you what Sangeeta told me today. Fawad will be so happy. She had a crush on him, she told me. She said he was funny.'

Rana got up from his seat, his hands on his head. 'Really?! Oh my God, he will be thrilled!'

'Who is this?' Amita asked lazily from the couch. 'The same Sangeeta who used to teach Esha?'

Indu nodded keenly.

'Ah the good, old days,' Amita said, staring dreamily into space, telling Rana, 'I had moved back into my home to study for some time, into Indu's room, in fact. I used to come to Number 7 with her, study all day, eat dinner with my parents, and then Indu and I would giggle and gossip about boys after dinner!'

'Really?' Rana asked chuckling. 'And who did you gossip about?'

'Well, she would talk about you so much,' Amita told him absent-mindedly. 'Who was that girl who started coming in for some time, the one with the short, curly hair . . . Renu or whatever. Yeah, Indu used to complain about her a lot . . .'

Indu widened her eyes at Amita, but her sister wasn't paying attention. Rana caught her eye but she looked away, pretending it wasn't true.

'Well, anyway, it was great because I had to see so little of Govind, you know. He can really be a pain.' She was silent before she said softly, 'I think there was a point where I could have loved him, but I lost that hope when I moved back in with him. Maybe what they say is right—it falls apart without the children . . .'

They sat in silence for some time, then, each lost in their own thoughts. At long last, it was close to eleven and they got ready for the arrival of the expected party.

At exactly 11 p.m., the bell rang.

Amita sat daintily on the sofa while Rana stood at the very back, the pictures snug in the pocket of his jacket and his arms crossed over it. Indu set the *dupatta* on her shoulder, gave a nod to Rana and Amita, and opened the door.

Dhar uncle stood outside, looking as tall as ever, dressed in a suit, immaculate. His pepper-grey hair shimmered in the glow of the light in the corridor, and he gave a slight nod, waiting for Indu to invite him in. Indu glanced swiftly behind him, and when she didn't see anyone, looked quizzically at him. Dhar uncle looked to his right and Fawad came into view, standing farther down the corridor.

The first thing that Indu saw was that he looked haggard; there were dark shadows beneath his eyes, his hair unevenly cut. A rough beard grew on his face, hiding his dimple, and his entire body seemed to have shrunk. The usual shine on his face was missing, but when he gave a small smile, he looked like a shadow of his old self. Indu wanted to take a step towards him to give him a hug, but stopped herself, and instead backed up so that they could enter Number 7.

When they walked in, Indu saw him and Rana exchange a friendly, wistful look. She then noticed that Fawad's wrists were still tied together. Dhar uncle looked at Indu.

'Let's sit here,' Amita called out from the sofa, making him jump—he hadn't noticed that there were more people there. 'My name is Amita, I'm Indu's sister,' she said and he nodded a greeting at her. He went over to the sofa and Fawad followed him.

'So,' said Indu.

Dhar uncle nodded.

'Would you like anything?' she asked uncertainly, 'um, water, tea or something?'

'Photographs, please,' Dhar uncle said, extending his hand.

'Fawad first,' Rana said from the back, and Dhar uncle looked up sharply at him. 'I have him here, you can see it. I still don't know whether you have the photographs.'

Rana stared at him for a few seconds, and then shook his head.

Dhar uncle looked at Indu in appeal, and she signalled to Rana that they could trust him.

Reluctantly, Rana walked over to Dhar uncle and handed him the brown package.

He took a good five minutes going through the pictures, inspecting each and every one of them, his eyebrows going higher and higher until they finally threatened to disappear into his pepper-grey hair. 'These are all your own pictures?' he asked.

Fawad spoke up for the first time. 'We put our lives on stake for them!'

'Are there any other photographs that aren't among these?' Dhar uncle asked.

Rana was indignant. 'I wouldn't do something as immoral as blackmailing you for something and then not holding up my end of the bargain, even if I did blackmail you in the first place.'

Dhar uncle stared at the three of them for a few seconds but didn't say anything.

He went through everything again while Fawad impatiently asked Rana to untie him. Rana had barely gotten up when the doorbell rang again.

Indu looked at Amita in alarm; no one was supposed to know they were even here. Unless it was Rajat. But why would Rajat not have arrived with Dhar uncle if he wanted to come? Indu put a finger to her lips to indicate to the others that no one should say anything. They all sat still and the bell rang again, thrice in a row, and then somebody banged on the door. Rana quietly suggested that everyone tiptoe into another room. Once everyone was in the other room, Indu went to the door and opened it, hoping it was just the little boy across the corridor.

Her heart turned to lead when she saw Roshan standing there with Govind *bhai*, and three men behind them.

'Good evening, Indu,' Govind *bhai* said, smiling at her dangerously. 'Aren't you supposed to be sleeping over at my house right now?'

When Indu didn't reply or move from the door, Roshan gave her a little shove and walked inside, with the others following him. Indu wanted to protest but suddenly had no voice left in her. She walked back, her body shaking, as Roshan shouted for the others to come out. Dhar uncle walked out and asked what was going on. Roshan ignored him and asked the other three men to go inside the room.

Next thing Indu knew, they had dragged Rana, Fawad and Amita out of the room. Indu yelled at Roshan to stop it, and he asked the third man to let Amita go.

'What the hell do you think you are doing?' Indu screamed, and perhaps it was the treble of her voice, but Roshan paused for a second and then asked his men to back off. They were now on one side, and Indu, Amita, Rana and Fawad on the other, while Dhar uncle stood in the middle, trying to understand what was going on.

Govind stepped to the front. He and Amita stared at each other for the longest time without saying anything, and just when Indu was about to speak up, Govind spoke. 'It was an interesting evening today,' he remarked mildly. 'I was going over some work at home when I got a visit from Roshan here, who introduced himself as Indu's fiancé's brother.'

When no one replied, he smiled and went on. 'I was completely taken aback, wondering why he was at my home, but I invited him in, of course. That's what decent people like us do. But then, he showed me a picture of this man—' he jerked his head towards Fawad, '—and asked me if I knew him. I said, of course I know him, he is the one who maligned my family, someone who should have been put in jail a long time back. Guess what Roshan told me then?'

Indu looked at her future brother-in-law, hating him; Govind clapped his hands. 'He told me that my wife, who's supposed to be at the home of her parents, is meeting him tonight!'

If Amita felt anything, she didn't show it. Her face did not betray emotion, apparently taking no note of the fact that Govind was now staring at her in intense dislike.

'I told you not to help her,' Roshan told Dhar uncle with menace.

'Your brother was fine with it,' Dhar uncle replied.

'My *brother*,' Roshan emphasized, 'was the one who told me about Govind and his problems with his wife. He was the one who advised me to talk to Amita's husband and ask him to put some sense into her. Who knew I would open a pandora's box? I mean, Govind told me that he had some unfinished business with the man that his wife was trying to get released! Wrote some things that put Govind's uncle in trouble, I am told.'

Indu couldn't believe that he had gone to this extent. 'I don't get your problem,' she said to Roshan brusquely. 'This is none of your business.'

'You are my problem,' he told her. 'See, I don't believe you actually care about my brother. Now I don't care if you're in love with this loafer here, but to actually ask my brother to *help* your boyfriend? That pissed me off. I suggested to Govind here that the same might be true for her sister. He didn't believe me when I said you'd be here. I asked him to come with me.'

While Amita remained unfazed, Indu felt a surge of anger; she stepped forward, her arms folded, now talking directly to Roshan. 'I've heard enough of your bullshit. You better get out of here. This is our house, and you have no right to step in here.'

Roshan smiled widely. 'Your house, is it? We'll go, but we are taking these two with us. Both of them should have been picked up together in the first place.'

She saw that he pointed at Rana and Fawad, at which point Rana laughed. He stepped forward and now he and Roshan were face to face.

'Sorry, but I am not interested in going anywhere with you. I don't like your look.'

Roshan smiled at Rana, and before Indu could figure out what was happening, they were locked in a fight. They pushed, shoved and punched each other, knocking over some books from a bookshelf. Fawad was trying to fend off the three other men, kicking and punching as hard as he could. Dhar uncle stood to one side, and both the sisters watched in horror. Indu was sure that it would be only a matter of minutes before someone came to the door. In desperation, she tried to call out to Rana, but to no avail. Then she saw his bag lying on the floor and picked it up, rummaging inside, gripping it when she found what she was looking for.

'Stop!' she yelled and when no one heard her, she decided she had no choice; gritting her teeth and making sure she hit the ceiling, she fired a shot upwards and there was a loud blast. Plaster fell to the ground. Silence fell as the scuffle ended suddenly.

'I'm going to say this once,' Indu said quietly. 'Leave, all five of you.'

'Or what?' Govind snarled, walking towards her. 'You're going to make your own sister a widow?'

'Watch me,' Indu replied to Govind, refusing to put the gun down.

Govind laughed and Roshan joined him. Roshan picked up a book and began flipping the pages. Indu wondered whether he had gone mad.

'I think it's a little too late, if you're looking to educate yourself,' Rana said to him; Roshan suddenly took out his lighter, set fire to the book and threw it to the floor.

'What kind of a child are you?' Indu hissed. 'You'll ruin my things if you can't have your way?'

He ignored her and looked at Govind now. 'Didn't you say this place was the cause of your broken marriage? Well, you should have done this already, then, don't you think?' he asked, as he added another book to the previous one, which started burning.

Dhar uncle told him to stop but Roshan ignored him, rattling the shelves so that books fell down with a clatter. Rana moved forward to make him stop but Roshan threw a burning book at him, so he backed off.

'Let's see,' he said manically, 'if Indu Narayan can protect her burning library.'

He added more books to the burning pile as Indu yelled at him to stop, that there were others in this building, but Roshan seemed to have lost all sense. 'I don't even know why my brother likes you,' he went on. 'Looking at your company, I can easily tell you're not going to be an honest woman, let alone an honest wife . . .'

Indu wasn't listening now; she moved and pointed the gun right at Roshan's face. Still, it was only when he could no longer stand the heat from the burning pile of books that he turned around and left, and the others followed him. Govind gave Amita a final, sweeping look. 'Now's the time to choose, Amita,' he said.

She turned away from him, towards Indu. 'I chose long ago.'

The gun fell from Indu's hands with a clatter as the men left the flat. 'Quick, we have to douse this!'

Rana and Fawad tried to put it out with their jackets, but the flames were too strong now. There was no bucket in the bathroom which she could fill with water and pour it on the books. They looked around wildly as the flames spread until a bookshelf fell right on the fire, burning alongside the books.

'We need to leave,' Amita said urgently.

'No! We have to douse the fire!' But the fire was now past containing, and they dragged Indu out of the door. 'We'll have to call the fire brigade!' Rana yelled. 'Indu, come!'

There were already clouds of black smoke in the house as Indu and Rana went into the corridor. She saw her sister through the smoke, clutching Fawad's arm as they held themselves against the wall, trying to shield themselves from the heat. She saw Rana look around in panic and then at her; he took her *dupatta* and threw it far from them. 'We must warn,' Indu panted, 'the neighbours.' With her right arm, Indu covered her nose as her eyes watered from the smoke, and she struggled to keep them open but gave up, blindly being pulled by Rana as they crossed the corridor, and Dhar Uncle followed them.

Amita covered her nose with the skirt of her *kurta* as all five of them coughed helplessly, unable to keep their eyes open for longer than a few seconds. She could now see a burning cabinet through the door of Number 7, and she banged on the Sardar's door. The father came to the door, groggy and confused, and Indu asked them to evacuate. Smoke was emerging from the door of Number 7 now, and Rana, Fawad and her sister were backed up in the corridor, waiting for Indu; Dhar uncle was on the stairs. 'You two have to go,' she said to them, as a fit of coughing overcame her. 'Dhar uncle . . . please. You have the pictures. These two can't be seen here.'

'Come,' he said to them urgently. Rana opened his mouth to protest but was pulled away by Fawad, and she just saw a fleeting glimpse of him stumbling down the stairs. Indu and Amita got out of the building as more heads began to emerge from the windows and cries of 'fire, fire!' echoed from the flats. Indu held Amita's hand and just about managed not to collapse on the ground.

21

'Where to, madame?' Natty asked as Indu stepped inside the Ambassador.

'Masterji,' Indu answered listlessly.

With a prompt 'yes, madame', Natty set off and Indu leant her head against the window, occasionally looking outside at the people. There was a slight nip in the air and so Indu kept the window shut.

Tonelessly, Natty began singing '*Tera mujhse hai pehle ka naata koi*' and Indu listened quietly, noticing how he glanced at the rear-view mirror frequently when she didn't comment. His singing went from bad to worse but Indu didn't say anything, so he finally stopped, looking curiously at her.

'Seems like you have finally learnt to appreciate my singing, Indu madame,' Natty said, and Indu gave a slight laugh, but still didn't say anything. After that, Natty fell quiet. When they arrived, Indu quietly got out of the car and went up to the masterji's boutique.

As usual, there were rolls of fabric at the back of the shop, standing against each other. On the wall, there was a large calendar with a Ganeshji on it. Masterji's words broke through Indu's thoughts, 'Some *thanda*, madame? Campa? *Shikanji*?'

He was as short and hunched as ever, bristles of white beard covering his face, a slab of sky-blue chalk placed safely above his right ear.

'Madame? Madame?'

Indu shook her head slowly and he waited for her to talk, but when she didn't, he admitted guiltily, 'Your blouses aren't ready yet, madame.'

He folded his hands, his head bent, waiting for Indu's disapproving snipes, but when she didn't say anything, he looked up quizzically. 'Just give me two more days, madame. In two days it will be done. Think of it as already done.'

How many times have I told you to be more efficient with your work than with your words, masterji, Indu's own voice rang out to her. She knew what was going to happen next—of course she did.

'Whose wedding is it, madame?' masterji asked her.

Indu looked up at his face as if seeing it for the first time.

'My own,' she replied, and barely heard his exclamations and apologies, hardly listening as he promised the delivery of these blouses within the next two days.

She placed her *dupatta* neatly on her shoulder and spotted Natty across the road. As if on cue, she looked up at the building with the huge poster. It wasn't Rajesh Khanna and Sharmila Tagore this time, Indu realized with a jolt; it was a poster of *Kabhi Kabhie.* The poster featured Amitabh Bachchan and Waheeda Rehman, and Indu stared at it wistfully, as if just her stare would change Amitabh Bachchan to Rajesh Khanna. She almost bumped into a man on a bicycle and heard nothing when he hurled an insult at her.

Sitting in the Ambassador, she asked carefully, 'Natty, can you tell me about this movie *Kabhi Kabhie?*

If Natty found her question odd, he did nothing to show that and only asked, 'What about this movie, madame?'

'This movie, what happens in it? Do Waheeda Rehman and Amitabh Bachchan marry or . . . or what?'

'Oh,' Natty said, comprehension dawning on his face. 'Well, I'm not sure you want to hear it, madame. It's a bit sad.'

'I want to hear it.'

'Well, what happens is, madame, Amitabh Bachchan and Waheeda Rehman have to marry each other, madame, because of family and what not. But they don't love each other. Many years later, they meet the people they once loved and then some . . . but they should have married the people they loved, see. It only makes sense.'

Indu heard him but didn't have anything more to say.

Yes, you look like Waheeda Rehman, a voice rang out in Indu's ears, *if the lights are off.*

'Stop, stop, *stop*, Natty!' Indu yelled, and he stopped the car with a jolt.

'Wait, did you mean the car or the singing, madame?'

She ignored the question.

Things were rather stiff. Supriya aunty and Balwant uncle sat in the drawing room of their house while Indu's parents made casual conversation. Amita flitted in and out of the room as the phone rang for her constantly. When Indu arrived, she was told that Rajat was arriving soon, so she went up to her room to get ready. Her sister joined her after a few minutes, and smiled at Indu.

'It's done,' she said smiling.

'Seriously?' Indu asked.

Amita nodded.

'And you're sure?'

Amita nodded again and said, 'The papers will arrive soon.'

Indu nodded too and clutched the side of a table to steady her beating heart. Would she remember this moment years later? Would she remember it as Amitabh Bachchan and Waheeda Rehman had done, would she remember it with sadness and regret? Rajesh Khanna, her own words echoed in her ears, *the original superstar* . . .

In a few minutes, Amita told her that Rajat had arrived and Indu brought him straight up to her room.

Indu shut the door behind them and Rajat looked around, staring at the painting, the one of Indu with the jasmines in her hair. 'Nice painting,' he commented, nodding at it.

Indu shook her head and hugged him tightly.

'I'm sorry to have dragged you into this mess. Really, I mean it—I know you didn't ask for any of it.'

He nodded curtly, and she saw that he wore this expression, one of long suffering. She couldn't exactly blame him.

'Did you tell Roshan about Govind *bhai* and Amita?'

The colour suddenly drained from his face. 'Listen, Indu, I told you, I'm sorry about what he did. We promised not to reveal each other's secrets. You won't tell anyone that it was Roshan who burnt Number 7 and I—as in we—won't reveal all that you've been doing with Rana and Fawad.'

'But did you tell Roshan—did you put the idea in his head to try to bring Govind *bhai*, to manipulate him into thinking wrongly about Amita, to gather support? To have Govind *bhai* with him when he arrived at Number 7?'

Rajat shook his head vigorously. 'Of course not! That's, well, Roshan is a bit of a maniac. He gets overprotective sometimes. I did tell him about Govind in general, but I would never do this, Indu.'

Indu didn't reply and instead sat on the edge of the bed, her head in her hands.

'What—what is it, Indu? It's all over, everything will be fine now, we're moving . . .'

She shook her head as she cried some more, and now his eyes widened and he took a step towards her. She shook her head some more and he took another step forward.

'Indu, what are you saying, we—we can go . . .'

'I can't,' she told him tearfully, 'I just can't. I don't want to. I can't.'

He stopped where he was now. 'Are you saying you don't want to marry me?'

Now Indu nodded, and a wave of relief washed over her as she finally said it; as if all of her being wanted only to assert that one thing.

He opened and closed his mouth several times, taking a step back, and finally sat down on the edge of the bed.

'I'm sorry,' Indu said in a small voice, but he did not seem to hear it. Indu shook her head again, rushing to explain. 'I don't know you. We have nothing in common. How can I imagine spending a lifetime with you? I know I have been unfair and a horrible person to you, but don't you see? It's . . . clearly, it's not enough! The situations of two people are not enough to determine if they should be married, if they can be together. Everything is perfect, you will have a beautiful home in a new city, lovely parents, and you're a nice person, I'm sure—but I feel nothing for you. Marriage has to be more than that. It has to be more than us fitting together on the outside. Look at what happened to my sister, you know it now, what with your brother and her husband joining leagues—have you seen her wedding picture, though? Wait, I'll show you.'

Indu ran to her shelf and took the wedding picture of Amita and Govind, so beautiful and so widely distributed. She took the frame and thrust it in his bewildered hands. 'Look! Look at them! Don't they look perfect? Can you tell that they would be divorced in a few years? Do you see the lie?'

He stared at it because she asked him to, and then shook his head. 'It doesn't have to be like that.'

'I don't want to take that chance.'

Putting the frame on the bed, he got up and walked away while Indu followed him. She felt sorry for everything, but weak with relief at the same time.

'Let's go,' she heard Rajat call out to Balwant uncle and Supriya aunty, but when he walked straight out of the house without saying anything, his parents looked at Indu accusingly.

All four of them sat down again, the reality of what had happened hitting them. None of them spoke for some time until Indu's mother asked, 'What will you do now?'

'Father said we'll see if Number 7 can be restored,' she said.

'We will,' he replied, 'and we'll also look into other things. What you want to study, work . . . there is so much to do.'

Indu sat all afternoon, ruminating about her decision, looking back on the last few days. Nothing seemed to make sense. All her life, Indu had revered a leader; that leader had caused a crisis, the end of which Indu could not see. Indu's encounter with the resistance to this leader had been as unfavourable. It did not seem to care for an individual life if the greater goal could be achieved. And then those with whom she would have been bound by marriage hadn't turned out any better than the others.

Now her father was openly against the party's policy and that divided everyone into two camps—those who were afraid of saying anything and those who had already acted. For the first

time ever, he and Shashi uncle were on opposite sides. While a
lot of it had to do with Amita and Govind's crumbling marriage,
their ideological differences had also become too wide.

Yet, she couldn't stop thinking about Amita and how
she was a doctor now, and come what may, would forever be
a doctor. That was the strength of being something; it didn't
matter whether Govind *bhai* was in her life or not. There was
nobody in the world who could take this away from her, and
despite her parents' initial hesitation about her wishes, there was
no one who boasted about it more, no one who was prouder.
They were already talking about setting up a clinic for Amita in
the next few years.

More than anything else, Indu decided, that was what she
wanted.

'Indu, there's someone waiting for you outside!' her father
said, standing at the door to her room, interrupting her reverie,
while her mother laughed standing next to him.

She looked up. 'Who?'

'Rana,' her father said.

When she didn't reply, her father continued, 'We had a chat
this morning.'

'About what?'

'He was seeking advice. He said he had been offered a job
at this particular firm, and he wanted to check the "political
leanings" of this place.'

Rana had gone to speak to her father that morning and
hadn't even informed her. Classic Rana, she fumed to herself;
they hadn't met since parting that night after the fire, and here
he was, already making new plans for himself . . .

The Ambassador's honk sounded as she made her way
outside.

Rana stood beside Natty in front of the car and when she appeared, walked into the garden towards her, holding his hands behind his back. He had recently cut his hair and wore a white shirt, his teeth matching the colour as he grinned. He held out his palm to Indu, and a couple of white jasmines lay on it.

'I remember what you had said once,' Indu said, looking at him. 'It's just flowers, you had said, it's not my love.'

Rana laughed at that, but Indu didn't let it go. 'You meant it then.'

'What I meant was, it's only flowers, nothing as special as my love.'

'I hope so,' Indu said. 'Or you know what.'

'What?'

'I'll crush the flowers.'

'You'll never crush my love.'

'It could do with some crushing, to be honest.'

He held her other hand, the one without the flowers, in both of his.

'What if there's a Runjhun again?'

'She will pale in front of your fury.'

'And the Emergency?'

His face darkened. 'I know. But I will never leave you again, no matter what. In fact, I told your father some of my plans.'

'What plans? And why didn't you tell me you went to speak to him?'

'Fawad was upset about the photographs,' Rana said, 'but then our talk with your dad cheered us up.'

'What talk?'

'Of course, what would be great, the cherry on the cake, is if you could have Fawad meet Sangeeta.'

'*What are you talking about, Rana—*'

'We have exciting things to look forward to,' he said, 'but first, we need to watch a movie. Natty, shall we?'

Natty gave a deep bow. 'There is no Rajesh Khanna movie, sir. And madame only watches Rajesh Khanna movies.'

Rana laughed, 'Madame will still be watching Rajesh Khanna, Natty. I'm going with her.'

When Indu gave Rana an indignant look, he put up his hands in defence. 'I told you I am as close to Rajesh Khanna as you'll ever get . . .'

THE END

Acknowledgements

I t might take a writer to write a book, but it takes a village to raise a writer.

I have wanted to be a writer all my life and perhaps no one knows it better than my father. Every single moment I have received nothing but encouragement, motivation and great advice. In life, you need one person to be irrationally crazy about you and your dreams, and my father has been that and, more, working so hard and inspiring me to do the same. I would have been nothing without you.

My big debt towards my mother, who took care of me in ways that only a mother can, by putting me ahead of herself, every day, and being the perfect example of resilience and indomitable spirit.

My sister Rose, who is my absolute favourite person in the entire world, and, in all honesty, the one responsible for being the cool person I am today (you were just an excuse to compliment myself, *hehe*). There is no one else on Earth who means more to me.

The reason why this book is dedicated to a city rather than a person is because it would never have been written if I hadn't moved to Edinburgh. The moment I took my first steps around the city and got hit by cold blasts of wind, I knew it was something special. Over the course of the year I met wonderful people who, in the cheesiest sense, really taught me how to live again.

My professor R.A. Jamieson, who encouraged me profusely when I presented this novel as my dissertation proposal. And oh how it has changed now.

My dearest soul sister Isabel, the godmother of this book, who, living next to me, had the unfortunate duty of keeping an eye over me to making sure I keep writing and studying, giving me company on my cooking escapades and being her incredible true self, which never ceases to amaze me.

My adopted mother Martina, who might be the craziest person I have ever met; you truly are my mother Marti, and I hope I keep following your footsteps in making the world a little more fun.

Martin, who inspired me in every way a girl can be inspired; of course I knew I am an Indian spice, but you reminded me of the devilish, rascal sparkle in my eyes.

And my coolest *malaka* Elena; they truly don't make girls like you any more.

A big thank you to my wonderful and super-sharp editor Roshini Dadhlani, who not only believed in my writing, but also never hesitated from telling me whenever Indu sounded too cruel, and Rana too lame.

My gratitude to Milee Ashwarya as well, who opened the doors for me that writers so often find themselves stuck behind.

Many thanks to my Juggernaut girls for their invaluable suggestions. I must be the luckiest girl in the world, for I had not one but two publishing houses taking care of me. I also owe Chiki Sarkar so much. Being the phenomenon that she is,

I learn so much about publishing simply by being in the same space as her.

Saving the best bite for the end: a lifetime of thanks is not enough for Sharan, who has stood by me at every step in my life, with a pat on my back. He owns an infinite pool of patience and encouragement, supporting me blindly and unconditionally. But of course the hardest part of the journey is putting up with me. This is just the beginning.

To you, dear reader, for giving me the greatest joy of my life—the joy of being read.

And finally, gratitude for the One Who creates and runs everything, in Whose shadow we become what we are.